AMBUSH

AMBUSH

A Steve Flynn Thriller

Nick Oldham

This first world edition published 2016
in Great Britain and the USA by
SEVERN HOUSE PUBLISHERS LTD of
19 Cedar Road, Sutton, Surrey, England, SM2 5DA.
Trade paperback edition first published
in Great Britain and the USA 2016 by
SEVERN HOUSE PUBLISHERS LTD

British Library Cataloguing in Publication Data
A CIP catalogue record for this title is available from the British Library.

ISBN-13: 978-0-7278-8634-7 (cased)
ISBN-13: 978-1-84751-739-5 (trade paper)
ISBN-13: 978-1-78010-803-2 (e-book)

All Severn House titles are printed on acid-free paper.

Severn House Publishers support the Forest Stewardship Council™ [FSC™],
the leading international forest certification organisation.
All our titles that are printed on FSC certified paper carry the FSC logo.

Typeset by Palimpsest Book Production Ltd.,
Falkirk, Stirlingshire, Scotland.
Printed and bound in Great Britain by
TJ International, Padstow, Cornwall.

To the memory of my brother, Peter. A true gent.

ONE

'Oh, yeah, I'm a murderer, a mad axeman, actually. A double murderer at that. I killed two – my partner and his lover after I'd found out about their, y'know, affair.' The man called Felix Loveday tweaked his fingers in invisible air speech marks around the word 'affair'. He paused and frowned at the thought, the memory. 'I didn't know I had such rage in me,' he continued. His voice was at a conversational level and as he spoke he pulled up his right shirtsleeve to display his forearm just above the wrist and the simple, home-inflicted tattoo that said the name 'Trevor'. Loveday swallowed as he gazed at the name. 'I found them both in bed, actually. Suspected something and there he was.' He tapped the name on his forearm. 'Up to his nuts, the maker's name, in that utter whore who I thought was my friend, Jon Dunson. I can still see 'em,' he recalled wistfully. 'Obviously they didn't expect me to turn up. I watched 'em through a crack in the bedroom door. I mean, even now' – he splayed his right hand over his chest – 'I can feel how my heart was pounding at the sight, how I couldn't get my breath . . . and then' – his eyes became evil, his voice dramatic – 'that sudden, all-consuming rage that kinda poured over me like molten metal.'

'Very descriptive,' the man sitting opposite him said. The two were playing cards – pontoon – with two others, and they were listening attentively to the opening up and sudden honesty of Loveday.

Loveday picked up the two cards he had just been dealt and added up their value.

There was a pile of matches in the centre of the small card table and each man had a small stack next to him, the stakes for what appeared to be a fairly innocent game.

The man directly opposite Loveday, the one who had made the dry comment, was called Brian Tasker. At first Tasker had not been too interested in the confession and was just listening because he had nowhere else to go, no one else to play with.

And because all four men were in prison.

But as Loveday revealed all, Tasker frowned and became a little more interested. 'What happened next?' he asked.

Loveday inspected his cards. 'Twist,' he said to the dealer on his right, who flipped over a card. 'Twist again,' Loveday said. Another card was revealed and Loveday scraped both into his hand and pushed four matches confidently into the central pile. Each match represented a debt of some sort and the overall winner that night would be able to choose to call them in whenever he felt like it.

So far, the largest pile of winnings was next to Tasker.

'What happened next?' Loveday echoed, raising his eye line across the top rim of his cards. 'I closed the door quietly, then I snuck downstairs and went into the shed and found the axe. In those days we had a wood-burning stove, so we were always chopping wood. Never once did I dream I'd use an axe for anything other than that. I remember picking it up and running my finger over the blade and thinking, "Not sharp enough" . . . so I sharpened it on one of those sharpener things.' He looked at the other men. 'What're they called?'

'An axe-stone?' one suggested.

Loveday shrugged. 'Something like that. Anyway, I sharpened it, then snuck back upstairs, and they were still at it.' He shivered with revulsion at the memory. 'Anyway, Trevor's back was to the door . . . I can still see his naked arse . . . and I snuck in and went for it – his head, by the way, not his arse. I remember that first blow as if it was only yesterday. Right into the back of his skull. And it was one of those, y'know, like when you slam an axe into a log, then you can't get it out because it's stuck, and you have to rive it free?'

The other three card players visualized it, seemingly horrified.

'Anyway, to cut a long story short, I got it out, then really started whacking him with it. Went bananas.' He snorted a laugh. 'Jon managed to do a runner – naked and shrieking like a woman down the stairs, running like a right pansy. Started off with a hard-on, too. Anyway, I went after him but he'd got to the front door and I was still on the stairs, so I had to chuck the axe at him. I suppose it could have gone either way, but I got lucky. If it'd missed him or hit him and bounced off, he would've got out on to the street. But God was on my side and I struck lucky.' He chortled at his own wit. 'It was almost the perfect throw. Like in a cowboy film, a Cherokee throwing an axe that whizzes through the air like a cartwheel. The point didn't stick in him, but the blunt end embedded itself in the back of his head and he went down on his knees before he could get the door open. I just pulled it out, stood over him and started hacking like a lumberjack chopping wood. Blood fucking everywhere.' He looked at his cards and said, 'Twist.'

Tasker said, 'Then what?'

Loveday gave a cheeky grin. 'By the time the cops landed I'd dismembered and disembowelled both of them. I was sitting there with Trevor's severed head in my lap, stroking his hair, covered in blood and guts, whimpering like a puppy with body parts all over the house. Bit of a mess,' he admitted with huge understatement.

'Shit,' one of the other card players said, blanching and rubbing his neck.

'I admitted it, got life – twice, concurrently. Judge threw away the key, called me a deranged individual,' Loveday said.

Tasker's eyes narrowed thoughtfully. 'How long ago was that?' he asked, thinking Loveday would say ten or twelve years maybe.

'Uh . . . 1985 . . . thirty years ago.'

'You've been in clink for thirty years?' one of the others said in disbelief.

Loveday nodded philosophically. 'Yes. The judge said minimum thirty, which I thought was a bit harsh, but I don't regret what I did. Both of the sneaky, cheating bastards got what was coming to them and I got what was coming to me. Yin, yang.'

'So how old were you when you did it?'

'Nineteen.'

'Nineteen eighty-five, eh?' Tasker said. He would have been fourteen years old that year. 'Did they have DNA back then?' he asked. 'You know, cops sampling, like they do now?'

'Nah. Fingerprints was about it. They took my blood, they could do that, but that was about it.'

'And they never took your DNA then, swabbed your mouth?'

'Nope.'

''Bout you, guys?' Tasker asked the other two.

Both had had their DNA taken.

'Yeah, me too,' Tasker said.

'After my time, DNA,' Loveday said. 'I'm a pre-DNA guy.'

Tasker's bottom lip jutted out as he nodded and digested the information, realizing that big things often come from chance conversations. 'But you're up for parole now, I hear? After all these years.'

'Yeah.'

'And are you going for it?' Tasker asked. 'I mean, aren't you institutionalized after thirty frickin' years?'

'Probably I am, but I'm going for it. Did the crime, done the time, now I need to find out how the world has changed while I've still got some breath in me. I reckon I've got a lot of years left—'

'To shag some arse,' one of the others quipped.

'Oh, yes, baby . . . my final hearing's next week. No reason why I shouldn't walk,' he said confidently. 'I've been a good boy.'

'No reason whatsoever,' Tasker agreed. 'Stick, by the way.'

In his hand he had an ace and a king. Pontoon.

Ten days later Tasker invited Loveday into his cell. Both men were smiling broadly.

'Good news, I hear,' Tasker said.

'Yeah, yeah . . . all that good behaviour has paid off . . . just got to cross the "t"s and dot the "i"s, but it looks like I'll be walking out through those doors this time next week.'

'That,' Tasker said, 'is the best news I've heard in years. Congratulations.'

'Thank you.' Loveday was becoming quite emotional.

Tasker turned around and picked up two plastic mugs from his bedside cabinet, handing one to his fellow inmate.

'Illicit hooch, but good stuff,' Tasker said. 'To freedom.'

They touched mugs, a dull 'thuck' rather than a 'dink', and drank the bitter-tasting spirit.

'Your family will be pleased,' Tasker said, wiping his mouth.

'No family. Parents dead, no brothers or sisters, no aunts, uncles.'

'Oh, sad . . . so no one to greet you?'

'Nah, but that's OK . . . visit the probation office and that's about it . . . as a lifer I'm on licence for ever, obviously. Anyway, to freedom.' He raised his mug again, then swallowed the remaining liquor, which spread down into his chest like wildfire.

The same four card players assembled the night before Loveday's release in Tasker's cell. They settled down for a quiet couple of hours of poker and pontoon with some booze and cigarettes supplied by a tame prison guard.

It was the way Loveday wanted it, no fuss, just a bit of time with a few people he had come to regard as friends.

His moment of murderous frenzy thirty years before had been the only moment of complete madness in his life and he had paid his judicial dues quietly in several prisons across the north of England. This one – Lancashire Prison, just a few miles west of the town of Leyland – was to be his final one. He had spent six years here, existing fairly peacefully, causing no problems and getting on with his life behind bars, not making any waves. He had learned quickly how to survive, to cultivate non-sexual relationships, to kowtow to the duality of the prison hierarchy – the inmates and the staff – and never to flaunt his gayness in any way. Occasionally he took a considered chance with it, but only when he knew it was safe to do so.

All he wanted to do on that last evening of captivity was stay under the radar, unnoticed; spend time with a few other inmates he'd got to know, play cards, have a drink, then tootle back to his cell and, virtually, wake up a free man – bar the painful, bureaucratic procedure of being released.

The evening went to plan.

Cards were played, matches won and lost, and a variety of liquids consumed. Prison officers passed the open cell door infrequently; some looked in and genuinely wished Loveday well for tomorrow and the future, but none interfered with the civilized night until the lights out warning bell sounded at ten forty-five p.m. for the eleven p.m. lockdown.

The playing cards were stacked and all debts for that night were written off good-naturedly.

Then the four men stood around the card table and raised their mugs for the final drink and a toast to Loveday and freedom.

A prison officer appeared at the cell door and caught Tasker's eye – at which precise moment Loveday's eyeballs rolled back in their sockets and his knees buckled. He dropped his mug, swayed, but just before he pitched forward two of the card players grabbed him, one on each side, before he hit the hard cell floor, ensuring he did not injure himself.

The prison officer stepped in, pulled the door to but did not close it.

Tasker stepped aside as the drugged Loveday was eased unconscious on to the lower bunk and laid out on it.

Five minutes later, the scene was prepared and ready.

TWO

Three months later

D etective Chief Inspector Craig Alford was the first of the targets, the first of the five programmed to die.

There was no specific reason for him to be first; he just happened to be first alphabetically and also the easiest to find, watch, follow and, of course, kill.

But there was a specific reason why the last name on the list was the final one.

On the day he died, Alford had been at work since seven a.m., coordinating a series of drugs raids across the county of Lancashire from the new communications room at police headquarters situated in Hutton, about four miles south of Preston. Alford was on Lancashire Constabulary's Serious and Organized Crime Unit (SOCU) based in the Pavilion Building at HQ (built, literally, on the site of the old cricket pavilion on the playing fields opposite the headquarters building, hence the adopted name).

That morning's raids were the culmination of months of fastidious intelligence gathering, use of sources (aka informants) and good targeting. Alford had grafted hard to make the operation, codenamed 'Aquarius', a success. Drugs raids were ten a penny, most not having any effect on the trade, and Alford wanted his to be different – to make a difference.

There would be no crashing through the bedsit doors of low level street dealers, smashing their soil pipes with sledgehammers to catch any drugs being hurriedly flushed down the bog, and then seizures of a few grams of coke and a few unhealthy cannabis plants.

Today Alford, as per his enviable cop history as a man hunter, was going to catch some very big fish and close down a massive drug-running operation – which, he knew realistically, would have an effect for a good week before the next drug lord stepped into the vacuum.

If, that was, all things came together.

He had four major, interlinked traffickers in his sights. The intel he and his team had gathered consisted of financial dealings, property ownership, legit fronts for illegal activities and, best of all, the prospect of catching all four main players with drugs, money and guns in their possession.

Alford could probably have struck much earlier and got a decent enough result, but he had resisted pressure from above and below because, as he succinctly summarized, 'I can't see the whites of their eyes yet.' Had he bowed to that pressure he would always have known that he should have waited just a tad longer to strike.

It was like waiting for Jupiter to align with Mars, he insisted – hence the name of the operation.

Things had to come together, to converge.

Drugs had to be at a particular location. Money had to be there. The guns had to be there. The targets had to be there and the police resources had to be ready to jump. Fast.

The waiting all became worthwhile when, from his perch in the comms room, Alford listened to the radio transmissions on the secure encrypted channel being used exclusively for Aquarius, watched the live video/audio feeds from cop-cams attached to various officers' shoulder pads and headgear and made on-the-spot decisions, finally giving the 'Go, go, go' order.

Four suspects. Four synchronized raids. Forty cops and support staff.

Jupiter, Mars.

'Gustav Holst,' Alford mused.

Twenty minutes after seven, twelve arrests had actually been made, because a few of the bit-part players were picked up along with the four main people, three men and one woman.

Eight million pounds' worth of cocaine was seized, and maybe about one million in drug-tainted sterling and euros plus four Heckler & Koch machine pistols, two Glock handguns and several Russian-made pistols, with ammunition and lots of documents.

The comms room, now known as the contact centre, was newly opened, and Alford's manic dance and high-fives with some members of his team were the first to be enacted on the new carpet, around the consoles of several bemused, wide-eyed comms operators.

None of this was of any interest to the man parked in a layby on the dual carriageway, the A59, that ran past the police headquarters campus, Preston to the north, Liverpool well to the south.

The man had been sitting there patiently since four p.m., had brought a flask and sandwiches with him, knowing that Alford usually finished work around five thirty, though occasionally he left at five. Often he stayed in until seven or eight p.m.

It was now just after eight p.m., but the man was certain Alford was still in work. He knew there was a pretty big police operation going on and had been expecting, but not assuming, that Alford would stay late.

Although there was always the faint possibility of the detective using another route when he left, Alford had driven out of headquarters this way on every other occasion this man had watched and waited, and although he was working later than normal, the man in the car did not think Alford would change his route home that day. Alford lived in a nice house on the north side of Preston, but because there was no right turn out of HQ on to the dual carriageway he would have to turn left towards Liverpool, then exit about quarter of a mile up, loop under the carriageway and rejoin it to travel north towards Preston. It was a pain for all the staff working there. Many years before, it had been possible to turn right through a gap in the central barrier, but the A59 was a straight, fast road at that point, and because of the number of serious and fatal crashes and near misses the Highways Department had decided to close the gap.

The man in the car had only been given a short brief: watch and report using a new pay-as-you-go mobile phone on each occasion. He had been instructed – over the phone, by someone he had never seen, did not know – to wait for Alford to drive past, then text the word 'YES' to a particular number and discard the phone carefully.

That was all. He didn't even need to follow the cop.

A hundred pounds a shot.

Ten shots so far.

Easy money.

So he sat back and waited, knowing this would be the last time of doing this, though he did not know why he was doing it. But he did not give a shit. A grand was a grand.

The day had been long, intense, nerve-racking and tiring, requiring complete concentration, and by the end of it Alford was ready for home. Aquarius had been a resounding success. A dozen arrests and all the prisoners scattered around police cells in Lancashire to keep them separate, now being attended to by well-briefed, experienced interview teams. Alford knew the raids were actually only the beginning of a long process of interviews, house and business premises searches, forensic and financial checks, liaison with the Crown Prosecution Service and numerous court appearances. He had to be totally on the ball for the next two weeks but was confident everything was covered. These drug dealers would not set foot on the streets again for at least fifteen years. That was his ultimate aim: disruption and incarceration.

As he pulled out of headquarters at eight fifteen p.m., then turned left on to the dual carriageway, Alford took a few moments to call home. His wife was also a detective, a DC based on a child protection unit. There was no response on either the home landline or her mobile phone, though this did not unduly trouble him. He knew she was busy with a particularly nasty case of child neglect and cruelty. At the moment their lives were not in synch, but everything always came back on line and they had plans for the weekend, staying at their favourite little pub in Arnside and doing some walking. Nor was he concerned that neither of the children answered the home phone. They were plagued by Payment Protection Insurance callers and the girls, now seventeen and nineteen, ignored the phone unless they happened to be standing by it and saw that the caller display showed a number they recognized.

He flicked off the Bluetooth and his Jaguar sped up the road, turning left and then looping back under the bridge to come back down towards Preston. He never even noticed the car in the layby because, as soon as he ended his attempts to call home, his mind whirred with everything 'Aquarius' and with what needed sorting next day, which, he had already decided, would commence at six a.m.

The man in the car sank low in his seat as Alford's sleek black car zipped by. Then he sent the text – just a simple 'YES' – and immediately began to dismantle his phone.

Alford's house was on the A6 north of Preston, just beyond the village of Broughton. Detached and standing in its own grounds, it was hidden from the busy main road by high fencing and hedging and was not overlooked by any of the neighbouring houses.

The hooded man heard the text drop on to his phone. He drew it out of his back pocket and read it, just that single word, 'YES', then slid the phone back in and smiled down at the three people lying in front of him, their hands bound with duct tape around their backs, ankles also bound and a J-cloth stuffed into each of their mouths and then taped over.

'Not long now, ladies,' he said. What he did next indicated that none of them would leave this scenario alive.

He pinched the top of his hood firmly between his finger and thumb and slowly pulled it off, revealing his face.

Now they had seen him.

Now they would die.

Alford's route home took him around the western perimeter of Preston, using Tom Benson Way, an old railway line which was now an arterial road connecting with the A6 north of the city. Then he was under the motorway bridge at Broughton, through the crossroads, and about a couple of minutes later he slowed down, indicated right and turned into his curved driveway. His thoughts about Aquarius were now dismissed and he was eagerly looking forward to chilling and eating with his family, whom he adored.

He did give a brief pout of puzzlement when he saw his wife's car was on the wide drive, behind the two cars belonging to his daughters. He wondered why none of them had answered the phone.

He shrugged and climbed out of the Jag. It was almost six years old but still a quietly magnificent car. He walked to the front door of the house which, twenty years earlier, when he'd been a detective constable and his wife had been in uniform, had almost crippled them with mortgage repayments, but which was now worth probably four times what they had initially paid for it. He was immensely proud of it and his family, and of what he and his wife had achieved over the years through hard graft and working at a brilliant marriage.

He stopped abruptly at the front door, which he saw was ever so slightly open, just resting on the door frame.

At first he wondered if it was a birthday or anniversary he had forgotten, or maybe there was a surprise waiting inside and they were all about to ambush him. Just a fleeting thought. He knew there was nothing pending, and he did not miss stuff like that anyway.

But for some reason the open door was slightly unsettling, though he could not say why.

It wasn't a feeling based on evidence, just a cop's instinct.

His mouth went dry. He pushed the door open with the tip of his right forefinger.

It swung noiselessly.

There was no one in the tiled hallway.

The kitchen door at the far end was open, lights on.

The door to the lounge on the left was closed.

The house was silent.

Unusual. He frowned.

Normally the place was throbbing with life and the aroma of good cooking because the ladies of this house were bubbly, exuberant people who always had food on and music blaring. They looked after him, he looked after them.

He tried to shake off this weird feeling. It was nothing. Surely he had come home to this before? A quiet house.

He stepped across the threshold and called tentatively, 'Hello? I'm home. Is anyone else?'

A tiny part of him still expected all three women in his life to leap out in camouflaged onesies and surround him because, surely, he must have forgotten something. Was it his own birthday?

The dog's birthday?

Where the hell was the dog? The slavering Labrador that always greeted him and tried to knock him over and lick him clean.

'Stuff this,' he thought. Even the bloody dog was being held back for the big ta-dah!

He took a few steps along the hallway and opened the lounge door.

He had perhaps one second to take in the horrific tableau that greeted his shocked eyes: his wife, his daughters, trussed up, bound and gagged on the carpet between the settee and the armchairs. Their terrified eyes.

The stunning blow to his head instantly dropped him where he stood, withering to his knees and tipping forward across his wife. And into complete blackness.

THREE

Santa Eulalia, Ibiza

Steve Flynn looked twice at the young man hunched in the dark recess of the doorway, but didn't make his second glance too obvious. The first was just the normal jerk of the head – what anyone might do while walking past and half-spotting a figure lurking in the shadows. Most people would probably just walk on and forget they had seen anything, and Flynn would have done so too except that at his first glance his sharp eyes, their vision honed by many years of hard use, noticed something as they pierced the darkness.

They saw the outline of a hooded man, his face hidden by the shadow, but also the glint of something in the man's right hand down by his thigh.

That was what Flynn registered on the first look.

The second look, just a flick of his eyes as he walked on, merely confirmed the fact.

The man was armed.

Flynn continued to stroll on because that was what he was doing, simply making his way through the resort of Santa Eulalia, enjoying a stroll, slowly but surely making his way down to the marina for a late dinner. He felt the arm of the woman walking alongside him looped into the crook of his right arm. A good feeling. Like an old married couple. He walked on as though he had not seen anything.

But to the woman he hissed out of the corner of his mouth, 'We need to call the cops.'

'*Sí* . . . yes, we do,' she agreed.

Flynn could not help the shimmer of a smile on his lips.

She too had seen the figure in the doorway and had probably done exactly the same subtle double-take as him.

'You're good,' he complimented her.

'*Sí, muy bien*,' she purred.

They stopped maybe fifty metres along from the doorway and backed into their own alcove, the doorway of a clothes shop recently closed for business that evening. From here, looking through the angle in the shop window, Flynn could see back along the narrow street, which was called Carrer de Sant Vicent. Flynn slid his left arm around the shoulders of his companion and she fumbled for and extracted her mobile phone from her shoulder bag.

'He has a gun,' she said.

'An old-looking revolver,' Flynn said, glancing back along the building line, able to see the darkness of the doorway but not the figure in it. Then he said, 'Shit.'

'What?'

'Two of them.'

The second guy was in a doorway almost directly opposite the hooded man, the entrance to apartments above the shops. Flynn had seen movement in the gloom, then, briefly, a white face peeking out before disappearing quickly.

'You are certain?'

'Yep.'

'What are they doing?'

Flynn weighed it up.

Further back along the street, on the corner of the next junction, was one of those small, ubiquitous Spar shops, a convenience store selling groceries, booze, water and other essentials. Flynn and his companion had walked past it a minute earlier. He had registered that the shop was in the process of closing for the night. The window shutters had already been pulled down and padlocked, but the shutter over the front door was only a quarter of the way down and a couple of customers were still at the till. The message was clear – we're closing and no one else is coming in, *gracias*. Flynn had spotted just two members of staff, a young girl on the till, probably in her mid-teens, and another, slightly older woman hovering by the door, key and padlock in hand, discouraging would-be shoppers.

It was one of several Spar shops in the resort. But they were dotted all over the island too, and Spain, and the world. Good, steady businesses mainly serving self-catering holiday makers and mostly taking cash.

'The corner shop,' he said. 'Easy target.'

Both lurking figures were still hidden in their respective doorways.

'How are you doing?' Flynn asked the woman he was with. Her name was Maria Santiago. Her smart phone was pressed to her right ear.

'Calling,' she answered.

Flynn nodded. The last two customers, a man and a woman, ducked out of the shop under the partly lowered shutter, followed by the assistant with the padlock.

'Still ringing,' Santiago said.

'Shit,' Flynn mumbled.

The woman in the shop said *'Buenas noches'* to the customers and reached up to the metal door with a thin hooked rod, attached it and began to unravel the door to close it.

Flynn removed his arm from Santiago's shoulders.

She glanced worriedly at him. 'Still ringing.'

'Anything like the cops in England, you'll end up talking to some call centre in Madrid.'

'I know.'

If a robbery was on the cards – something quite rare in this resort, indeed on the island – it was going to have to start now, just as the shutter was being drawn down, because once it touched the ground it would become a whole lot more complicated.

Flynn stepped out of the doorway at the exact moment the two figures emerged from theirs and started to sprint towards the shop. Each had a gun in his hand.

'Flynn, no,' Santiago blurted, knowing him all too well.

He gave her a helpless shrug and began to move. He was no sprinter now, his heavily muscled frame ensured that, but he didn't have far to run.

The first hooded guy, the one Flynn had originally spotted, dashed diagonally across the narrow street and slammed his body into the shop assistant dealing with the door. His arms enfolded her and he bundled her roughly back through the decreasing gap as the shutter descended.

Flynn saw the plan: first one through grabs whoever is locking up for the night; second one drags the shutter door down behind him, and then they have time to operate without interruption. Hold the hapless staff hostage at gunpoint, empty the tills, then force the women into the back office and empty any cash boxes kept there. Unless they'd banked earlier that day – which the robbers would know if they'd done their homework – Flynn guessed they could easily be looking at a haul in the region of 3,000 euros, give, take. Not a bad amount for about six minutes' work, if they were organized, not drugged up to their eyeballs, and meant what they did. If they were a good duo they could be in and out, business done and away – with no one hurt. Which was the thought that almost slowed Flynn down. Let them go, let them get away with it. Unfortunately he was hard-wired to react and intervene. The best part of twenty years as a cop and a few years before that as a Royal Marine had mainlined something into him that still hadn't quite evaporated, even all these years after leaving the cops behind.

Drilled into him: a need to intervene.

He pounded across the narrow street.

Ahead, the first guy had done as expected and he and the woman (now stunned but terrified) were inside the shop. Guy number two was already starting to pull down the shutter door which, as Flynn rocked up, was about a metre from closing.

The door was a medium security shutter of the type that

allowed people to see through slats into the shop even when closed. It was made of fairly strong aluminium and was controlled manually.

The second guy, in the process of pulling it down from the inside, was surprised when Flynn appeared on the opposite side with his big fingers curled underneath the bottom edge of the door. The two men were both bent over, face to face, eyeball to eyeball, inches apart, glaring at each other through the holes in the horizontal slats and pushing in opposite directions.

The man pressed down harder, panicking.

Flynn took the weight easily, now with both hands holding the door. He started to heave up.

In the shop beyond he saw at a glance that guy number one was holding the collar of the woman's work blouse and was pointing his handgun at the girl sitting motionless at the checkout till, screaming at her, not aware of the tug of war at the door.

He was shouting in English.

The face of Flynn's current opponent in the test of strength was stretched to bursting with the tension and effort of pushing down against Flynn. It was not a fair contest. The guy was thin, without any real muscle, whereas Flynn was pretty much the polar opposite: well built, muscled, strong.

The door, inexorably, inevitably, started to rise.

Flynn and the felon were virtually nose to nose, separated only by the thin door. Their eyes stayed in contact.

Flynn gave him a lopsided grin and then a wink.

Without warning, sensing he could not win this, the guy released the door and stepped away.

The tactic caught Flynn slightly off balance. Suddenly there was no resistance and the door shot upwards on its rollers and clattered open. He teetered back a step and the man he'd been door-wrestling with had his small revolver – something similar to a two-inch-barrelled Smith & Wesson detective special – coming around hurriedly to aim at Flynn.

He came back on balance almost instantaneously.

Flynn's life for the last ten years or so had revolved around keeping his footing on the sportfishing boat he skippered, so tripping up was not something he did and, despite his size, he moved around the boat with the grace of a ballet dancer. He was also accustomed to grabbing and dealing with fast-moving, thrashing, dangerous fish such as sharks with very sharp teeth and marlin with lethal swords, so he had no problem covering the distance between him and the guy with the gun in a micro-flash. He drove his right fist into the man's face before the gun even came around. The face disintegrated as Flynn's brick-like fist connected with the bridge of the nose. The guy dropped straight away as the impact closed down all brain function with an implosion like the formation of a black hole. His knees buckled, he fell as though he had stepped into an open manhole. The gun dropped out of his hand and clattered away across the tiled shop floor under a mobile shelf displaying suntan lotion.

Flynn strode over the unconscious man, his posture filling out threateningly.

The first guy had dragged the screaming hostage up tight against him like a shield. He jacked his forearm across her throat like an iron bar, squeezing her windpipe.

The girl on the till had her hands to her face, peering out through splayed fingers.

Flynn, keeping his eyes blazing at the robber, jerked his thumb at her. 'Go.'

She fled, leaving Flynn to face the guy he had first glimpsed in the doorway, with the woman pinned between them.

From the wild, wet eyes and hateful expression and the running nose, Flynn could tell the guy was drugged up after all. Speed, coke, a combination, whatever . . . it meant his metabolism was running at perilous levels, as was his mental state, making him dangerous and unpredictable.

'What're you? What're you?' the guy demanded of Flynn, waving the gun, which looked heavy and old but nonetheless lethal. 'Some kind-o fuckin' hero?'

'Put the gun down, let the lady go,' Flynn said calmly. The woman's fingers gripped the man's forearm at her throat as she gagged for breath. 'This doesn't have to get worse,' Flynn added, although he was pretty sure it would. He used his large hands with nice slow placating downward gestures, not aggressive.

Instead of taking Flynn's advice, the guy skewered the muzzle of the revolver into the woman's neck, twisting it painfully as if

he was trying to drill it into her. She screamed. Flynn could see
the whites of her eyes, her terror-stricken features.

At the same time, from the expression on the guy's face, he
could see the myriad of thoughts crashing through his head as
panic began to rise when his eyes lit on the sight of his partner
in crime splayed out, laid out, blood gushing, bleeding profusely
by the suntan display and the big, unafraid, menacing man who
had done that.

He pulled the gun away from the woman's neck and aimed it
at Flynn. The barrel wobbled unsteadily.

'Even under ideal conditions most folk can't hit a barn door at
six feet, especially with one of those heavy things,' Flynn advised
– not completely truthfully.

'Fuckin' good job you're bigger than a barn door, then,' the
guy snarled, adjusting and readjusting his aim. Then he jammed
the gun back into the woman's head. 'Won't miss this bitch, then,
will I?' he threatened. Flynn again saw the wild eyes, the bad
teeth and gums, the terrible complexion as pock-marked as the
moon, the snivelling nose.

'Put the gun down,' he said, soft and firm. In the distance he
heard the approach of sirens, cocked his head and flickered his
eyebrows meaningfully. 'Two minutes, cops'll be here, and if that's
still in your hand, you're a dead man,' he promised.

Indecision.

Flynn nodded to confirm his prediction. Behind he heard footsteps running up to him. He did not turn but kept his eyes firmly
on the robber and the gun. He sensed it was Santiago behind him.
The guy's eyes swivelled to the new arrival on the scene.

'Bastard!' He shoved the woman forward, propelling her
with the flat of his hand at the centre of her back. She stumbled
against the checkout counter with a scream, then crashed to her
knees, dragging an e-cigarette display over with her. Then the guy
aimed unsteadily at Flynn again, holding the weapon sideways,
parallel to the floor, like all misinformed villains who had no idea
how to hold a handgun properly. Flynn gritted his teeth and
clenched his stomach muscles, bracing himself for the impact of
the bullet. The man pulled the trigger back.

Flynn's world slowed down nauseatingly. He saw the hammer
move back, the cylinder start to rotate; he could also see the tips

of the bullets in their chambers, deadly missiles in their silos. With the exception of one. The chamber that was next to align with the barrel.

It was empty.

The hammer slammed down and the firing pin hit thin air and nothing happened.

Flynn's sickly world of treacle suddenly became one of ridiculous speed.

He saw his chance, reacted and launched himself at the guy, who was momentarily stunned by the misfire.

The guy looked beyond the gun as Flynn hurtled towards him.

In further panic he yanked the trigger back again.

This time the gun fired. But it was badly aimed, essentially pointed at the ceiling above the front door. The round tore into the brittle polystyrene tiles above Santiago. She ducked instinctively as the ceiling disintegrated and fell like dirty snow. At the same time the bullet, by chance, sliced through a coil of electrical cable and instantly plunged the shop into darkness.

Flynn tripped on something – a mop resting against the checkout – and slid sideways, missing the man, who sidestepped and leapt across the aisle to the opposite side of the checkout. He sprinted for the door.

Though covered in dust, Santiago unhesitatingly stepped into his path, holding out her hands, palms out, to stop him.

But he was thin, wiry, and had momentum and drugs on his side and probably a lifetime of evading capture. He zigzagged under her grasp, leaving her clutching air, and was gone like a wisp. She turned as Flynn, recovered from his slip 'n' trip over the mop, went after him, oblivious to Santiago's shouted plea to let him go, let the cops have the problem when they arrived.

Flynn was furious and focused. Not least because he'd been shot at. He knew from experience of chasing villains on foot that if they got out of sight there was every chance of not seeing them again, and Flynn had no intention of allowing this man to keep his liberty.

As he swung out of the shop door, using the frame to propel himself, he saw the guy leg it diagonally across the narrow street and swerve into the Passeig de s'Alamera, the wide, picturesque avenue running down to the sea front. Flynn upped his pace.

He was too big to be a fast runner, but his advantage lay in stamina and tenacity. He ran with the lope of a hunting dog, knowing that if he kept his prey in view he would eventually wear him down because, with few exceptions, guys like this robber were usually unfit. Flynn had caught up on many people coughing up their innards, clinging to walls and pleading for a cigarette.

The guy was out of sight for a couple of seconds but as Flynn turned into the avenue he was still there ahead, racing down the middle of this pretty feature with its beautifully lit multi-coloured fountains down each side and market stalls in the centre selling mainly jewellery, clothing and bric-a-brac.

It was still quite busy, although some of the stall holders were starting to pack up for the night.

The robber glanced desperately over his shoulder, spotted Flynn.

Recklessly, he fired the gun. The sound, though a little like a car backfiring, was unmistakably that of a gun being discharged.

Reaction was instant as people ducked, dived for cover and screamed.

It was a badly aimed shot, on the run, over his shoulder. It missed Flynn, who prayed it hadn't hit anyone else by mistake. Flynn took a hurried glance and saw no one had obviously fallen, at least not within his line of vision.

It also meant there were, at most, three rounds left in the revolver.

The robber ran straight into a woman. He threw her sideways, then grabbed the awning of one of the market stalls and dragged it down. The stall, flimsy at best, collapsed and the man ran on.

Flynn kept going, not nimbly but managing to veer around the scattered goods consisting of loofahs, wrist bands and tacky jewellery. He was still behind the guy, who dodged between strolling people, screaming at them and brandishing the gun, until he emerged on to the promenade, skittering and accelerating left, still throwing frantic backward looks, horrified to see that his pursuer was a relentless bastard.

Flynn pounded on, a half-smile playing on his lips. This was an easy run for him. He jogged four miles minimum per day anyway. He could tell the guy was flagging, even after only a couple of hundred metres.

It was just a matter of time – and dodging bullets.

The guy ran towards the port with one of the largest marinas in the Balearic Islands. It had over 750 berths, mainly for luxury boats, yachts and cruisers.

Flynn got the impression that there was no strategy in the guy's addled mind, simply the forlorn hope that his hunter would either lose him or give up; neither was going to happen.

He ran around the headland close to the ferry terminals, down the steps and through the tables set outside the Mirage Restaurant, which occupied a corner plot by the marina. The tables were packed with customers enjoying food and drink and a two-piece rock combo belting out a variety of Sixties classics.

It was then that the man's legs seemed to become increasingly heavy, like tree trunks. He crashed into one table, overturned another, scattering a family of four. Then he staggered, breathless, his lungs working ineffectively, towards a row of cars parked on the marina edge, one being a banana-coloured VW Beetle emblazoned with the logo of a well-known Ibizan nightclub and clothing range. He fell against this car and slithered to his knees, his smoke-ravaged lungs rasping for breath as he clung to the vehicle.

As Flynn approached with caution, the guy slumped on to his backside, wheezing and devoid of strength, unable to raise the gun. Flynn came at him from the side and quickly wrestled the revolver out of his grasp by the barrel.

The guy's head lolled with exhaustion but his eyes glowed malevolently at Flynn, his lips in a snarl.

'Up,' Flynn ordered him, not remotely out of breath, even though blood pounded through his veins. He flipped the gun into his right hand, thumbed the cylinder release and let the shells fall out into his left palm. Two discharged, three remaining.

The guy swore, too shattered to move.

Flynn pocketed the ammunition, grabbed the guy's hoodie by the collar and easily hauled him to his feet, holding him like a marionette. He was nothing more than skin and bone.

At the far corner, where the port road did a ninety-degree left turn, a police car with blue lights flashing careered around, scattering holiday makers, and accelerated towards Flynn and the robber.

Still keeping a tight grip on the man, Flynn bent over and laid the gun on the ground, then carefully placed his right foot on the barrel. He raised his left hand to show he was unarmed and dangled the man from his right so that he was on tiptoes, as if hanging from a hook.

Once more the man looked malignantly at him. He said, 'I know you, don't I?'

FOUR

It had been a long day for DC Jerry Tope over 1,000 miles away from Ibiza, up in deepest Lancashire.

Tope had been one of the officers involved in the drugs raids overseen by DCI Craig Alford that day, but Tope's involvement, like Alford's, had been for much longer than the day itself.

Tope was an intelligence analyst. It was a job he loved because it meant he could sit in front of a computer all day and delve. For the last three months he had been part of the Aquarius team, painstakingly assembling what amounted essentially to a 5,000-piece jigsaw of information and intelligence which, with other Aquarius data, culminated in that day's coordinated raids, seizures and arrests. Even so, Tope did have the feeling that not all the pieces were in place; he just could not find the missing ones.

But anyway, it had been a very good day indeed.

Although it was very much unlike him, Tope had been one of the officers dancing a jig with Alford around the new contact centre, much to the dismay of the communications operators.

He had left work a few minutes after Alford, following the senior detective's route for part of the journey – up the A59, under the bridge, then back towards Preston. Whereas Alford went north of the city, Tope cut west to his home in the suburb of Lea where he arrived home to an empty house, his wife Marina being away visiting her mother in London. He'd had two days of bachelor living and, weary though he was, he felt the need to get out for a drink. After a quick shower and change of clothes he jumped back into his car and headed for the Sitting Goose, a pub out in the countryside which he frequented, where he settled back with a pint of lager and a tub of salted peanuts and began to chill.

On his third sip his mobile phone rang.

'Where are you?'

Tope frowned as he recognized the voice of Detective Superintendent Rik Dean, one of the three detective supers heading the Force Major Investigation Team (FMIT), based at police head-quarters. The remit of FMIT was to investigate and run inquiries involving murder and other very serious crimes such as stranger rape and armed robberies. Dean was quite new in post, but Tope knew him well.

'Pint, peanuts, pub. Some sort of European footy match on big screen TV,' Tope answered.

'I need you to turn out now, Jerry.'

'Me?' Tope was a desk jockey of the highest order. His forays into the real world of front line policing were few and far between, something to be avoided if at all possible unless it involved a jolly. 'I do intel,' he said, but realized that a direct call from an FMIT superintendent was unusual.

'How much have you drunk?' Dean asked.

'Third of a pint. Just sat down.'

'Leave it . . . I'll reimburse you out of my own pocket. This is urgent, all hands on the tiller and all that shit.'

'OK, what is it?'

Fifteen minutes later Jerry Tope knew exactly why he did not like turning out to jobs. He had made his way straight from the Sitting Goose to Craig Alford's house on the A6 with a terrible churning sensation in the pit of his guts. There was a row of police cars, all makes, liveries and departments, parked on the roadside and a police crime scene tape stretched across the entrance to Alford's driveway.

Tope parked about quarter of a mile distant so as not to get in the way, then walked back with growing trepidation, his legs feeling like sloppy jelly.

He registered his name with the uniformed PC at the gate, the one recording all the coming and goings and preventing any unauthorized access. He was directed to the Scientific Support van, where he was issued with a white forensic suit with elasticated slipovers for his shoes, a hood and a surgeon's mask and latex gloves; basically he was covered from head to toe. He was ready to enter.

He had never been to Craig Alford's house, although he had known the guy for the best part of fifteen years. Alford had been an ambitious detective with his eye, ultimately, on becoming a superintendent whereas Tope was content to search around computer databases and analyse information. Also, Tope was not the most sociable of men; nerds like him rarely were. And although he had been invited to a couple of 'bashes' at Alford's over the years, he had never quite made it to the door, even though he quite liked the man and knew that his wife, Carrie, was also a detective. Tope had worked with Alford on a few protracted, high-profile investigations over the years.

His walk up the driveway seemed to take for ever until he finally reached the front door. Across this there was more tape, but at a height that made it possible to duck underneath easily enough.

Tope stopped on the top step and looked through the open door.

A besuited crime scene investigator was peering closely at the frame of the lounge door to the left, his powerful digital camera hanging from his neck. Incredibly, he was using a magnifying glass.

The CSI stood aside and allowed someone to come out of the lounge, also in one of the forensic suits.

Rik Dean pulled the hood from his head and breathed out long and slow.

Even in those few moments, Tope saw that Dean was deeply affected by whatever horror was in the room he'd just stepped out of – a room Tope now did not wish to enter.

Dean wiped his brow with his forearm, then clocked Tope on the doorstep on the other side of the tape. He made towards him.

Tope watched him approach – another detective he had known for a good number of years. Rik Dean had begun his service, as all cops did, as a uniformed PC, having joined from the Customs and Excise people, as they then were. He had been a brilliant thief taker, his skill recognized, and he was headhunted on to the CID. Here he blossomed and, proving that as well as being an exceptional detective he was also a good manager and leader, worked his way up the ladder of rank to become a superintendent and a Senior Investigating Officer (SIO) on FMIT. Tope knew, though, that Dean was not finding the new job easy, having underestimated how tough it was at that level.

'You were quick,' Dean said to Tope.

'Came straight from the pub.'

'This is a bad one,' Dean said bleakly.

'Uh – why am I here?' Tope asked. Analysts usually came into their own later.

'Because I want you here from the get-go. I want you to feel part of this, not even slightly detached from it, OK?'

Tope nodded.

Dean raised the tape, Tope ducked under. He traipsed behind the superintendent down the hallway to the lounge door.

Tope's experience of terrible crime scenes was mostly from CSI photographs and videos, which did give a certain detachment; to be at an actual scene was something very different.

'You were with DCI Alford in comms, I believe?' Dean asked.

'All day,' Tope confirmed.

'Were you there when he left for home?'

'I was . . . I left a few minutes after him, just after eight.'

This snippet of dialogue took place in the hallway just in front of the closed lounge door and before Tope was given a view of what lay beyond.

The bloodbath.

'Presumably you took the same route as he did into Preston?'

Tope shrugged. 'It's a presumption. I never actually saw which way he went.'

'But, assuming you did take the same route, and I'm not saying you did, did you see anything suspicious?'

Tope quickly spun the journey through his mind's eye, then shook his head. 'Nothing . . . do you think this is connected to Aquarius? We've locked up some very bad people today.'

'Don't know yet,' Dean admitted. 'We don't know anything . . . other than Craig Alford drove home after work and he and his family were executed. Excuse us,' he said to the CSI, who was still using his magnifying glass on the door frame. The man stood aside.

Dean's hands were in tight-fitting latex gloves, as were Tope's. Dean pushed the door open with the knuckles of his right hand and stepped into the room.

Tope took a breath to steady himself and followed tentatively.

The room was the sort of lounge Tope would have expected that a reasonably high-ranking cop and his wife would have. Quite big, a comfortable three-piece suite, big screen TV in one corner with an expensive-looking DVD player and sound system; nice pictures on the walls – signed, limited editions of Lancashire landscapes by local painters; a display cabinet with mainly police-related medals and certificates in it. There was a small upright piano in another corner and, beyond, the whole thing opened out into a pleasant dining room and conservatory.

Tope caught sight of a large, framed, professionally taken Alford family photo above the fireplace. Genuine, happy-looking people in it, spoiled for ever by the arc of blood splatter right across it.

There was a gap between the coffee table and the hearth.

This was where four bodies lay. In a pile, one on top of the other. A heap.

The two teenage girls were laid side by side on the bottom of the pile, slightly overlapping each other; Carrie Alford lay at right angles across them, and at right angles across her, and on the top of the heap, was Alford himself.

The floor underneath them was of genuine polished floorboards, and they were all lying in a huge pool of their own blood, thick and coagulating, becoming tar black as it congealed.

More blood was splattered across the hearth and up the walls.

Tope's mouth went very dry and he had to click and roll his tongue to induce saliva. He could taste the leftover alcohol from the few mouthfuls of lager he'd had earlier.

The two girls were lying face up.

The wife was face down, as was Alford across her.

The three females had all been shot through their faces. The entry wounds – two bullets each in the case of the daughters – were obvious, but because they were lying on their backs and had not yet been moved, the exit wounds were not visible.

But there were definitely exit wounds; as Tope glanced up he saw blood and brain residue across the big TV screen.

Alford's wife had also been shot in the face, but because she was lying face down over her daughters, the horrible exit wound was visible.

Tope ran his finger and thumb across his eyebrows.

Alford, unlike his family, had been shot through the back of his head and the entry wounds through his short-cropped grey hair were clear to see, but not the exits through the front of his face.

Tope swallowed, still drily, as his eyes came to rest on Alford's back. His police warrant card was laid on it.

'Have they been deliberately arranged like this?' he asked Dean.

'Don't know yet, too early to tell.'

'But it looks like it . . . and we do know they've been executed.'

'Yeah, we know that,' Dean confirmed.

Tope thought back to earlier in the evening and Craig Alford's jubilant face at the news of the success of Operation Aquarius, his dance of joy.

'Boss?' he said to Dean.

'Yeah?'

'I think I've seen enough . . . I really need to—' He gulped. 'Y'know?'

'Go for it.'

With his mouth clamped tightly shut and now attempting to control his gagging reflex, Tope spun, ducked under the tape, barged past the magnifying-glass-wielding CSI and headed for the front door.

He burst through the tape stretched across that opening like a runner, belted down the front steps (to the amazement of the cops in the area) and ran across the driveway, where he slumped on to his knees by the edge of the lawn and brought up what he had been keeping back.

Flynn sipped his Black Russian cocktail. Five parts vodka, two parts Kahlúa, drop of Coke, shaved ice.

It was his second one of the night and he knew that was probably enough for him because last time he'd drunk more than two he'd ended up dancing wildly to the song 'YMCA' and doing all the arm actions to it, always a few steps behind the beat.

A Black Russian certainly eliminated his natural shyness.

But he had acquired a bit of a taste for it, having been introduced to the drink by the bad influence that was Maria Santiago. Normally he was a lager man but since he had been in Ibiza, a couple of late night Black Russians had become a habit. And at five euros each, they were a bargain in this part of the world.

He was sitting on a very comfortable cane sofa in the 'Every cocktail 5 euros' bar squeezed amongst the many other bars and restaurants lining the Santa Eulalia marina, sipping the now favoured cocktail, drawing it into his mouth through a short stubby straw and watching the world go by.

He had eaten alone – not the plan – at the restaurant next to the cocktail bar, the Black Pirate, where he'd consumed a lovely seafood spaghetti; now he was idling before heading to bed, hoping Santiago would be able to catch up with him before his head hit the pillow.

It was a warm night, as ever in late July in Ibiza, and as much as he missed Gran Canaria – where he actually lived – he could not say that his life was awful.

Flynn was the owner/skipper of a sportfishing boat operating out of Puerto Rico on Gran Canaria – normally – but at the behest of an old friend he had relocated lock, stock and boat to Ibiza for the summer.

His friend had just started a boat charter business, hiring out skippers and boats, usually on a daily basis, to take out small groups of holiday makers from Santa Eulalia to spend lazy days exploring sea caves and secluded beaches around the island, swimming and snorkelling in the warm sea, and to provide customers with all the food and drink required for a great day out. The problem – a nice one – had been that Flynn's friend had overbooked for the season and suddenly, desperately, he had needed another boat and skipper for ten weeks. He had called Flynn.

Flynn had just bought a pre-owned but gorgeous forty-five-foot sportfisher he had named *Maria*, after Santiago, and berthed in Puerto Rico. Because of the fate of his previous boat he had only just started to pick up the pieces of the fishing business, and the lure of a guaranteed 1,000 euros each week for ten weeks, no matter what, including free servicing and fuel, had been too much to resist so he had upped sticks and decamped from the Atlantic to the Med. He had been forced to leave Santiago behind. At least in the short term, but she had now joined him for an extended period of leave from her job as a detective with the cops in the

Canary Islands, based on Gran Canaria, although her boss was now screaming for her return.

Flynn raised the second Black Russian of the night but paused with it halfway to his lips and reflected, for just a moment, on Santiago.

Things could have been very different.

He stared blankly as these thoughts crashed through his mind – the idea that Santiago could have been blown to pieces in a car bomb set by an Albanian gangster called Bashkim, intent on vengeance. It had only been the intervention of a crack FBI team led by a man called Karl Donaldson, a man Flynn half-knew from some previous encounters—

'*Hola!*'

Flynn shook himself out of his contemplation as Santiago waved a hand in front of his eyes, interrupting his thoughts.

'You look like your motor has run down,' she said, flopping next to him on the sofa.

'Just thinking,' he said, making light of his dark 'what-if' musings.

'About me?' she cooed, leaning into him, angling her face up and fluttering her brown eyes at him.

'Actually, yes,' he admitted, then took a pull of his Black Russian up the straw.

'I'll have one of those,' she said. She beckoned a waiter and ordered two more.

Flynn said, 'I'm OK, I've had enough.'

'Who said they were for you?'

'Oh,' he said warily. '"YMCA" time?'

In order to maximize the income over that summer period in Ibiza, Flynn had decided to live on board his boat berthed in Santa Eulalia. It was a windfall he wasn't expecting, but to rent a decent apartment for ten weeks would have been a big chunk out of the gross. When the contract was over, he wanted to be able to return to Gran Canaria with as much cash in his back pocket as possible to give him a cushion up to the end of the year while he got the deep sea fishing business up and running again.

Previously he had part-owned a boat with a business partner. When the partner had become embroiled with some seriously shady men Flynn had ultimately lost that boat in spectacular fashion but had acquired enough money to buy another and start again. The purchase had cost him virtually every penny of that cash, which was one of the reasons why living frugally in Ibiza for two and a half months was not to be sneered at.

He and Santiago had strolled back to his boat moored at one of the jetties and they sat on the rear deck, tired, but not yet wanting to go to bed.

They were sipping cheap whisky and Santiago was telling Flynn about the two armed robbers from the Spar shop.

Being a cop, albeit in Gran Canaria, she had felt it appropriate to spend some time with the local force while the two villains were processed. One was still under armed guard at the casualty unit being treated for the facial injury he had acquired courtesy of Flynn's fist; it was actually causing Flynn some pain too. It was amazing how hard another man's face could be.

'Both chancers,' Santiago was telling him. 'From the north of England.' Though Spanish, Santiago had spent her early years in the UK, where her father had worked in the nuclear industry in Lancashire, and she was completely bilingual. Occasionally Flynn could hear a Lancashire twang, which amused him. 'Your neck of the woods,' she said. 'Blackpool.'

'What are they doing here?'

'Dealing and robbing. Apparently two Spar shops, one in Ibiza Town and one in San Antonio, have been robbed in a similar fashion: closing time, just one or two members of staff in the shop, cash and goods stolen, mainly cigarettes and spirits. They've made about seven thousand euros and if they'd been successful tonight would have had two thousand more. Obviously they're favourites for the other jobs. The local cops are just trying to locate their apartment or wherever they're crashing out. They think it's in San Antonio.'

She was referring to the resort on the other side of the island which was very much the centre of the club culture for which Ibiza was famed.

'The one I chased said he knew me,' Flynn said. 'Not sure I know him . . . and the name you gave – Assheton – didn't ring a bell.'

Santiago frowned. 'He kept asking your name. Maybe you came across him when you were a cop?'

Flynn shook his head. 'That was over ten years ago and he would only just have been out of nappies. If I'd met him, I think I would remember.'

Santiago sat back on the sofa and exhaled happily.

The boat was quite luxurious and despite being a sportfisher it was not out of place amongst the luxury boats in the harbour. It made a great day boat as well as an excellent place in which to sleep; the huge bed in the stateroom was ideal for two, even if one was as large as Flynn, who often slept splayed out like a starfish.

He glanced at Santiago and grinned. She had initially come into his life thinking she might arrest him for murder but had ended up in his arms, and he was very happy about that. For some horrific moments he had thought he had lost her, but she had survived and he was in no mood to let her go, ever.

Steve Flynn, he almost hated to admit, was in love . . . again.

'Bed time,' he announced. 'Charter tomorrow, ten until four.'

'And unfortunately I need to phone my boss in Las Palmas. He's sent me too many texts to ignore . . . wants me back on something.'

'That's a shame.'

They knocked back their drinks, then, with their arms draped around each other, they headed for the stateroom.

Somewhere in the distance, Flynn could hear music playing.

Village People. 'YMCA'.

He gave Santiago a meaningful look and cocked his head.

'No. No, don't you dare.'

'But I love this tune,' he whined.

'Sometimes I wish I'd never introduced you to a Black Russian.'

It was at that moment that Flynn's mobile phone rang.

Flynn scowled at the caller display. As he pressed the 'answer' button – he was using an old Nokia – and gave a gruff 'Yeah?', Santiago's phone also rang.

They disengaged from each other's arms and concentrated on their individual calls.

'Steve, it's Jerry Tope.'

'What have I done to deserve this phone call? It's usually me harassing you, old mate,' Flynn jibed, but at the same time he had noticed an urgent tone in Tope's voice even in the few words spoken. It was very unusual, almost unknown, for Tope to call Flynn, since the former tried to avoid all contact if possible, their past history being a delicate one.

'Steve . . .' Tope's voice cracked.

Flynn walked to the stern. 'What's the matter?'

He glanced at Santiago, who also seemed to be having a serious conversation. As Flynn knew, no good ever came from phone calls in the middle of the night.

'It's Craig Alford . . . I thought you would want to know . . .'

'Know what?' Flynn asked, immediately thinking, *Heart attack*. Alford liked food and booze, but it was just an assumption on Flynn's part. He hadn't seen or heard from Alford in over ten years. For all he knew he could be slimmer of the year and running marathons now.

'Dead,' Tope blurted.

'Oh, God, sorry to hear that, mate.' The news did not really hit Flynn hard. 'What? Did he keel over, have a thromb?'

'No,' Tope gasped. 'Murdered. His whole family murdered, executed . . . looks like a gangland hit . . . excuse me.'

Flynn heard a rustling noise, the sound of footsteps, then a retching sound he guessed was Tope honking up his stomach contents. The connection went dead.

Flynn glowered at his phone, then looked up at Santiago, who had just finished her call. She was looking at the screen of her mobile, a smart phone, much more advanced than Flynn's little block of antiquated electronics. He recognized the sound of a text landing and saw her reaction to whatever it was: a sudden look of horror as her lips popped open and she pivoted her head to look at him.

'Uh, yeah?' he said.

Carrying the phone as if it was a block of gold, she came up to Flynn.

'That was the detective investigating the robbery at the shop. He found the apartment rented by the lads in San Antonio.'

'OK.'

'He sent me a photo of one of the items found.' She turned the phone around and showed him the full screen.

It was a photograph of a photograph.

And that photograph was of Steve Flynn.

*   *   *

About the same time as Flynn squinted, puzzled, at his picture on Santiago's phone, a series of photographs and a short video landed on another phone.

The recipient smiled grimly and with satisfaction at the images of four dead bodies, ruthlessly dispatched, then piled on top of each other like trash – exactly as the man had ordered, because that was what he believed. DCI Craig Alford and his family were garbage and needed to be put down like the dogs they were, but Alford himself had to witness the deaths of his family members first, before he himself was executed.

That was how true justice worked, the man thought.

And it had been a long time coming. Even so, it still felt fresh and tangy.

But it was just the beginning. More had yet to die.

The message underneath one of the photographs read, 'Instructions complied with. Continue?'

The man thumbed his response. 'Continue.'

FIVE

'Who was he to you?' Santiago asked Flynn.

They had decided to forgo bed for a little longer and were sitting on the rear deck of the boat, the night still warm enough for T-shirts and shorts, accompanied by a measure of decent whisky this time, watered down ever so slightly to bring out the flavour of the malt.

Flynn considered the question, screwed up his face, shook his head.

'To be fair, not a lot,' he admitted. 'He was a DI – detective inspector – when I was back in the job. I knew him reasonably well, we got on all right, but I wouldn't call him a friend as such. We worked on a special task force, two thousand two, three, for about six months. I was a drugs branch DS and he headed a small unit.' Flynn shrugged his shoulders. 'Beyond that, nothing . . . I suppose Jerry just wanted to tell me . . . he was part of that unit too. Even though Alford and I weren't close, it's still a big thing when a colleague dies, especially in such circumstances, as you know.'

Santiago nodded and delicately sipped her spirit. The effect of the Black Russians seemed to have worn off and both were now stone cold sober, not feeling the need for sleep.

The boat bobbed gently on the water. The resort of Santa Eulalia was shutting down for the night now. It was nothing like its vibrant, drug-fuelled sister, San Antonio. Santa Eulalia was aimed at young families and middle-aged people and did its job very well, but it also meant it was a much more subtle, gentle place, with a pace to match.

'Jerry isn't good at real life crime.' Flynn grinned. 'I can imagine the effect it would have had on him. He's got a queasy tum at the best of times.'

'I can imagine, too,' Santiago said. She knew Tope and had liaised with him earlier in the year over crimes and criminals in the Canary Islands – and had survived the same car bomb attack at the hands of the vicious Albanian gangster, Aleksander Bashkim.

Flynn sipped the whisky and said pensively, 'Craig Alford, dead.'

'Did you ask Jerry what Alford was currently investigating?'

'Didn't get a chance, but not really my business, I suppose.'

'Sounds like he's into something, ruffled some feathers.'

'It does,' Flynn agreed.

'And moving to the other issue of the night . . . why would a scumbag armed robber have a photograph of you in his apartment?'

'Let me look again.' Flynn waggled his fingers at Santiago, who picked up her phone, found the photo, handed it over.

It was definitely a photograph, a head-shot of Steve Flynn, about passport size. It was quite old, well over ten years. As he looked at it, something dawned on him.

It showed him with quite long, slightly unkempt hair, wearing an open-necked shirt and with very obvious stubble around his chin.

'This is an old warrant card photograph,' he declared, 'from my drug squad days – hence the haircut, clothes and lack of shaving—'

'And style,' Santiago quipped.

'That too,' he agreed. 'So the mystery is not only why did he have it, but also how did he get it?' Flynn pondered and tried to get his mind to work. It did not seem to want to solve anything. He'd had a long day with a charter, then the evening excitement of busting up a robbery had made it all drag out even more. He had a day trip later that morning, so he knew he needed to be properly rested for it. The party was due on board at ten until four, and before they even set foot on deck he had to prepare the boat. The latest he could start was eight a.m.

'There was a phone number scribbled on the back, a mobile,' she said.

'Did the detective ring it?'

'Yes . . . dead. A burner, probably,' she said, meaning a pay-as-you-go disposable.

'Right.'

Santiago watched Flynn's face, saw his eyelids droop.

She took her phone back and said, 'Bed.'

'Anything?'

Jerry Tope looked over his shoulder at Rik Dean, who was standing in the doorway of Craig Alford's tiny study on the first floor.

Tope was sitting at the desk, still in his forensic gear, latex gloves on, with Alford's personal laptop open in front of him. Four other laptops, two iPads and four iPhones had also been found in the house, belonging to the various members of the family. They were stacked on the desk and had been bagged as evidence for Tope and other techies to look at later. For the time being he had occupied himself with what he assumed was Alford's own laptop. Tope knew the DCI also had a desk computer, laptop and iPad at work which would all need investigating.

Tope shook his head in answer to Dean's query. 'This looks like a computer the family all had access to,' he said. 'Thousands of photos stored on it, holidays and such like . . . and it looks like Craig was trying to write a novel, working title *The Great British Cop Thriller*. Done one chapter . . . looks pretty good,' he said sadly. 'I've glanced through his personal emails, but nothing of interest stands out just yet, all crap and spam, mainly.'

'When was the computer last accessed?'

'Five p.m., day before yesterday.'

'No one's been on it since?'

'Not that I can tell.'

'Do you think this has anything to do with Operation Aquarius, Jerry?' Dean asked.

'Has to be a possibility, I suppose . . . we've been following some really bad people, but until yesterday morning none of them would or should have known that, unless we've got a mole in our midst. And even then,' – Tope's face looked pained – 'just seems so far-fetched, and to arrange something like this in that time scale . . . doesn't seem feasible to me.'

'Mm . . . we need to look at what else he's been involved in,' Dean said, musing out loud. 'You'd think it was connected to his job . . . maybe corruption.' Tope shot him a sharp look. 'Just surmising, Jerry, but it'll need following up.' Dean was trying to juggle together an investigative strategy, looking at all possible angles – and there were many, even at such an early stage. 'You keep looking, give it another half-hour, then go home, get a bit of kip, and we'll reconvene at HQ at eight. I'm going to run this from the Training Centre, it's as handy as anywhere.'

Dean turned, leaving Tope at the computer.

The screen in front of him was actually the one he had mentioned to Dean, the files containing thousands of downloaded digital or scanned photographs, all in separate folders, hundreds of them.

Tope had clicked on a few, and no doubt over the coming days as the murder investigation got under way, he – or preferably someone else – would have to skim through each file and photo.

He sighed, tabbed through the screen and was about to move on when he spotted something that stood out to him. A file named 'Ambush'. He hovered over it with the cursor and pressed 'open'.

There was only one photograph in the file and it was not a digital download as such, but a scanned copy of another photograph.

Jerry Tope remembered the picture being taken.

'Shit,' he said sadly, looking at the faces of the six men in it.

One of them had died two years earlier from cancer but the other five, to the best of Tope's knowledge, were still very much alive – with the exception now of Craig Alford, who stood in the centre of the smiling group.

'Those were the days,' Tope thought.

Tope himself was one of the group, as was his old colleague – he hesitated even to think the word 'friend' – Steve Flynn, whom he had phoned earlier to tell him about Alford's death. He had thought Flynn would have wanted to know because, after all, this lot had been through some things together.

But that was all a long time ago.

People had died since then, people had moved on, people were different, not least Flynn. That said, the photograph on the screen, one Tope had not seen for a very long time (although he had a copy of it in an album somewhere), evoked memories, a certain time, a certain place.

He printed off a copy, folded it and slid it into his back pocket, just for old times' sake.

It was three a.m. by the time Tope had finished his initial trawl through the computer, having found nothing of interest. He would need the actual thing in front of him at his work desk before he could dig deeper and find any hidden information or deleted files, though in all honesty he did not expect to find too much, and certainly nothing that would link to Alford's death. Even the visible browser history reeked of dull. Lots of searches about running a bed and breakfast or *gîte* in France, obviously Alford's retirement dream.

One which would never now be realized.

With sadness overwhelming him, Tope closed it down and reluctantly made his way downstairs, which was still a hive of police and forensic activity. He tiptoed out of the house without having to look into the lounge.

Outside he stripped off his forensic suit, bagged it and signed it back to the CSI van, then made his way back to his car. He sat in it for a long time before starting up and heading towards home.

With the air conditioning just ticking over, humming low, the boat was cool and comfortable but, even so, Flynn could not find his 'off' button.

Santiago slept soundly, almost instantly, emanating a cuddly purring sound that Flynn had learned to love and could usually fall asleep to. Usually.

He lay on his side and in the darkness of the stateroom watched Santiago sleep, hoping he wasn't being too creepy. He knew of men who sat up watching their girlfriends, wives, whoever, sleep, and found it quite unsettling, but the only reason he did it that night was because his mind was tumbling and criss-crossing with thoughts which would not settle.

First, about Santiago and how lucky he was to be lying here by her side . . . he recalled several months before leaning on the railings of a café in Puerto Rico, watching her drive away with Jerry Tope, and not many seconds later standing next to the man who was pressing 'send' on a mobile phone, an electronic message to a detonator inserted into a block of Semtex stuck under the car.

Cruelly, that man made Flynn watch and listen to an explosion maybe a quarter of a mile away in which Flynn believed the car Santiago was driving had exploded with her and Tope in it.

Flynn had then assumed he was about to die himself, the last thing on his mind as that man had pointed a gun at his head being the thought that he had lost Santiago. But before the man could pull the trigger he had been taken down by FBI agent Karl Donaldson.

Flynn had flinched, certain he was about to be killed, as the bullets from Donaldson's gun had been fired, but it had been the Albanian gangster who slid to his death in front of Flynn's eyes, the culmination of a terrible scenario involving Flynn, gangsters, corrupt cops and Santiago.

She was a Spanish detective, recently transferred to the Canary Islands, and had met Flynn as he was arrested and framed for a murder he had not committed. As the truth unravelled Flynn and Santiago had fallen in love and when her car blew up, Flynn truly believed that once again he had lost a woman in tragic circumstances just because she had been involved with him.

Donaldson melted away immediately after his execution of the gangster, and Flynn had launched himself towards the rising, crackling flames and smoke.

Santiago turned in bed, murmured something in her sleep, a Spanish word Flynn did not recognize.

He grinned in the darkness, recalling running the fastest quarter mile in his life, along the Doreste y Molina towards the town centre, running against a tide of people surging in the opposite direction, away from the explosion, until he skidded on to Avenida del Valle and there, in the middle of the road, was the car, blown to smithereens. Smoke rose from what little was left of it, the chassis and engine block, just a burned-out, almost unrecognizable shell of tangled, scorched metal. No one inside the car – or standing near it – could have survived the blast.

He had stared mesmerized in agonizing shock at the wreckage.

The occupants would have been incinerated instantly.

Flynn had sagged slightly, a shroud of nausea enveloping him.

Then he became aware of someone on his right hand side.

Aware of shaking slim fingers intertwining with his.

A ghost. Had to be.

And also someone else standing just by his left shoulder, then the sensation of a hand resting on it.

Another ghost.

Slowly Flynn's head rotated to the right.

Santiago, pale, ashen in spite of her dark Mediterranean complexion, stood there and she was no phantom, but a living, breathing human being.

The hand on his shoulder patted him.

Flynn's head cricked left to see Jerry Tope – the man who had been in the car alongside Santiago – standing there, equally shaken, his already pale colour now pure white.

'Fuck me, mate, that was close,' said Tope, trying to laugh, failing dismally. It came out more like the sound of a cockroach being crushed under a boot.

Santiago moved in the bed again.

From the rhythm of her breathing he could tell she was awake and her eyes opened, the glint of what little light there was reflecting in them.

'Are you looking at me?' she said softly.

'If the light was on, I would be.'

She shuffled towards him, pressing her hot naked body against his. He revelled in the wonderful sensation of her breasts crushed against his chest, could feel the hardness of her nipples.

'Cannot sleep?' she asked.

'Mind whirring a bit.'

'About your colleague dying or something else?'

'Something else entirely – you.'

But that was not strictly true because in the tumble of his thoughts he had not been thinking exclusively about her. He had been thinking about Craig Alford and was trying to get his head around the enormity of the murder. A whole family. Who, what sort of a bastard, killed a whole family? What could Alford have been involved in to bring about retribution of that magnitude?

The other slightly worrying thing preying on his mind was why his own mug shot should be in the possession of a toe-rag armed robber in Ibiza. That did not make much sense to him, though he speculated it might have had some connection with the Albanian gangsters he'd had a run-in with. But even that seemed unlikely. A low level crim from Lancashire, a nobody, having those connections seemed a bit ridiculous.

Santiago wriggled against him. He gasped when she took hold of him, rolled him on to his back, then sleepily straddled him.

In a time zone one hour behind the one Flynn was in, another person unable to sleep was Jerry Tope.

He had driven home, poured a large whisky, then sat in the living room staring blankly at the TV, sipping the fire-water, unable to rid his mind of the image of four stacked bodies, the lake of blood in which they lay, their own blood, creeping across the wooden floor.

He considered going to bed, yet, weary as he was, the prospect of climbing between cold sheets and into an empty bed was not enticing.

Instead he decided he needed air.

He placed his glass down – he would return later for the unfinished drink – stood up, grabbed his jacket and went out to the car.

They made love slow and easy. Soon after she was asleep again, rolling to the far edge of the bed, putting some distance between them in what was essentially a large, triangular bed. This allowed Flynn to slide out without disturbing her, pull on his shorts and head out to the rear deck, where he stretched out on the cushioned bench and closed his eyes. In moments he was asleep.

Tope drove down to Preston Docks, less than two miles from his home, feeling a need to clear his head. He pulled up in the car park at the Morrisons supermarket, then walked across Mariners Way on to the wide promenade that ran all the way around the big old rectangular Albert Edward Dock, part of which was now a small marina for leisure craft.

Tope leaned on the railings and looked down into the still water, which was a fairly unpleasant shade of green because the whole dock was infested by dreaded blue-green algae which discoloured the water and made it unsafe in several ways, for both animals and humans.

However, as dawn slowly approached, the water was actually looking good. Tope thought if he took a little exercise by walking swiftly around the perimeter of the dock it might just help him sleep.

He set off, turning right and heading west, crossing the dock via the swing bridge over Navigation Way, then walking past the series of converted warehouses, now apartments, along the southern edge, then past the multiplex cinema at the far end and turning back more or less to his starting point. There he paused again and leaned on the rails, feeling fresh in the cheeks now, watching the aerial acrobatics of some black-headed gulls.

His mind churned with the night's activities. He pulled out the photograph he had printed off, the one with the line-up including Alford, Flynn, Tope himself and other detectives. He unfolded it carefully, then took out his mobile phone and with the inbuilt camera took a photo of the photo.

He was concentrating on this task and never heard the soft-footed approach from behind.

As he pressed 'send' on his phone, he felt the muzzle of the handgun at the bottom of his skull, the point where his cranium rested on his spine.

He would never know it, but the barrel of the gun was angled slightly upwards so the trajectory would take the rounds up through his head, through his brain, and the hollow-pointed bullets would exit somewhere around his hairline. Which they did.

Tope had no time to react because, in the world of professional killers, conversations are rarely entered into. They are given a job. Sometimes they know the background of the target, some-times not.

As it happened, the man who had sneaked up silently behind

him did know the provenance of the contract, but even so it was not his job to chat about it.

His job was to kill efficiently, to exact revenge.

He fired two very quick shots into the back of Tope's head, both of which exited through his forehead, ripping away the top half of his face.

Tope slumped across the railings.

The killer had hoped he would somersault over them, but that wasn't to be. People being shot rarely respond spectacularly, and Tope simply fell limp across the railings, then slithered to the ground.

The killer kicked him over into the murky, infected water of the dock. His body slapped into it with a muted splash.

The photograph Tope had been holding had flapped to the ground. The killer picked it up, gave a short laugh and dropped it into the water, where Tope's body had already splayed out face down on the surface.

The photograph, purely by accident, floated down and rested on Tope's back like a leaf falling on an autumn day.

Very quickly the killer leaned over and took a few shots with his mobile phone, then was gone.

The sound of a message landing on his phone roused Flynn. He stirred and groaned. The Black Russians, the lovemaking and the excitement of the previous evening, which had initially made him unable to sleep, were now having the opposite effect and he was in a stupor as he fumbled for the phone and looked through bleary eyes at the message. It was just a photograph – no accompanying text – from Jerry Tope.

Flynn sat up, his head throbbing, and looked at the image.

He gave a short laugh and thought, 'Memories.'

At the same moment, a series of photographs and a short video landed on another phone.

A message underneath one of the photographs read, 'Second instructions complied with. Continue?'

The man thumbed his response.

'Continue.'

SIX

Flynn's response to Tope's photograph was to take and send a photograph of his own on his ageing Nokia, a view from the back of his boat, capturing the twinkling lights of the resort. He then tossed his phone down on to the sofa he'd been sleeping on.

He stood, stretched and yawned, rolling his neck muscles in an effort to eliminate the headache.

Everything seemed to have worked against him getting a half-decent night's rest and already there was more than a hint of dawn in the eastern sky. He knew it was pointless trying to sleep now.

He pulled on his ragged basketball vest and then his equally ragged trainers, took a long swig of water from a bottle, then with another, smaller, water bottle in hand crossed to the jetty and began a slow jog. He had it in mind to head along the coastal path in a north-easterly direction up to Es Canar, the resort where the famous weekly hippy market took place, and then back, a distance of about eight miles over variable terrain.

He knew it was the only way to get his blood pulsing, to clear his head for the coming day's work. By the end of it he knew he would be exhausted, but at least on the far side of it, and this time he should get a good night's sleep.

Moments later he was cutting past the Punta de s'Església Vella – the Old Church Point – and heading towards the bay known as Ses Roquettes.

Already his head was beginning to clear.

Rik Dean had always wanted to be a detective superintendent, his career goal to be a Senior Investigating Officer on FMIT. He had never imagined it would be as stressful as it turned out to be.

Being in charge of murder investigations was one thing, and he revelled in that. It was the other dross that came with the rank and role that dragged him down. The constant pressure from the hierarchy to get better results, the endless strategic and tactical meetings, locally and nationally, and then stuff like the Women's Institute and other such bodies constantly sucking him dry of time.

He often wondered how his predecessor had coped.

As much as Dean was horrified by the enormity of the brutal call-out to the killing of Craig Alford and his family – and Dean knew Alford well – there was also a frisson of excitement in him, because he knew this was a very big deal indeed. The execution of a police officer and his family by what seemed to be a professional hitman. Dean was savvy enough to know that a successful conclusion to it could define his career – just as failure could.

But Dean was in no mood to fail.

He had decided to run the investigation out of the force Training Centre at Hutton Hall, to commandeer a couple of classrooms and convert them into a major incident room. He could have chosen to run it from Preston police station, which was geographically closer to Alford's house, but for the sake of a few miles, the Training Centre offered easier access for vehicles coming and going, and specialists, such as the intel unit, were pretty much on tap.

Once he had done what he could at the scene, then entrusting it to an experienced crime scene manager, Dean returned to his office in the FMIT building at the Training Centre – a converted, refurbished accommodation block – and set about pulling his murder squad together while, with a DI, board-blasting the initial investigative strategy.

By ten a.m. on the morning after the Alford family murder he had secured two interconnecting classrooms on top of a training block close to FMIT, one of which would serve as a briefing/tasking room, and a mixed bag of cops had assembled in front of him.

Dean had watched them all filter in, trying to remain calm and composed on the surface and also wondering where Jerry Tope had got to. Dean knew Tope's computer-based investigatory skills would be invaluable.

He rang Tope's mobile number from his smart phone and got no response; it, and Tope's home number too, clicked on to voice-mail. Dean left a terse message on both – a 'Where the fuck are you, Jerry?' kind of terseness – then dialled through to the intel unit based in the headquarters building a short distance away. No one there had seen Jerry and his desk, apparently, looked the same as it had done when he'd left it: pristine.

'Fuck is he?' Dean muttered to himself and looked up across the gaggle of officers, all waiting patiently with serious faces, some sitting on the chairs provided, some lounging against the walls.

Two of their own had been taken and all wanted to catch the killer.

'Good morning, ladies and gentlemen,' Dean said after clearing his throat. 'I'd like to say welcome but you all know why you're here, and welcome doesn't seem an appropriate word to use. Two of our police family, DCI Craig Alford and his wife, the very popular DC Carrie Alford, and their two lovely children have been brutally – callously – murdered and it is our job to catch a very dangerous killer . . .'

Dean stopped his opening, unrehearsed, speech.

The door at the back of the classroom had opened and someone was edging through the assembled officers saying quietly, 'Excuse me, pardon me,' until he reached the front.

Dean scowled at the interruption by one of the detective constables who worked for him on FMIT, then his expression changed to one of puzzlement at the grim look on the younger man's face. He had a piece of paper in his hand which he held out to Dean.

'Boss . . . sorry to butt in,' he began.

Because Jerry Tope's body had floated tight up to the side of the dock wall, it was an hour before a passer-by, a man out walking his dog, paused for breath and happened to spot Tope's legs in the water below him. The police were on the scene less than ten minutes later, but after that it took some time to retrieve the body because the waterline of the dock was about ten feet below the level of the surrounding walkway. It was impractical to reach down with hooks or ropes, plus the first officer on the scene, having peered perilously over the edge, saw the wounds to the back of the floater's head and realized this could be something more than a simple drowning. His first thoughts were that the body of the man could have been the victim of a mugging.

Tope's body was eventually recovered by use of a Rigid Inflatable Boat owned by the chandlery at the opposite end of the dock and two CSIs and two uniformed constables dragged Tope on board and then brought him ashore on to one of the wooden jetties in the marina, which was then secured and cordoned off as a crime scene.

Rik Dean met the first officer on the scene at the point where Tope's body had been pointed out to him in the water. The PC indicated exactly where he had seen Tope floating face down in the water, explained how he had seen the wounds in the back of the head but had thought they could have been caused by a blunt instrument. It was only closer inspection that revealed they were bullet entry wounds, and it was only when Tope had been hauled into the RIB that the exit wounds had been seen and Tope identified.

Dean nodded gravely as he ingested the information, all the while looking across the port at the converted warehouses opposite with all those apartments and balconies and windows facing this way.

Then, rather than driving the quarter of a mile or so, he decided to walk along the dockside to where Tope's body had been drawn on to a jetty.

Although it was not a long walk, it felt so to Dean, but he wanted to do it to get a feel for the scene – even though this was an area he was familiar with.

He reached the small marina, populated by a few uninspiring motor boats, canal barges and small yachts. He was met by a PC at the security gate and allowed through after identifying himself.

Tope's body lay under a plastic sheet.

'Let's look,' Dean said to the CSI standing next to him.

The woman bent down, picked up a corner of the sheet and drew it back.

Dean stared down at Tope's body, hardly able to draw breath. His nostrils dilated and his heart hammered against his rib cage. The grinding of his teeth echoed around his cranium.

'This was floating on the water next to him,' the CSI said. She handed Dean a clear, sealed bag containing the sodden photograph of Craig Alford and others, all of whom Dean recognized. 'Don't know if it's relevant or not.'

Dean looked at it and shrugged. 'Inasmuch as two of the people in the photo are now dead in bloody quick time, you'd think it might be.'

Like his predecessor, the man into whose rather large shoes Dean had stepped, very much a mentor and patron to him over the years, Dean liked coincidences because, as that previous incumbent had once declared to him, 'Coincidences is clues.'

Steve Flynn ploughed through the day with his clients, a nice family group – mum, dad, two teenage kids – who had rented the boat with him as skipper; Santiago came along and helped with food and drinks and the social side of things, at which she was far more adept than Flynn.

He sailed north out of Santa Eulalia, stopping off at a few secluded bays to allow swimming and snorkelling and eating and drinking at a leisurely pace.

Apart from keeping everyone safe and allowing them to enjoy themselves it was an easy day's work, though by the time Flynn re-entered the port at five p.m. he was exhausted and politely declined the offer to join the family for an evening meal.

All he wanted to do was hose down the boat, prepare her for the next day, then get showered, hit a restaurant for a pizza, get back on board, chill and crash out: evening sorted.

He thought maybe he was getting old.

The wash-down took an hour, after which he and Santiago each took a shower – one at a time (they'd tried to double up on the boat before, but it hadn't been a great success because of the lack of space and Flynn's tendency to get over-excited). After washing their clothes and hanging them out to dry they changed into fresh gear and strolled along to the Mirage Restaurant, outside which he had cornered the armed robber on the previous evening.

It was a good meal, and he weakened; instead of a pizza he ordered sizzling chicken, Santiago having the same, and local lager.

Afterwards as darkness came they sat and watched boats returning to harbour, mainly very expensive motor yachts and big speed boats. He enjoyed watching experienced skippers manoeuvring their boats into tight moorings without a scrape.

'My boss has been on at me,' Santiago sighed. 'Needs me back, he says.'

'That's a shame . . . what've you told him?'

'That I'd get back to him.'

'That's my girl . . . don't suppose you've heard anything from your cop friends in Ibiza Town?'

'Nothing. They said they'll let me know if anything happens . . . you still worried about your photo in that man's possession?'

'Curious rather than worried.'

'I'd be worried,' she admitted.

'But I'm a big, tough guy. The only thing that worries me is trying to read long words and adding up numbers . . . other than that, nothing.'

She regarded him mock-cynically. She'd seen his soft underbelly and knew that although he had the outer swagger of a male lion, inside he was a kitty cat, especially when people he cared about were under threat. Then she laughed out loud, enjoying herself. She was here for the summer with Flynn and was thoroughly relishing it. She would try to keep her boss at arms' length for as long as possible. She did not want it to end.

They strolled back to the boat, arms entwined, easy with each other. Flynn, not for the first time, pointed out stars and constellations and named them all. She pretended to be impressed.

As they stepped on to the rear deck Flynn said, 'Just need to pay a visit.'

He went ahead of her, down the steps to the toilet, while she prepared a whisky nightcap, then sat on the rear deck.

Somewhere amongst the various strains of music around the resort, Santiago picked out the tones of Elvis, or at least someone purporting to be him.

She slid back, comfortable.

Flynn reappeared, took his drink and sat next to her.

They chinked glasses.

'Cheers,' he said. 'To us.'

'Really?' she asked, taken aback.

Flynn – alley cat, love 'em and leave 'em kind of guy – twisted around and gazed meaningfully and deeply into Santiago's eyes, which shimmered in the reflected light of the resort.

'Yeah. To us.'

With his left hand now dithering slightly he took a sip of

whisky, and was about to say something even more courageous to Santiago – whose heart had started to beat very quickly indeed – when the moment was interrupted by the ring tone of his mobile phone.

He swore softly, placed his glass on the coffee table and picked up the phone. The screen did not help much, telling him the number calling was international, nothing else.

'Hullo,' he answered gruffly.

'Can I ask who I'm speaking to?' asked a male voice.

'You can ask, but you should tell me first because you called me.'

'My name's Detective Superintendent Rik Dean from Lancashire Constabulary.'

'And I'm Steve Flynn.' He sat up.

'Ahh – we know each other.'

'We certainly do, Rik . . . how are you, and what do you want from me at this time of night?'

There was a pause. Flynn's brow furrowed. He knew Rik Dean well enough, had known him way back as a great thief-taking PC on the streets of Blackpool, then on and off as a detective. They had been involved with each other on a few occasions over the past few years when Flynn himself had been innocently dragged into scenarios he would rather have avoided.

'Er . . .'

'What's up, Rik? Is this about Craig Alford? I haven't seen the guy in years.'

'You know about his death?' Dean asked, surprised.

'Yeah.'

'May I ask how?'

'Hey, look, I don't want to get anyone into any trouble.'

'You won't. Did you hear about it from Jerry Tope?'

Hoping it would do no harm, Flynn said, 'Guilty. He wanted me to know because he and I and some others worked on a special task force with Craig way back. But like I said, I haven't seen or heard from Craig in a very long time.'

'OK, I get that.'

'So why phone? I'm pretty sure I can't offer any help.'

'When, exactly, were you in contact with Jerry?'

Flynn swallowed, not liking the tone of Rik Dean's voice now

at all. 'Like I said, I don't want to get anyone into trouble . . .
Jerry was only telling me because—'

'Steve,' Dean cut in sharply. 'No one's getting into trouble here.
Jerry can't get into trouble . . .' His voice faltered.

'What do you mean?' Flynn stiffened.

Rik Dean told him.

The disease had crept up slowly on Dave Carver. He was only
fifty-six when the first 'real' symptoms were noticed, first by
himself, then gradually by others. Seven years later its progression
speeded up and it was virtually impossible for his family to care
for a once proud, quick-witted intelligent man who no longer
recognized any of them, who could not dress himself in the right
order and whose eruptions of violent temper petrified his wife and
grown-up children. He was sixty-three when he was placed in a
home specializing in the care of dementia sufferers.

The only comfort for his family was that most of the time Dave
Carver did not remotely comprehend anything that was happening
to him.

If, indeed, that was a comfort.

It made no odds to the gently smiling man standing patiently at
the reception desk of the care home, waiting for someone to appear.
In fact, his smile was the only thing that could clearly be seen of
the man's face, because most of it was obscured by the shadow
under the pulled-down peak of his baseball cap.

'You can come through now.' A woman beckoned as she opened
the secure door by the desk. She was dressed in the smart uniform
of the care home.

'Thank you.'

The two walked along a corridor.

'We haven't seen you here before,' the woman said, chattily.

'Bit of a black sheep of the family,' the man murmured. 'Live
down south . . . lots of family baggage, you know? But I couldn't
not come up here and see the old guy, even though I know he
won't recognize me.' He sighed sadly.

'I know. It's a terrible disease.'

'Yes it is.'

She led him along the corridor, up a set of stairs to the first
floor, a level of patients' rooms only.

The man kept his head tilted low, particularly when passing or approaching the very obviously placed and quite old-looking CCTV cameras on some of the ceilings. They were clearly not up to date, yet the man knew they could still be damning and were something to be wary of, work around.

'This is your father's room.'

The man said, 'Can I ask the patient–staff ratio?'

'Well, we have thirty patients and a core of four staff on at all times and then a number of very reliable part time staff and volunteers who come in to bolster up numbers. Now, for example, there are four full time staff on duty – myself and three others – plus three part timers.'

'That sounds adequate,' said the man, as though he was satisfied by the statistics. 'How much care, time-wise, do you give Dad?'

'Depends. Mainly he's self-sufficient between meals and toilet breaks . . . like now, he'll be sat in here reading.'

'Reading?' The man tried to sound interested and surprised.

'He reads a lot . . . but then . . .'

'Doesn't know what he's read?' the man guessed.

'Correct.'

They smiled sadly at each other, then the woman said, 'You don't look much like him.'

He shrugged. 'Like I said . . .'

'Black sheep.'

If she had not made that comment she might have lived. Her additional, 'You have a sort of eastern European look to you, if you don't mind me saying,' only added to the certainty.

'Not at all.' The man grinned.

She smiled and gestured. 'Shall we?'

'After you,' he said gallantly. Already his right hand was sliding inside his leather jacket.

The woman opened the door and stepped through into Carver's room, the man, just behind her, closing the door.

Carver was sitting in an armchair by the side of his bed, fully clothed with a book on his lap. He was, however, staring vacantly into space. It took a few moments for him to catch his concentration and bring his eyes to focus on the two people who had just entered the room.

'Dave?' the lady said. 'Your son is here to see you.' She stepped sideways to reveal the man.

Carver blinked uncomprehendingly, no flicker of recognition. 'Never seen either of you before,' he blurted harshly. 'Get out.'

'Mr Carver . . . Dave,' the woman cooed, and stepped towards him. She had a genuine, caring smile on her face.

That was the moment when the man drew the small automatic pistol from the holster under his right armpit. With a smooth action he simply placed the muzzle of the noise-suppressed barrel to the back of her head and squeezed the trigger twice.

She reacted as though she had been hit by a baseball bat, staggering forward to her knees before splaying out on her front.

The .22 bullets did not exit her skull but careened around in her brain, destroying the organ instantly. Blood fountained from the entry wounds like a double geyser and gouts of it cascaded from her mouth and nostrils.

Carver watched the killing, then looked at the man.

Something cleared in his eyes, in his brain.

'You've come for me, not her,' he said. 'He's sent you.'

The man nodded. 'Yes.'

'I always thought he would. It was always at the back of my mind.'

'I thought you were senile.'

'I have moments of clarity, like now.'

Carver hurled his book at the man, throwing it like a Frisbee. It was a hardback novel. It swirled through the air, catching the man unawares, and connected with his right arm.

Carver also moved quickly. He followed the path of the book as all his latent and dying instincts surfaced in a powerful primal need to survive.

But though the charge was unexpected a gap of two metres was too much for him to cover. The man's reactions were far quicker and more honed. He pivoted like a matador and pushed Carver headlong into the radiator, where he crumpled helplessly to the floor and into the half-world he inhabited, understanding nothing.

The man simply straddled him and put two bullets into his head, killing him instantly. Then he stood there for a moment and said, 'I think I've done you a favour, my friend.' He slid the gun back into the holster and took out his iPhone.

SEVEN

Flynn exhaled slowly, very unsteadily, after thumbing the 'end call' button on his phone and sank just as slowly on to the fighting chair on the rear deck of the boat. The phone slid out of his hand, hitting the deck with a thud. He brought up his left hand to his forehead and sat there in numb disbelief.

Rik Dean had described his day to Flynn, one of those from Hades. From having been turned out to the murder of Craig Alford – and the rest of the family – the night before, which had been bad enough, to beginning the first, crucial briefing for the murder team and wondering where the hell Jerry Tope was, how a DC had interrupted with the next bit of awful news: Tope's body had been found floating in Preston Docks and it looked as though he had been executed in much the same manner as Craig and his family.

Rik Dean had called Flynn because one of the first things he'd done was to call out the underwater search team to dive into the docks in the vicinity of where Tope had been found. It had proved to be a fortuitous decision because the divers had fairly quickly found Tope's iPhone on the bottom and, incredibly, after some drying out and TLC from the tech people, it still worked. From it Dean discovered that Tope had spoken to Flynn recently and had also sent him a photograph of the Operation Ambush team, at least the Lancashire contingent; ironically, Flynn had always thought that Ambush was, ultimately, the worst named operation ever. The phone also showed a blurred photograph of the marina at Santa Eulalia that Flynn had sent to Tope.

Dean had quizzed Flynn about the significance of the photograph, but he didn't really have anything to suggest. It was just an old photo he assumed Tope had dug out, one of his mementoes, after returning home from Craig's house and maybe feeling depressed.

'Yeah, I get that,' Dean had said. 'Memories.'

'Exactly.'

'Mm,' Dean muttered. Flynn could almost hear the cogs whirring and clanking in the SIO's head, trying to work it all out. He had Flynn's sympathy, because he knew that being a good SIO required an extraordinary level of skill, knowledge and abilities that only come from many years of detective work. Dean had gone on, 'He and Craig were working on an operation together.'

'Which was?'

'Big drug trafficking thing . . . made several high-profile arrests yesterday, a really good job involving some very top line, nasty crims.'

'Sounds like a starting point,' Flynn suggested, but Dean already knew that, as well as the suggestion that he shouldn't discount Craig's wife as a possible target in her own right. She was, after all, a cop too.

'In the mix,' Dean said, 'but thanks. The last thing I need on this is tunnel vision.'

'Both Craig and Jerry have been involved in incarcerating a lot of bad people over the years in various operations, so you've got your work cut out. Don't envy you. These sound like professional hits – with a touch of the personal,' Flynn concluded. 'Does Marina know, Jerry's wife?'

'I'm on it. We think she's away in London. We have a number.' Dean paused. 'That photo . . .?'

'Yeah.' Flynn picked up on his train of thought. 'You need to check if everyone else in it is OK.'

'I think it would be wise, just to warn them, but not spook them . . . by the way, a copy of it was found floating near Jerry's body . . .' Dean stopped talking, clearly emotional.

There was silence on the line.

'Shit,' Flynn said. 'Did he have it in his hand when he died?'

'I don't know . . . I really don't know.'

'Well, you know who they are, don't you?'

'I think so . . . but you could remind me,' Dean said, like a good SIO: let others do the telling.

'Well, this is just the Lancashire guys who were on Operation Ambush. There were plenty of others from other forces, but this lot – us – we were the main drivers.' Flynn reeled off the names and told Dean he hadn't been in recent contact with any of them except Tope. In fact, not long after the photo had been taken, a year maybe, Flynn had left the cops under his own cloud of recrimination.

'I'll get it followed up,' Dean said.

'I don't envy you.'

'Nah, not as such,' Dean said with a sigh. Flynn could hear heavy weariness in his voice. But, like anyone else who was or had been a cop, Flynn did envy him being involved in such an investigation. Every detective in Lancashire would be clawing to get on to it now because it had become personal.

That was pretty much where the phone call ended, and Flynn slid into the fighting chair as the enormity of the news struck him like a wrecking ball in the lower gut.

He felt the touch of Santiago's fingers on his shoulder. She had been half-listening to his part of the conversation, but going by the occasional glance he'd shared with her, she hadn't fully understood what it was all about.

She had known Tope briefly.

They had almost lost their lives together.

They had a connection, a bond.

And so had Flynn.

He had known him almost thirty years, having joined the cops at around the same time, been posted to the same town and been on the same shift for a while. Flynn had even covered for him after the stupid one-night stand Tope had been daft enough to have, which could have cost him his marriage. When Flynn had quit the cops their friendship had become a fairly distant memory, and they had only come back into contact when Flynn had wanted some information from him and had cruelly used the knowledge of the one-night stand as a bargaining chip. *Tell me what I want to know and I won't tell your wife you were unfaithful.* Since then they had always skated on thin ice with each other, although things had got better recently when, via Flynn, Tope got some huge kudos by dismantling an Albanian crime gang and discovering the whereabouts of a Mexican cartel member and millions of dollars of drug money.

Flynn would go so far as to say they had a friendship. Of sorts.

Tope might have said something different.

But now he could not say anything because someone had blown his brains out and it didn't take a mastermind to work out it was something linked to his line of work as a very talented intelligence analyst. Flynn was already sure that he had died because of what he knew or in revenge for something he had done, and the same applied to Alford.

Flynn touched Santiago's fingers with his and tried to find words. He knew it would be useless to say anything other than the truth, to try and sugar-coat the awful news. It was always best to deliver it upfront, firmly, compassionately.

He turned in the chair and looked into those amazing eyes again.

'What is it?' she whispered. 'Something more about Craig Alford?'

Flynn shook his head.

'Jerry Tope's dead. Murdered,' he said, and the hand he'd had on his forehead slid around to the back of his neck. Suddenly he was short of breath and he drew Santiago close in to him and held her very tightly.

They both needed a drink. Flynn secured the boat – although security in the port was a fairly vague concept because crime was very rare – so they had no qualms about leaving a few things out in the open. They went on to the quayside and back to the Mirage, where he bought a large beer and whisky chaser, and a tequila sunrise and whisky chaser for Santiago.

They sat on the edge of the patio area, silent, for a long time, deep in thought.

'Do you want to talk?' Santiago offered.

He screwed up his nose, a little offhand, then apologized for the gesture.

He fished out his phone and found the photo Tope had sent which, Flynn had worked out from what Dean had told him, must have been sent by Tope almost immediately before he was shot.

He had sent this to Flynn, possibly the last thing he had ever done in his life.

Flynn shook his head sadly, passed the phone to Santiago and showed her the image. She peered closely at it. The old Nokia wasn't the best to see photos clearly on, but she could work out the faces.

'Jerry is on it. And you. You look younger.'

'Twelve years ago, maybe longer, not sure. Operation Ambush.'

'Think there's a connection?'

Flynn winced and shrugged at the same time. 'Probably not, but I do know one thing . . . this is one of those jobs that comes back to haunt me.'

EIGHT

Detective Sergeant Steve Flynn peered through the driving rain flooding the car windscreen, making the wipers trudge through the downpour in an effort to keep the screen clear. Flynn's left hand clung to the inner door handle and his fingers tightened their grip as he glanced across and down at the speedometer and saw the needle hovering just below 120 miles per hour.

He had done some ridiculous things in his time and, at that moment in late 2002, he put travelling at stupid miles per hour in a torrential downpour up there among the highlights.

One slip, one moment of broken concentration, one swerve or bad move by any other driver who could not comprehend just how fast this car was travelling in these treacherous conditions, would end in disaster, possibly death.

In simultaneous thought, he visualized taking off over the central reservation of the M6 motorway and landing on the opposite carriageway. Upside down. It would be chaos.

Flynn smiled grimly, glad that he wasn't driving, then looked at the profile of the man behind the wheel.

His hands rested lightly on the steering wheel. Flynn saw that his eyes were constantly moving, looking ahead, checking his mirrors – even though the possibility of anyone coming up from behind was remote. He gave the impression of being chilled beyond ice and totally in control, which was what Flynn was glad about.

'You OK?' Flynn asked him.

'Good to go,' responded his partner, Jack Hoyle, keeping his eyes on the road.

Flynn grinned again. He knew Jack was a brilliant, highly skilled driver, better than Flynn – though that wasn't too difficult – and he was in good hands.

Flynn peered through the windscreen.

There it was. The only car on the motorway travelling at anywhere near their speed, and even through the sheets of rain Flynn could identify it because the rear nearside light was out. Flynn himself had seen to that, because he knew it was always best to have some sort of advantage on a long surveillance operation that entailed any night time following and, additionally, terrible weather.

The car they were tailing had been parked up the night before in a secure compound in north London. Dressed in black, Flynn had scaled the barbed-wire-topped walls and braved a sleepy watchdog to sneak up to the car, disable the light (without smashing it, which would have been just a tad obvious) and also fit a tracking device underneath a rear wheel arch. There had been a few hairy moments after that, with the appearance of two men from the Portakabin parked in one corner of the yard, who had scoured the yard with flashlights and woken the dog properly, but Flynn had managed to roll underneath another car and had not been spotted or sniffed out. The men had returned to the warmth of the cabin and the dog had sauntered across the yard straight to Flynn, who fed it a treat, patted its head, then made his way at a crouch and scrambled back over the wall without being detected or having his backside ripped out by an angry mutt.

The 'follow' had started late next evening. Flynn and Hoyle suspected there was a huge stash of drugs and money in the car, a Mercedes, including a quarter of a million ecstasy tablets, heroin and cocaine, valued together at in the region of £3 million on the streets.

The police hierarchy had needed a lot of convincing to allow the surveillance operation to take place. The higher ranks were always nervy about the possibility of losing track of such a lucrative consignment, but Flynn and Hoyle, both detective sergeants on Lancashire Constabulary's drug squad (a branch of the Serious and Organized Crime Unit), had argued the case: their information was that the drugs were due to be purchased by an unknown buyer somewhere in Preston and the two detectives, both with an outstanding track record (which they used mercilessly to win their pitch), had wanted to catch the money men as well as the suppliers with their hands on the product.

They had won the argument after much wrangling, but were

left in no doubt that if the operation went awry, they would be gobbled up by the organization and spat out as uniformed sergeants working busy custody offices.

It was a risk they were happy to take.

It had all gone well, pretty much up to the point where the Mercedes drove out of the compound and jumped on to the M1 northbound with three surveillance vehicles behind it and a healthy signal emanating from the tracker on to the monitors on the dashboards of all the followers.

It was eight p.m.

By eight fifteen p.m. the tracking device had been dislodged and fallen off the vehicle, before they were even north of Watford.

Flynn knew this for certain because at the exact moment it came off he was driving the first following car, Alpha One, and was positioned directly behind the target vehicle, Tango One, and close enough actually to see the tracker drop off behind the drug-filled car. He instinctively ducked as – almost sarcastically, it seemed – the device bounced twice off the motorway surface. The third bounce hit the bonnet of his car and the fourth hit the windscreen, from which it shot off at an acute angle, leaving a chip in the glass. It ended up crunched under the wheels of a heavy goods vehicle behind.

Had he been quick enough, he could have opened his window and caught the thing, but since he was travelling at eighty miles per hour, the whole incident was over in less than a couple of seconds.

The signal from the tracker died instantly on the monitors in all three following cars.

'Who the fuck attached it?' Hoyle laughed, having also seen its demise.

Although it was a rhetorical question, Flynn answered, 'That'd be me.'

'And five hundred quid down the Swanee,' Hoyle added, that being the cost of the tracker.

'Alpha Two to Alpha One . . .' The personal radios came to life, the operation having a dedicated, encrypted radio channel. 'Tracking signal has just withered on the vine.'

'Box fell off,' Hoyle transmitted. 'Box fell off . . . fitter has been bollocked . . . now all visual, guys 'n' gals.'

At this news, snorts of derisory laughter and cutting comments came over the air from the occupants of the two other cars, but it meant that the three-car follow had just got much harder and everything now rested on their skills, the rear light being out on Tango One and the hope (probably forlorn) that the target was not too surveillance conscious.

The car they were following was a high-powered Mercedes, about three years old, clean and fast, and was starting to average speeds around the ninety miles per hour mark, so full concentration was demanded from all of the followers.

So far the people on board Tango One had not obviously adopted any anti-surveillance tactics, but the journey had only just begun. There was plenty of time for shenanigans.

The first leg was fairly uneventful and, apart from losing the tracker, they reached Birmingham without incident. Corley Services was where the first stop of the journey was made, on the M6 just to the east of Birmingham and before the tangle of Spaghetti Junction.

Although the following positions had changed several times, Flynn and Hoyle were in the first car behind the Mercedes as it slowed, pulled off the motorway and stopped in the car park close to the service building. Flynn, at the wheel at that point, pulled into a space fifty metres away. Both of the sergeants were tense, as were the crews of the other surveillance cars, because this scenario could easily be the one to blow apart the whole operation if Tango One had any inkling of being tailed. Flynn and Hoyle had to rely on the occupants of the other cars to act normally too, as they had been well trained to do. If Tango One was jumpy and simply pulling in to check who appeared in the car park behind it and saw three cars park one after the other, the game would be over. But first, Flynn and Hoyle had to look normal – which meant that although neither of the two people in the Mercedes had yet moved, they would have to. To make it look realistic, they would get out of their car and stroll over to the service area where the toilets and café were situated, because that was what normal people did.

The other two cars would split. One to the petrol station, to refuel and then take up position on the other side of the lorry park to give quick access back on to the motorway; the other car to park up well away from the Mercedes, but in a position to keep it in view at all times, even if no one appeared to be in it, just in case something happened; there might be a handover, or it might turn out that there was a third person secreted in it.

Flynn and Hoyle climbed out of their Vauxhall Vectra Sport, a car confiscated from a drug dealer in Newcastle, and strolled over to the building.

The two men in the Mercedes got out of their car.

Flynn clocked them, recognized one but not the other. The one he knew was a low level drug dealer, courier and enforcer from the Blackpool area, and he guessed the other one would be much the same level. If the cops moved in on them now, each could expect up to ten years inside, or more, based on the drugs they were (hopefully) carrying. The guy Flynn recognized was also known to carry firearms and other weapons, which would add to the sentence.

They were clearly a pair of dangerous individuals but, as Flynn strolled across the car park with Hoyle, he pretended to pay them no heed and saw that they did not appear to be interested in him and Hoyle. They were both craning their necks, checking the car park.

'Jingle bells,' Flynn said.

'Yep,' Hoyle agreed, meaning alarm bells were ringing for the detectives.

Like every member of the surveillance team, Flynn had a personal radio strapped out of sight in a sling under his arm with a 'transmit' button running up a sleeve from the set to the palm of his hand, operated by his thumb; the mike, looking like a small badge, was pinned to his jacket collar which could be hunched up by the side of his mouth to talk into. The earpiece was tiny, flesh-coloured. He pressed the 'transmit' button and spoke.

'They're eyeballing, guys . . . we could've been rumbled . . . be on your toes.'

That was all he said before discreetly removing the earpiece and tucking it inside his collar. It was small, but also visible close up. It would not stand up to any inspection and was an obvious giveaway to a jumpy crim. Hoyle did the same.

They walked into the services, closely followed by their targets.

Flynn even held the door open for them, but the only response to his smile was a surly scowl as the men shouldered their way in. Flynn returned the look and added, 'My pleasure, guys.'

They heard but ignored the remark, and both turned into the toilets.

Flynn and Hoyle split up. The latter followed the two men into the gents. Flynn went into the café, ordered two large frothy coffees and took them to a table to await Hoyle's return, quickly checking up on the status of the rest of the surveillance team. All were fine. They'd relieved themselves by their cars and Flynn knew they all had flasks of coffee and sandwiches.

'Anything?' Flynn asked Hoyle as he sat down opposite him.

'Nah. One had a wee, the other went for a number two. Here they are now.'

Flynn raised his eye line past Hoyle's shoulder and watched the targets enter the café and go to the servery for food and drink.

'You know the other guy?' Flynn asked, referring to the one he did not recognize.

'No, but I picked up a London twang . . . could be interesting,' Hoyle mused.

'And we could be here for a while,' Flynn said, watching them at the counter but not watching them. He sipped his coffee, wiping foam from his top lip and stubble that was close to becoming a moustache, the rest of it perilously close to becoming a beard. Both cops looked unkempt after four days on the road, practically living in their car like the other team members. Flynn needed a bath and some proper sleep but knew this was unlikely to happen over the next few hours until this delicate part of the operation reached its conclusion.

'You OK?' Hoyle asked him.

As ever, Flynn thought his partner looked pristine – even though he was as unshaven and weary as himself – the diamond to Flynn's 'rough' in the partnership.

Flynn screwed up his face but said nothing. He wasn't prone to opening up much, but Hoyle seemed to sense something was or had been troubling him.

'What's up?'

'Dunno,' Flynn said, scratching his untidy mop of hair, almost a necessity for a drug squad officer on the ground. Not long, just fashionably unkempt. Then he said, 'Wife.'

Hoyle's frothy coffee paused part way to his mouth, then got there. He took a sip, wiped his mouth with finger and thumb. 'What do you mean, wife?'

Flynn shrugged uncomfortably. 'Not sure. Something going on.'

'Like what?' Hoyle frowned. He leaned forward, concerned.

Again Flynn shrugged. 'She just seems a bit different, distant . . .'

'I haven't noticed anything,' Hoyle said brazenly. The relationship between these two men went beyond work and into friendship in their private lives. They were drinking buddies and often went out as couples with their respective spouses. They saw a lot of each other, on and off duty.

'She's always bloody cross with me, short-tempered, always in bed before me these days and asleep before I get in. Or at least she pretends to be.'

'Just a phase,' Hoyle said knowledgeably. 'Women're like that. Faye's a good lass.'

'I know, I know.'

'When did you two last go away?'

'When we went with you and Marge, that week in Majorca.'

'Do you know how long ago that was?' Hoyle said. 'A long time ago . . . why don't you sweep her off her feet and zoom away with her somewhere? Surprise her?'

'Surprise isn't in my armoury,' Flynn admitted.

'Maybe it should be. Get romantic with her.'

'Mm, maybe.' Flynn's mind whirled with possibilities. His eyes lifted and he saw the two drug runners were getting towards the end of their snacks and brews. 'Need to make a move.'

As they left the café, Flynn was on the radio to the other team members. Flynn was essentially running the show, so he decided that the plan was to get ahead of Tango One on the motorway with two slow-moving cars – Alphas One and Two – and leave the third surveillance car to slot in behind the target as it left the service area. That way there would be one behind and two in front and they could work on formation and changes from that position.

As Flynn and Hoyle stepped out into the night and Flynn tossed the car keys to his partner, rain began to blast down.

* * *

The torrential rain slowed all the traffic on the motorway right down and reduced visibility dramatically.

'Alpha One, Alpha Three,' Flynn called on the radio.

There was no response from Three, the double-crewed car that had remained in the motorway services in order to follow Tango One back on to the motorway.

Flynn's car and Alpha Two had been on the motorway now for almost five minutes and had expected to have heard something from Three by now.

'Alpha One to Alpha Two,' Flynn tried. 'You receiving this transmission?'

'Loud and clear, Flynnie.'

'Have you seen or had contact with Three?'

'Negative.'

Flynn's eyes narrowed. The team had done a quick comms check as the surveillance was about to resume from the service area and everything had worked fine. Flynn had expected an update as soon as Three eyeballed the target vehicle about to move, but there had been no further transmission. Occasionally communications did go down and that was a problem surveillance teams had to contend with. But it was quite rare with modern radios.

Flynn tried again. 'One to Three, receiving?'

Nothing.

The next resort was the mobile phone. Flynn tried the numbers of both officers in Alpha Three, one after the other. There was no answer from either. Flynn looked at his phone and saw the signal was strong.

'Odd,' he said, but he wasn't too worried at the moment. Everyone involved in this job was skilled and experienced, not just as surveillance officers but as cops. Flynn himself had once been out of contact for almost eight hours on an operation, but you just had to go with the flow.

They were now seven minutes north of Corley Services.

Alpha Two was a quarter of a mile behind.

And no matter how much Flynn reassured himself that the two cops in Three would be OK, he began to feel a huge sense of responsibility and disquiet – feelings compounded when Tango One overtook them in the fast lane, travelling at about ninety miles per hour.

'One to Two, see what I see?' Flynn called quickly over the radio.

'Eyeballed it.'

'Any sign of Three?'

'Negative.'

'Shit, don't like,' Flynn said to Hoyle, who was now driving and had increased speed.

'Alpha Two to—'

'One interrupting,' Flynn said quickly. 'End transmission,' he barked. 'Radio silence.'

He shuffled his mobile phone into his right hand and called up both officers in Alpha Three again and once more got no response. Next he called one of the officers in Alpha Two and got through immediately. 'Burt, I want you to come off at the next junction, loop around and head back to Corley Services. I might be over-reacting, but I don't like this scenario. It might be nothing, and if it is, then it's on my head.'

'Will do . . . what about Tango One?'

'Leave him to us.' Flynn ended the call.

'What are you thinking?' Hoyle asked, and pushed up the speed of the Vectra a couple of notches.

Flynn's jaw rotated. 'Not sure, but we need to play it safe, Jack. If it's worst case scenario, it's possible these two guys have somehow neutralized Alpha Three and could be in possession of their radios, in which case they know at least two more cars are on their tail.'

'Yeah,' Hoyle agreed, grimly tightening his grip on the steering wheel.

The Mercedes cruised easily through the downpour in the fast lane.

Birmingham was on the left and they were headed in the general direction of Wolverhampton now, which, as the M6 curved due north, would soon be on their left too.

'Whatever,' Flynn said, 'we're on our own now.'

The Mercedes continued to travel quickly, relentlessly, into the weather, which worsened unremittingly.

At the wheel of the police car, Hoyle remained calm, his concentration total, while Flynn fretted about the whereabouts of and lack of contact with Alpha Three. He prayed something simple, mechanical, had happened, or maybe the radio had just packed up and the mobile phones, all at once.

One car, two radios, two mobile phones.

All at once.

He could not even begin to convince himself of that one, unless they'd been involved in a catastrophic accident as soon as they had rejoined the motorway. Not that he wished that to be the case; he just really needed an answer.

His mind was running riot with bleak possibilities.

Despite the speed, the time seemed to pass with excruciating slowness while he waited for an update. But as he and Hoyle drove relentlessly north, Flynn could not help but feel the threads of this operation unravelling. The next transmission over the radio simply confirmed this when a voice growled, 'Fucking cop bastards.'

Santiago had taken a long time to fall asleep. She had cried a little for Jerry Tope in Flynn's arms and he had cradled her until she finally dropped off into what Flynn could tell was a fitful doze.

He could not sleep again.

His mind was far too busy reliving that night, so many years before, sitting alongside Jack Hoyle as they followed a car full of drugs and money up the M6 in awful weather, and remembering the sudden breakdown in communication with one of the other surveillance cars.

In spite of the air conditioning on the boat, Flynn sweated as he recalled those dreadful words over the radio, though they weren't the only bad things he recalled from that night in 2002.

The first thing was that he could remember exactly, word for word, syllable by syllable, the seemingly mundane conversation he'd had with Jack Hoyle in the motorway café while they watched the targets drink their coffees and eat their snacks. At the time it had seemed to be insignificant – just a reluctant Flynn opening up to his best friend over concerns about his wife and his worries about her behaviour. Just a mate talking to another mate, normal, everyday, innocuous.

Even now Flynn could see the look in Jack Hoyle's eyes, because now he could interpret what he saw.

Lying there with Santiago, Flynn ground his teeth as in his

mind, like a TV screen on pause, he stared at Jack Hoyle's deceitful eyes.

'Bastard.' Flynn's lips moved almost silently.

But then he shook away the image and moved on.

Jack Hoyle back at the wheel of the surveillance car. The rain. The target vehicle ahead with just the one rear light.

One hundred miles per hour. Speeding through a lake.

The motorway signs indicating Stafford.

Flynn's mobile rang.

'Steve, it's Burt Tucker.' Tucker was one of the pair who made up the team Alpha Two, the unit sent by Flynn to go back and investigate the reason for Alpha Three's sudden breakdown in communication.

'Fire away.'

'We've found them, Steve.'

'Thank God for that.' Flynn's relief was all in his voice.

The phone connection went silent. Flynn thought the signal had dropped, but it had not.

Burt Tucker said, 'No, Steve, not thank God.'

NINE

They lost the car somewhere between Junctions 28 and 31 of the M6 when a combination of the terrible weather and volume of traffic brought the whole northbound motorway to a halt. At one point, Flynn and Hoyle were directly behind the target, nose to tail, uncomfortably so, with all three lanes at a standstill.

Flynn was raging.

'I'm gonna get out and drag those two bastards out now,' he growled. The fingers of his left hand touched the door handle.

'You'll get killed,' Hoyle said, 'either by them or by the traffic.'

Flynn was not listening.

He started to open the door, fury consuming him and his judgement; the red mist he could rarely control was now in front of his eyes.

'We need to grab them.'

'I know, I know,' Hoyle said sympathetically. He too was bubbling but trying to remain sensible and rein in Flynn, who was well known for flying off the handle. 'We've got traffic cars coming together further up the motorway on the M55. We'll stop them there, we're pretty sure they're going that way.'

'Pretty sure isn't a certainty. Suppose our gen is wrong?'

'It won't be,' Hoyle tried to reassure him.

'I'm going,' said Flynn impetuously.

He dragged open the door handle.

The men in the car – the identity of one known, the other not – were now hot murder suspects. They had gravitated from being drug runners to cop killers.

Burt Tucker, the detective constable, and his partner Jane Raw, who together made up Alpha Two, had done a turn-around back to Corley Services to try and discover why Alpha Three had gone off the grid. They had discovered the two-man team – Alpha Three – in the same spot where they had parked when they had come off the motorway and where they had stayed put with the intention of following Tango One back on to the M6.

Three had never moved.

Tucker and Raw from Alpha Two drew in behind the surveillance car and as their headlights swept across the car, they saw their worst fears confirmed.

Both detectives were dead, each shot brutally through the head, slumped down and sideways in their seats with terrible entry and exit wounds and blood-soaked sandwiches on their knees. The driver's window was fully open and the first assumption to be made was that whoever had killed them had somehow enticed the driver – DC Dave Crump – to open his window to talk.

Flynn was certain the offenders were in the car ahead.

Had to be.

On hearing the report from Burt Tucker, Flynn had immediately contacted the control room at Lancashire Police HQ and begun to arrange for traffic cars and Armed Response Vehicles to lay a trap somewhere ahead so the Mercedes could be pulled, the occupants arrested. When, shunting in the almost immobile traffic on the motorway, he and Hoyle had found themselves by accident directly behind the Mercedes, Flynn could not resist going for it.

Though he was unarmed and in an extremely dangerous situation, he was in a fury at the thought that two colleagues and friends were now dead, and a hundred per cent certain the killers were less than twenty feet away from him.

A man like Flynn could not do anything but act. It was in his DNA.

As his door opened, he cracked open his extendable ASP baton to its full length and was instantly drenched by a shower of heavy rain.

Then, as often happens in motorway traffic jams, a gap suddenly opened next to the Mercedes and immediately the car jinked sideways into it. Almost as suddenly the gap then closed tight and the middle lane moved on, leaving the fast lane at a standstill. Hoyle had no chance of following.

Flynn slammed his door shut and swore. 'Make sure you don't lose him,' he growled at Hoyle.

'I'm going nowhere,' Hoyle said sullenly. Then the inside lane moved again, but the fast lane stayed where it was.

Peering through the dark blanketing rain Flynn saw the one-tail-lighted Mercedes swerve across into another gap that had opened up on the inside lane; then, as the middle lane shuffled forward again – but without any gaps opening up – he lost sight of the car.

Hoyle edged the Vauxhall across, indicating.

Flynn opened his window and leaned out, gesticulating at other drivers to let them in, but nothing much happened except that he got even wetter. It was hard for anyone to see at best and his rude gestures did not endear him to other drivers caught up in the jam.

Eventually Hoyle crept into the centre lane.

Which stopped dead, no escape either side, although the lane he'd just left began to move.

'Well, at least he won't be going far either.'

Flynn could feel the muscles in his neck coiling like steel rope as he tried to keep himself from detonating.

He phoned control room, told them their position and what had happened. He was assured that traffic and ARV patrols were now hovering on the M55, waiting for the Mercedes to show up.

As he simmered, his radio came to life and the same voice

he'd heard before taunted him with a cackling laugh and 'Useless cunts.'

Flynn took a few breaths, then picked up the mike and said slowly, 'I know who you are and I'm coming for you. Make the most of your freedom. It won't last long.'

There was a further laugh, then the radio went dead and there were no more transmissions, even in response to more of Flynn's threats.

The traffic jam broke up gradually as they approached Junction 28, the exit for Leyland. Hoyle began to make more progress until he was back in the sixty to seventy miles per hour region, about the maximum he could reach with the heavy traffic still around him.

Even so, they never saw the Mercedes on the motorway again and when they reached Junction 32 and bore left on to the M55 westbound for Blackpool there was no sign of it. Both traffic and ARVs reported that they had not seen it either.

That was the moment Flynn's mobile phone rang and his boss, a DCI on the Serious and Organized Crime Unit, demanded to know what was going on and ordered Flynn and Hoyle to return immediately to headquarters and start to answer some pretty fucking nooky questions.

Flynn tried to explain, but the DCI – who apparently had the chief constable standing right behind him – gave Flynn no option.

'You come in now, Steve,' he insisted. 'End of.'

'Sorry boss . . . you're breaking up . . .'

'Don't fuck with me, sergeant,' the DCI said.

'Can't quite . . . hear . . . you . . . bad reception area . . .'

Flynn thumbed the 'end call' and looked at Hoyle, who demanded worriedly, 'What the hell are you playing at?'

'I don't know about you, mate, but I want to catch the people who've just killed two cops, two of our mates.'

'You can't be certain it's them.'

'If it's not, I'll dust 'em down and send 'em on their way, even blow smoke up their arses.' He looked dangerously at Hoyle. 'But you and I both know it is . . . two cops sitting in a motorway service area eating their butties don't just get their heads blown off randomly.'

'But we don't even know where to start looking.'

'In that case,' Flynn said, his right hand in a tight fist and making a twisting gesture, 'let's squeeze a few testicles to find out.'

Flynn and Hoyle had both started their police careers on the streets of Blackpool, on foot and mobile. They had been on separate shifts in their early days but knew each other well, and both had ambitions to become drug squad officers. To that end, they made it their mission to get to know as many people as they could in the big underbelly of that resort who were connected in any way to the drug trade – which was, and remains, rife.

Of course that meant almost all criminals they came across in their day-to-day duties, because virtually all low level acquisitional crime funded drug activity. Shoplifters stole goods in order to sell them to buy drugs with the cash; burglars' ill-gotten gains were also used to buy drugs. And so it went.

Flynn had seen this early in his career and it was also very well documented.

He realized that arresting petty criminals, leaning on them and then perhaps letting them off for the crimes they had committed (completely unofficially) in exchange for information about drug dealers, and others further up the ladder, would be a good way for him to start to build a reputation both inside and outside the cops. This would eventually lead him to a job on the drugs squad and quite possibly the chance to bust some big time dealers. He spent a lot of time staking out locations for well-known street dealers and would often pounce, then bleed them for information.

It was a fairly ad hoc approach and not always successful, but it was something he enjoyed immensely.

Most people who bought drugs did not want to upset their supplier, usually because they were terrified to do so; most low level suppliers would not squeal on their line-supplier either, for the same reason. This became even more dangerous higher up the chain: a low level dealer might just beat up a junkie he was not happy with, but further up the chain the beatings got more serious, and a nasty death was always a possibility.

Flynn and Hoyle were quite patient, though.

They understood the hopes and fears of the people they were dealing with, most of whom existed on the bread line and were more afraid of their suppliers than of the cops. But occasionally they struck lucky and moved a rung or two up the chain of command and because the two cops treated the low levels with a reasonable amount of decency and respect they put together a very nice bunch of informants, or sources, from whom they occasionally got snippets of gold which led to decent arrests while also protecting the informants.

One informant they nurtured was called Janie Miller, a young lady who lived in a shit-hole of a bedsit and stuck dirty needles into her veins, but who actually came from a good family that could not control her. She had dropped out of college and begun life on the streets; she stole to feed an out of control drug habit that, if Flynn had not acted, would have killed her before the age of eighteen.

He met her when she had been living rough for just less than two years, although 'met' was perhaps not the best way to describe their first encounter.

Flynn almost killed her.

He was a patrol PC back then, working a response car in Blackpool Central, one of the busiest policing locations in the country, comprising the Golden Mile, Blackpool's heaving sea front where the Tower could be found, and the immediate hinterland which was a hotspot of bars, clubs, theatres, amusement arcades, the bedsit world, shoddy hotels, drugs and violence.

Flynn loved it, revelled in it.

An eight- or twelve-hour tour of duty flew by, job after job pouring in, especially during the summer months when visitors surged into the resort in their millions. Long days, short hot nights. And wonderful to be a young cop.

The report of a robbery in progress on the street behind Blackpool Tower came in on the treble-nine system.

Cops in cars and on foot were dispatched, including Flynn, who at the time of the shout was in the kitchen of an Indian restaurant savouring a hot curry. He ran to his car, a liveried Astra, flicked on the blue light and sped out of the back alley in which he was parked.

He dinked through all the short cuts, criss-crossing town through all the rat runs he knew like the back of his hand way back then, some alleyways just wide enough, but only if he aimed his car correctly. When he was within spitting distance of the robbery he skidded into another back alley – the last short cut – which, as it was almost midnight, was black.

He drove his right foot down on to the accelerator, flipped the headlights on to main beam and saw the prostrate figure laid out across the alley just ahead of him.

With a scream and curse combined, Flynn slammed on and slithered to a halt on the oily cobbles. His front bumper rocked just an inch above the body.

Drunks splayed out in alleys were a common sight in Blackpool, and this is what Flynn thought he had encountered.

He beeped his horn and leaned out of the window, shouting angrily for whoever it was to get shifted.

No response.

He jumped out, intending simply to drag the inebriate to the side of the alley and get on his way. He had hoped to be first on the scene of the robbery and was maddened to think that that pleasure was now going to fall to one of his colleagues.

His eyes took in the shape under the glow of his headlights.

A thin, scantily clad young girl, maybe seventeen, white legs and arms, hair matted and caked over her face. She seemed to be dead.

Flynn saw the blood-filled hypodermic needle hanging loosely from the soft flesh inside her right arm, a belt used as a tourniquet wrapped around her bicep.

And the dribble of vomit from her mouth.

'Shit.'

Flynn dropped to his knees beside her, turned her gently on to her side and stuck two fingers into her throat to clear her airway of the porridge-like sick. There was no retching and Flynn saw the girl wasn't breathing at all. She had flopped like a shattered doll. He rolled her back on to her back, checked for a pulse: none.

For Flynn the next few minutes were an autopilot blur of using the CPR training that had been drilled into him, pounding her chest, breathing into her mouth, watching the chest rise and fall, checking the pulse, while at the same time shouting for an ambulance over the radio.

He was later told that the time which elapsed between his first frantic transmission and the arrival of the ambulance was twenty-two minutes. During that period, the passage of time for him varied considerably. Sometimes it felt as though he was being swept away in a vortex and the seconds raced by; other times were like treading through thick, warm Blackpool rock as time slowed, almost stopped, even seemed to go backwards.

He pushed. He breathed. He spat out her sick, retching himself, but he kept going, willing the girl to live and never once contemplating the medical implications for himself – the possibility of contracting a horrible disease or infection.

And a year later – or was it just seconds? – the ambulance did arrive, and still he kept going until the paramedics eased him away and took over with breathing devices, defibrillators and cool skills. Flynn liked paramedics.

He slumped back, watching, gasping for his own breath, feeling his pounding heart crashing against his insides like waves before eventually subsiding to normal, though he sat there in the alley feeling more exhausted than if he'd just completed one of his tri-weekly workouts.

The remainder of the shift was a blur of police activity. Flynn was run ragged by a succession of incidents, including bursting into a bedsit with other officers to arrest a suspected robber. While doing all this Flynn ensured that comms kept a check on the progress of the girl from the alley and kept him up to date since, unless something transpired that meant he had to go to the hospital on another job, he was too busy to get there and check himself.

He finished his tour at seven a.m., bleary-eyed and wanting bed. But first he decided to check on the girl. He drove up to A&E at Blackpool Victoria Hospital, tucking his car tightly into the space reserved for ambulances only.

Flynn was a well-known figure at the hospital.

He had purposely nurtured the A&E staff so he had a regular brew spot which could also double as a good source of information. Many of the nurses, male and female, went weak-kneed at the sight of him – and not just because he could be charming. He had also made it his business to get to know the very harassed and overworked doctors.

'Heroin overdose,' the junior doctor explained. They were standing in one of the cubicles looking at the girl whose life he

had saved. She was linked to monitors reading her vital signs and
drips were inserted via cannulas into veins in both her arms. She
was not moving and had a deathly pallor and if the monitors hadn't
said otherwise, Flynn would have thought he was looking at a
corpse. 'And a lot of booze,' the doctor added.

'Thought I tasted whisky,' Flynn said, making a smacking noise
with his tongue and recalling spitting out a lot of unpleasantness.
'Did I do OK?' he asked.

'You did exactly the right thing . . . well done,' the doctor said.
'You saved her life.'

'That's OK, then.'

The doctor checked her watch. 'I'm off duty in ten minutes.'
She eyed Flynn lustfully. 'You could save my life too, if you
wanted.'

Inwardly he cringed. This was an ongoing, playful thing he had
with this rather gorgeous lady doctor. Both knew it would never
happen, even though they had exchanged numbers before.

'Sorry,' he said. 'Happily married.'

The older Flynn, the tough-as-nails sportfishing skipper, now recol-
lected that comment with sad cynicism.

He had thought he was happily married; at that point in his life
he was certain of it.

He had left Santiago sleeping again and was walking along
the promenade in Santa Eulalia, unable to put his thoughts into
logical order. The news of Jerry Tope's death had completely
smashed him.

He had got to thinking about Janie Miller, the zapped-out drug
addict he'd saved from certain death in an alleyway in Blackpool,
and her tenuous link to Operation Ambush.

After that night shift and ducking the advances of the lovely
doctor, the young Flynn slept well for eight hours. In those days,
he did sleep very well. He was up before four in the afternoon
and before he began his next shift at seven p.m. he went back to
BVH to check on the girl. He found she had been transferred to a
ward.

She was propped up and looked very weak but better than when
he'd found her. There was a tint of colour in her cheeks, but little
else.

Flynn introduced himself. 'Thought I'd see how you were getting on.'

'You saved me,' she whispered. Her voice had a rasp to it.

He shrugged modestly. Now, with fluids inside her, despite the prominent cheekbones – the result of addiction rather than bone structure – he saw she was pretty and had wonderful, deep blue eyes.

'I assume it wasn't an intentional overdose?' he guessed.

'I don't know. Maybe. Not sure. Could have been.'

'At least you're alive to fight another day.'

'Whatever,' she sighed. 'How can I thank you? We can fuck when I'm out of here, if you want. Free.'

Flynn laughed. 'No . . . you can thank me by going into rehab . . . I'm told counsellors are queuing up to see you. I know there's a place at Marton Hall . . . please take it.'

'OK, I will,' she promised.

Flynn held her gaze. 'But I do want something else.'

'What?' she whispered hoarsely, afraid, knowing.

'The name of your dealer.'

She never told him, but she did become a good informant for him and although she did attempt rehab, she never kicked the habit either. She had a good in-depth knowledge of the local drug scene, who the low level dealers were, a few names further up the food chain, and she occasionally fed Flynn tasty scraps about dealers not directly connected to her.

She had been the one who, several years later, when Flynn had become a hard-arsed DS on the drug squad, had given him the information about a drugs pick-up in London, bound for Lancashire. She claimed her information had simply been an overheard conversation in a pub called Fat Billy's and, though pressed, she had remained tight-lipped about names and identities.

She lived on the top floor of a council block on the Shoreside estate, one of Blackpool's poorest, most deprived areas.

Since Flynn had first met her, Janie Miller had gone unsuccessfully through numerous rehab schemes, emerging clean and full of hope for a few days until she slid back into the life, then plunged downhill like a skier. She had lived with several abusive men and had three children by three different fathers; she was not sure which child belonged to which man, though she did not really care.

Flynn never gave up on her though he did realize she was a lost cause and beyond help, but when he burst into her flat on the night his two colleagues were murdered, his patience with her had all but evaporated.

As his six-three frame crashed through the flimsy door, kicking it off its hinges, her current man friend rose to the challenge of the intruder.

Flynn put him down with one blow – a cross punch – and stepped over his moaning body as the unfortunate man clutched his crushed nose. He grabbed Janie from the tatty sofa and carried her into the bedroom, slamming her against the wall, which moved like dodgy scenery. 'Names,' he snarled into her face.

She begged for mercy, pleaded innocence, sobbing with big, body-racking gulps.

He slammed her again. Everything rattled, even the bones in her skinny body.

'Two of my mates are dead, Janie . . . I need names, now.'

'I don't know, I don't know . . .'

Flynn lifted her so their faces were aligned. He could smell her body odours, cheap perfume, her breath.

'I fuckin' swallowed your vomit to save your life. Names, Janie, or every shithouse drug dealer in this town will know you've been my snitch for the last ten years . . . two cops shot dead.'

'Let me go, let me go.'

Flynn released her with a contemptuous flick of his fingers. She slithered down the wall, her tiny skirt rising up above her thighs to reveal a lack of underwear.

'Fuck you,' he said, turning away. No matter how much he wanted to, he could not hurt her.

As he reached the door, she gasped, 'Brian Tasker.'

'Who the hell's Brian Tasker?' He turned back.

'Biggest drug lord in the country. He kills people.'

'Tell me.' Flynn squatted in front of her and dragged a pillow from the bed so she could cover herself.

'He's expanding . . . taking over . . . his gang, his organization, whatever you want to call it . . . honest, I did, I just heard a conversation . . . I was shooting up in a gents' cubicle in a bog in a pub in town . . . they didn't know I was there. They shoulda checked the shitters, but they didn't.'

'Who?'

'It were Don Braceford and this Tasker guy . . . he'd been about a bit . . . he were a big deal. Half o' what they said I couldn't remember anyway, except the name of the yard because it were my name – Miller's Yard. And I'd heard of Tottenham and I just passed it on to you. Rest were down to you. Said Will Carney were going down with Tasker.'

Flynn nodded. Carney was the low level shithead he'd recognized in the motorway service area – now one of the killers.

'You won't tell Braceford, will you?'

'Where can I find him?'

Flynn knew Braceford, but their paths had yet to cross. Braceford had been the subject of numerous unsuccessful police operations because he was a tricky, devious bastard. He was close to the top of Flynn's to-do list, a well-known quality dealer on the Fylde coast, the area of Lancashire encompassing Lytham, St Annes, Blackpool and all the way up to Fleetwood.

Flynn returned to the living room, where Janie's current beau was sitting up looking very sorry for himself, with a tea towel pressed to his face. He cowered as Flynn stepped towards him.

Jack Hoyle lounged by the broken front door. He arched his eyebrows questioningly at Flynn, who nodded.

As they left the flat Flynn took out his mobile phone and called Jerry Tope.

TEN

Those were the days when Flynn had no need to hold the sword of revelation (concerning infidelity) over Jerry Tope's head. Both were cops, and Flynn had every right to access information about villains via the intelligence system, unless it was restricted for some reason.

That said, Flynn's phone call at that particular time of day was still unwelcome.

Tope was busy in his spare room, the one doubling as a study-cum-mini-brewery. He was dealing with some delicate ingredient mixing, putting together his favourite home-brewed wine of dandelion and nettle, and disinfecting bottles.

As Flynn and Hoyle ran from Janie's flat and leapt into their tired, well-travelled Vauxhall, which was almost devoid of fuel after their long, fast journey from London, Flynn had his phone to his ear, calling Tope's home number. He knew Tope – completely unofficially, and way ahead of the rest of the force back then – had remote access to Lancashire Constabulary's computer mainframe from his house. At that time the organization was terrified of the internet and staff were only gradually being given permission on a very limited basis to access the World Wide Web from their work stations, let alone their homes. Unless, of course, you were called Jerry Tope, who bypassed everything because he could. He was way ahead in the internet game, already able to use it to access the mainframe from home, something which would come eventually for other officers, mainly those of higher rank. If he had been found out, it could have meant being disciplined and might even have cost him his job.

Flynn only knew this big secret because Tope had become very loose-lipped one night on his home brew. And it was going to prove useful now for a bit of quick out-of-hours digging.

'Jerry? Me,' Flynn said breathlessly as the phones connected.

'Do you know what time it is?' Tope responded instantly. 'I'm busy disinfecting.'

'I know the time, you shiny-arsed bastard,' Flynn responded, using the cute colloquial term for headquarters-based office wallahs. 'Two cops are dead and I need some information now.'

'Two cops?' Flynn heard something clatter in the background. 'Do I know them?'

Flynn said yes, told him their names.

'Shit, what can I do?' Tope asked.

'You can plug that dinky computer of yours into the mains, or whatever you do, and get me some information now.'

'I'm not at my desk, you know,' Tope said coyly. 'I'm at home.'

'Don't bullshit me, Jerry. I know you can get into the system from there; you told me, remember?'

'Oh, yeah,' Tope muttered unhappily. 'You haven't told anyone else, have you?'

'Not yet. Now get on the laptop and do some gardening. I need addresses for Don Braceford and I want you to dig into a guy called Brian Tasker, could be from London.'

'Got it. Give me five minutes. I need to log in.'

'I'll call you back in ten,' Flynn said and ended the call.

He looked at Hoyle, who said, 'What do we do?'

'All night Maccie Dees on Preston New Road. I need fast food fast and we need to fuel up too.'

They decided to catch a breather at McDonald's and instead of driving through they parked outside and walked into the restaurant.

It was relatively quiet, just a few customers, but they included a rowdy table of young men clearly the worse for alcohol who, when they spotted Flynn and Hoyle enter, dropped their loud-mouthed chatter and watched the two cops with surly expressions. Flynn noticed them and wondered if the lads had 'made' him and Hoyle as cops or were simply responding in the primal way of many males of that age in Blackpool – and elsewhere, of course. Flynn and Hoyle looked rough and tough, so there was an immediate challenge, even though neither of the cops paid the lads any heed.

They ordered burgers, chips and coffees and sat at a table as far away as possible from the four guys who, Flynn noted, were huddled in discussion, their eyes constantly checking them.

'We should eat and go,' Hoyle said, also having observed the glances. 'Last thing we want is trouble.' He had picked up the undercurrent of threat.

'I know,' Flynn said. He had his phone out and was looking through the numerous missed calls on the screen from the DCI. 'I need to call the DCI.'

'Good idea. Appease him.'

Flynn made the call, held the phone away from his ear at the bashing it got from a furious boss. He then explained why he and Hoyle had not stopped moving and had disobeyed orders. He said he hoped to have some good information on the offenders within minutes, and when he got it he would call in and arrange for back-up – although he knew he wouldn't. This promise placated the boss somewhat, but not much. Cops were dead. Things were messy. Other forces were involved and screaming down the line at him. The chief was still literally breathing down his collar. Things had to be done properly.

As the conversation ended, Flynn looked up.

The four lads at the rowdy table were pushing themselves up with looks of determination.

'Trouble,' Hoyle said out of the side of his mouth.

The obvious ringleader led the way and stood, swaying slightly but attempting to tower with menace over the detectives. They looked up blandly, unaffected by the presence.

'Phones,' the lad said.

'Pardon?' Flynn asked.

'We want your mobiles, now.'

'Go away, guys,' Flynn advised, stuffing a handful of chips into his mouth. 'We're busy.'

The ringleader sneered, then leaned on the table with two hands and glared at Flynn, who could smell his beer-reek breath. 'Phones, now, or you both get the living shite kicked out of you and then we steal your phones and empty your fucking wallets.'

Unfortunately for him he had positioned his face within striking distance of Flynn's right fist. Flynn hardly had to move to slam the brick-like structure of his knuckles and bones into the young guy's nose. Way back then, Flynn was all-round fit and strong and lightning quick, sometimes too quick for his own good.

The young guy's head jerked back as his face dissolved and his whole body flipped backwards against his three surprised mates, blood spraying out of his flattened nostrils. Flynn slid another chip lengthways into his pursed lips and sucked it in before saying, 'Next,' and rising slowly. Hoyle was getting up as well. Though not anywhere near as tall, broad and physically imposing as Flynn, he was also a commanding presence. And he knew how to fight, too.

'Jeez,' one of them said in awe, kneeling next to his injured friend.

'Get him out of here and you all get lost,' Flynn growled, 'otherwise we congregate outside and take it much further.' He sipped his coffee through the hole in the plastic lid.

None seemed willing for more trouble.

Four versus two had begun as good odds, especially with the

hard-man gang leader ready to mix it. Three on two was not so appealing. Already they knew that within a second it would be two against two. They dragged their mate out of the restaurant, with Flynn and Hoyle hovering behind them, then piled into a van and skidded away.

'Bloody hell,' Flynn breathed, flexing his fingers. That was the second blow he had delivered in a very short space of time and both had hurt his hand. The noses he had connected with might have squelched on impact, but Flynn's knuckles had also hit hard bone.

His mobile phone rang. It was Jerry Tope.

They did not have to go far.

Tope had accessed all the files he could on Don Braceford and pulled out several addresses, including houses and business premises, all in the South Shore area of Blackpool. The first address was a basement flat below a terraced house also converted into flats. This was close to the Pleasure Beach, Blackpool's big amusement and ride park, a place Flynn loathed. The plunging, twisting rides terrified him because he was not in control. They did a quick cruise of the surrounding streets and alleys for the Mercedes, but there was no sign of it.

Hoyle stopped outside the flat and Flynn climbed out of the police car to peer over the railings by the steps leading down to the door. Lights were out, the place was in darkness.

Flynn jumped back in. 'Next one.'

This was another South Shore flat Braceford was known to own. That too was in darkness and there was no sign of the Mercedes.

Next they drove past a seedy club Braceford part-owned with another Blackpool low life, but it was closed and there was no sign of the car.

'Doesn't mean no one's home,' Hoyle commented.

'Or that the car isn't in a garage,' Flynn added.

They cruised slowly around the streets but did not see the Mercedes.

'What's next?' Hoyle asked.

Flynn peered at the last address he'd scribbled down on the palm of his hand in black ballpoint. 'Jerry said he didn't know what this was.' Flynn switched on the inner light to squint at what

he'd written. 'Something in Marton Industrial Park,' he said, referring to the largest industrial park in Blackpool, close to the end
of the M55. It was a huge mishmash of businesses large and small,
legit and shady. It was shaped like a huge lung and fed by a
complex inner road system; finding some of the smaller business
on its outskirts could be difficult.

'It refers to a big scrapyard on the edge of the Spen Dyke
Road and the info is that one of Braceford's cars had been seen
outside it, nothing more. Jerry didn't know if this was any use
or not. Just a snippet a patrol PC had submitted to the Field
Intelligence Officer a while back, no further action taken on it.'

'Spen Dyke Road, here we come,' Hoyle announced. He knew
Marton Industrial Park well enough. He spun the car around and
cut across the resort. Less than five minutes later they were creeping
slowly around the estate. Both knew it was a base for various
illegitimate businesses in amongst the legitimate ones. It was a
fairly badly signposted place but Hoyle quickly found Spen Dyke
Road on the outer rim of the park, backing on to open farmland
adjacent to the M55. As he turned into it, the first businesses on
either side looked to be good quality, thriving concerns – an HGV
dealership, a large car sales forecourt, a small office block and an
immense cash and carry warehouse outside which several lorries
were parked, delivering goods. As the two detectives made their
way along the road, the enterprises became steadily grubbier and
seedier away from the glare of the lights.

'Did he give a business name?' Hoyle asked.

'No, just that it was a scrapyard or car breaker.'

Hoyle nodded.

The street lights petered out.

The car continued to creep slowly and the rain, which had eased
for a time, began to thrash down again.

Flynn's sharp eyes surveyed each side of the road, peering at
and between parked vehicles and at business names on units,
fences and walls. Then he spotted an open gate and beyond it
the stacked, rain-glistening broken hulks of scrap cars.

'Could be the one.'

Hoyle pulled in fifty metres down the road.

'We going in?' he asked Flynn.

'Be rude not to.'

Flynn scrambled out and went to the boot. He gave Hoyle a ballistic vest and put one on himself, then put his short zip-up jacket over it and pulled his hood over his head. Hoyle did likewise and both men slid their extendable batons into their belt rings. Both had mini Maglite torches in their hands.

With Flynn trotting ahead, they reached the open mesh gates of the scrapyard and saw the name 'Fylde Scrappers' on a sign with a phone number underneath.

'Dog,' Hoyle hissed over Flynn's shoulder and gestured with his torch.

The shape of a muscular-looking canine could just about be made out, chained to a post ten metres inside the gate.

Flynn stopped.

The dog wasn't moving, which was odd. Flynn did not know of any dog that would willingly lie on cold, wet ground. They were creatures that liked warmth and comfort.

Then he saw the reason for the lack of movement as he took a couple of tentative steps towards the beast.

'Dead dog,' he said.

A bullet in the head and one in the side of the chest.

Flynn unconsciously took hold of his baton.

'Not good,' Hoyle whispered.

Beyond the gate was the yard, crammed full of scrap cars waiting their turn to be crushed, a car transporter and beyond that a portable office with a light on inside and the door open, but no sign of life. Behind the cabin were crushed and flattened cars, stacked precariously in high towers, thousands of them, like a science fiction city set in a dystopian future.

And in front of Flynn and Hoyle was the Mercedes they had followed all the way from London. Parked alongside it was a Range Rover, almost new with smoked-out windows at the back and its front passenger door wide open.

Crouching, the detectives walked slowly towards the Mercedes, their senses in overdrive. They stopped at the boot of the car and looked through the rear windscreen. Flynn could make out a figure hunched over the steering wheel. A man, unmoving.

Flynn circled sideways for a better view.

He could not see the man's face because his head was twisted sideways on the wheel, but through the non-existent driver's door window he could see that, like the dog, the man was dead, shot through the back of the head.

'Check the boot,' he told Hoyle, who backed off and opened it.

'Spare wheel, nothing else.'

From somewhere inside the high-rise city of dead vehicles came two distinctive sounds.

Gunshots.

Flynn's head jerked around.

'We need back-up,' Hoyle said.

'Yeah, we do, but we also need to check it out.' Flynn knew his partner was right but also that it was not in his own nature not to bowl in, armed or otherwise.

By this time he'd been a cop a long time and the need to help people was part of the way he was, even at the cost of his own safety.

'That said,' Flynn muttered to himself. He opened the driver's door of the Mercedes, went on to his haunches by the dead driver. Although he could not see his face properly, he believed him to be Will Carney, one of the two men he'd observed in the motorway café. Without touching anything, Flynn leaned in and immediately found what he'd thought might be there – a handgun lying between the feet of the dead man, under the pedals of the car.

He lifted it out carefully.

'What you doing?' Hoyle asked anxiously.

'What's it look like?'

It was a Browning 9mm semi-automatic pistol, a weapon Flynn had known well in his military days. Way back then it was the preferred weapon, although in 2002 it wasn't used so much in Europe, having been replaced by lighter, easier to use handguns such as Glocks.

Flynn checked it. There was a bullet in the breech and the magazine, he guessed from its weight, was about half-full, possibly six bullets in it. Flynn had learned to estimate the weight of weapons by handling them, a skill he'd acquired in the Marines and then the SBS. It was quite hard with older weapons, which were heavier to start with, but newer ones made of plastics and carbon fibre were easier to judge.

'Might come in useful,' Flynn said.

'Shit.' Hoyle did not like this. Then he said, 'OK.'

Flynn jogged towards the cabin, keeping quiet as he went with his back against the outer wall, Hoyle behind him. Flynn gestured him to keep quiet, then stepped up to the open door in a combat stance with the gun pointing ahead of him, his arms locked in an isosceles triangle, with the weapon as its point.

It was empty. Just rubbish furniture – a desk and two plastic chairs and a rusting filing cabinet.

'Clear,' Flynn declared, dropping outside again, beckoning Hoyle to follow him.

Two more bangs, quick succession, double-taps, cracked through the night from somewhere within the stacks of cars.

Flynn ran on and found a gap and plunged in with Hoyle, a track into this city between two finely balanced towers of crushed vehicles. It was a scary journey into a creepy place where it felt as if the stacks of vehicles, creaking and groaning, were alive and might fall and crush them to death at any moment.

Flynn followed what seemed to be a prepared route, straight in, left, right, as dark as the floor of a tropical rain forest, then suddenly emerged into a clearing, again as if in a jungle, a quadrangle about twenty metres square. Dead ahead across the square were three stacks of vehicles side by side, forming an impenetrable barrier, but facing him were steps leading into the back of an open truck just above ground level.

'What is it?' Hoyle said.

'Secret hidey-hole, I reckon.' Flynn moved cautiously across the flat square, mounted the steel steps and entered the back of the truck. Beyond this at the far end of the container, and obviously underneath hundreds of stacked vehicles, was another door into a narrow passageway held up by steel lintels and girders holding up a weight that was probably in excess of 10,000 tons, lit by a string of light bulbs. It was like the entrance to an old gold mine.

Above, the vehicles creaked ominously. Rain dribbled through the gaps.

'Someone's gone to a lot of trouble,' Flynn whispered. Hoyle grunted agreement.

They began to walk cautiously along this corridor until they finally turned left and hit a dead end. Except it wasn't a dead end, it was another steel door leading into a steel container.

Flynn heaved it open.

Even years later he remembered vividly the sight that greeted his eyes.

The inside of the container was illuminated by another strand of weak, swaying light bulbs hanging on wires from the roof, but only dimly lit for that.

A blood-soaked man stood astride the body of another man with his head massively damaged by gunshot wounds, his mouth agape.

The man held an automatic pistol in his right hand, which started to rise in Flynn's direction. In his left he was holding something that Flynn did not instantly identify. Something rubbery, short, fat, squat and very bloody.

Then he knew what it was.

A tongue.

'Police!' Flynn screamed, swinging the Browning up as he dropped into the combat firing position. Already his brain was churning with everything, the equivalent of a crazy mind map.

The lighting, the distance, the angles. Should I move? Throw myself to one side? But would that also expose Jack to danger behind me? Where should I shoot the man? What if he's quicker? What would a bullet penetrating me feel like if it hit me anywhere apart from on the vest? What would it feel like if it hit the vest?

And alongside those practical thoughts of survival, other things somersaulted through his mind.

How do I explain the gun in my hand to my bosses and the Crown Prosecution Service? How will it look? Do I still want to be a cop? If I do, then pulling this trigger won't do me any favours. It complicates things so much. I'd be better off throwing it down and getting shot.

And.

A fucking tongue!

Shit!

His finger curled on the trigger.

He would use it, he knew he would. He would be able to explain it away, defend himself now and later.

Self-defence. Reasonable force.

Shit again.

'Drop the weapon!' Flynn shouted.

Flynn saw there was no chance of that happening.

And at that moment, Flynn actually froze as indecision racked him. The man's gun came up and he fired.

Flynn compacted his body mass, ready for the impact, the hot lance of a 9mm slug travelling at 1,500 miles per hour.

But nothing came.

The hammer crashed hollowly on to an empty breech. He had fired his last bullet.

The two men shared a moment of realization.

But he had not finished. The man flicked his thumb and the magazine dropped out of the stock and hit the steel floor with a metallic clatter. He hurled the bloody tongue at Flynn and then his left hand went to his jacket pocket to reach for a new magazine to reload.

Flynn reacted instantly now. He was back on firmer territory.

He dinked as the tongue cartwheeled past his head, feeling blood splatter on his cheeks, then launched himself at the man and connected with him at the moment the man's hand found the new magazine.

The man responded quickly, slicing the gun horizontally through the air, intending to smack Flynn across the head.

He missed. Flynn was moving low and fast.

He powered into the man's torso just below his rib cage, doubled him over with the impact and continued with the momentum until he had him pinned against the wall of the container.

Even trapped as he was, the man pounded Flynn remorselessly with the side of his gun against his face, smashing it into his cheekbone and jaw. Flynn held on grimly, knowing he was in a fight for his life and wondering where the fuck Jack Hoyle had gone.

That question was suddenly answered when, unexpectedly, the battering of his face ceased.

Hoyle had been behind his friend, desperate to help. His baton was out, extended, and he wanted to bring it down on the gunman's head but not smash Flynn in error.

He connected just right.

The baton arced and smashed the gunman on the left temple with a crashing, well-delivered blow that instantly knocked him unconscious for about four seconds. His grip on Flynn opened and he slid down the container wall stunned, but regaining his senses as his backside landed.

Hoyle pulled Flynn away and launched himself on the gunman. Although smaller than Flynn, he was strong and agile and within moments had the man face down on the floor, kneeling between his shoulder blades and forcing his arms around his back, peeling the gun out of his grip and throwing it aside. He kept him pinned there as he cuffed him even though he was now struggling violently, bucking like a horse.

Flynn had dragged himself away on all fours and was spitting blood from the cuts inside his mouth where his teeth had sliced open the soft inner flesh, and also spitting out a tooth, which he picked up and slid into a pocket. He shook his head like a hound dog, then crawled back to the struggling gunman and sat on his legs.

As the detectives held him down, they looked around at the poorly lit scene of murder and mutilation on which they had stumbled. They caught each other's eyes, disbelief and horror on their faces.

Flynn ordered another beer from the waitress at the Mirage. He had considered a Black Russian but singing and dancing the 'YMCA' did not seem appropriate that evening. Beer did not make him do strange things, as far as he knew.

Santiago ordered a vodka tonic.

She had listened to his retelling of events and as he drew to a close she said, 'That sounds horrific,' as she imagined the fight and the brutal deaths that occurred that night.

Flynn touched his face, just below his right eye. 'Still sore sometimes,' he said of his eye socket. 'Especially in cold weather – which is why I live in a hot climate.' He laughed.

'There are other reasons for that too.'

'There are,' he concurred.

Their drinks came. On stage inside the Mirage the act for the night started their second set of old rock 'n' roll songs. Their show was beamed to large screen TVs hanging outside the bar.

Flynn sipped his lager meditatively.

It had been another long day on the boat, with an annoying rich guy making silly demands of him, but at least he'd got through it and even pocketed a 500-euro tip.

'I can see how the operation would have affected you,' Santiago said softly. 'Keep you awake at nights.'

'Yeah, yeah . . . my tough guy image is breaking up like pixels,' he complained.

'Tough guy with a heart . . . my tough guy with a heart,' she said tenderly.

He looked at her. 'Mm, he gave me a good whacking with that gun . . . and I've been trying for years to get in a good joke about a tongue-lashing, but it's always eluded me.'

Santiago shuddered with revulsion.

'One day,' Flynn promised.

'So who was this guy, this Brian Tasker? A name, I have to say, not designed to strike fear into anyone's heart . . . so ordinary.'

'Which makes it all the worse, a wimpy name attached to a raving psychopath . . . a dangerous, dangerous guy.'

'But you got him. Ultimately, Operation Ambush was a success!'

Flynn uttered a short laugh. 'Yes and no . . . what I've just told you about for the last hour . . . that wasn't Operation Ambush.'

ELEVEN

Flynn spent most of the remainder of that night in 2002 in A&E at Blackpool Victoria Hospital being X-rayed and treated for his facial wounds, none of which were too serious, although there was a tiny crack in his cheekbone about which nothing could be done, other than to allow it to heal by itself. He had lost a tooth from the front row, he was cut and grazed to bits and two of his head wounds required butterfly stitching. (At this point, as he retold the tale to Santiago over their drinks, he leaned over and parted his short hair to show her one of the cuts which, years later, was just a faintly visible white line.)

During his hospital treatment he made a phone call to his wife, Faye, but the voice of the electronic lady told him that the person he was trying to call 'was on the line'. He actually doubted that, even though it slightly puzzled him. He guessed she was more likely to be tucked up in bed with her phone switched off.

And despite himself he kept an eye out for his favourite lady doctor who had half-propositioned him some years before. He knew she was now a consultant, married with kids, and still worked on A&E, but she was nowhere to be seen. He shrugged mentally, slightly disappointed.

Throughout the course of his treatment, Jack Hoyle popped his head into Flynn's cubicle from time to time to keep a check on him. Hoyle was also keeping an eye on the man they had arrested, who was now under armed guard in a separate treatment area. He had been admitted because of the whack Hoyle had given him across the skull during the violent arrest. The prisoner's X-rays were fine but his head did need stitching.

Hoyle kept Flynn up to date with progress, until finally he came to tell him that the prisoner – now identified formally as Brian Tasker – was being discharged from hospital and about to be conveyed to Blackpool nick by a section van, followed closely by an Armed Response Vehicle. Until they knew more about this man, the cops were taking no chances with him now.

Flynn slid off his bed. 'They haven't quite finished with me yet, apparently,' he told Hoyle. His face was swollen and puffy around his damaged cheekbone. 'Well done, mate, thanks for hitting him. I'd lost it,' he admitted.

'We're in it together.' Hoyle shrugged modestly.

'You're a great mate and partner,' Flynn said genuinely. 'I owe you one.'

'Cheers, pal.'

There was a moment of awkwardness when they could possibly have given each other a man-hug, but Hoyle's radio squawked: the section van had arrived and the escorting cops were about to walk the prisoner out of the hospital. Hoyle turned away and Flynn walked out of his cubicle to the end of the A&E ward where a central corridor ran through the department, knowing the prisoner would have to be brought past him.

He wanted a good look at the man he believed had killed two cops and two of his own partners in crime, cutting out the tongue of one of them.

There was a scuffling noise. A side door further along the

corridor opened and the prisoner was led out by a PC holding his hands, secured by rigid handcuffs, in front of him. The PC's hand was clasped on the solid bar between the wrists, giving the officer immediate control should it be required. One turn and the cuffs would cut into the nerve endings around the wrists and the prisoner would be on his knees, screaming in agony. Another PC was behind the prisoner and behind him were two armed cops with their Heckler & Koch MP5s slung diagonally across their chests.

Jack Hoyle brought up the rear.

Flynn, Hoyle and the prisoner were still in the same clothes they had been wearing during the arrest, all three soaked in blood up their arms, across their chests.

A few nurses and a doctor came to gawp at the slow procession, fascinated by the sight of an individual who could murder someone and then cut out their tongue. It reminded Flynn of something medieval and he half-expected rotten fruit to be hurled.

Tasker wasn't a big man but lithe, fit-looking, early thirties.

His eyes were pinned to the floor watching his own feet as they shuffled along but as he drew alongside Flynn his gaze rose, his head rotated slightly sideways and he looked straight at Flynn, and in that moment the detective was treated to a view deep into the darkness of that man's soul. It was not a pleasant sight.

Then he was gone and that was the last time Flynn saw him for another four months.

He returned to his cubicle and sat down stiffly on the edge of the bed.

'Long time, no see.'

Flynn looked up and the lady doctor, who he had thought was off duty or working somewhere else, was in front of him, clipboard and white gown, very prim and proper.

'You look a mess,' she said truthfully.

'You don't.'

'I hadn't made the name connection when my informant told me,' Flynn said to Santiago. They strolled arm in arm along the marina, then past the Hotel Ses Estaques towards the Ses Savines restaurant where they were going to sit and share a bottle of wine. 'The Tasker family were – and still are, as far as I know – one of the biggest crime families operating out of north London.'

'The name rings a bell,' Santiago said. 'I think I've heard of them.'

After showing her his skull scar, he had then delighted her by unscrewing his tooth from his top set, refitted at huge expense by a very skilled dentist. He had given her a gap-toothed grin from which she had recoiled.

Flynn went on, 'I'm not surprised, you know. They're into everything from gambling to prostitution, drugs, people trafficking, you name it. Very wealthy, international, but also fairly discreet except when things erupt, as they tend to from time to time in their world. They prefer negotiation with other gangs, but if they have to they'll don their balaclavas, grab their shotguns and hang people up on meat hooks . . . but that's all pretty rare.'

He continued, 'That said, Brian is or was the son from hell they wish they'd never had. He wanted to run the business but in a very different way. Apparently he was obsessed by the way in which the Central American cartels operated, ruthlessly murdering and dismembering or decapitating their rivals or anyone else who got in their way, including cops. Thought it was brilliant – apparently Brian junior was a cat strangler – and hated the almost genteel, gentlemanly way the Tasker family operated. Which, of course, they didn't really. But Brian wanted brutal expansionism and to become mega-rich, not just rich. His methods didn't fit with the way the family wanted to operate.'

They had reached Ses Savines and found a cane sofa outside the restaurant which gave them a view, through olive trees, of the bay of Santa Eulalia. Flynn ordered a bottle of wine.

'For the family he did some bad things to rivals. A spate of killings in London and the south, four or five guys shot in the face, then smashed flat with a spade, and one beheaded with the same tool.'

Santiago winced.

'No one was ever arrested and the Tasker family did close ranks around him, but the heat was on and they had to cut him loose. Too wild, too uncontrollable, too psychotic, too dangerous, someone who could jeopardize years of careful business building in one blow.

'So he set up on his own, which is pretty much where we came in.'

*   *   *

It was good to get to bed with Santiago and in the air-conditioned berth they again made very slow love, after which Flynn lay awake thinking about Brian Tasker, Jerry Tope and others.

As much as the cops thought they were being careful that night with regards to transporting Brian Tasker from the hospital to the police station, they were not careful enough. And, of course, a police escort can be very vulnerable.

It was a journey that should have taken five minutes, tops.

Tasker was led out of the A&E unit and shoved into the back of the waiting section van, a Ford Transit. He was locked inside the inner cage, which under normal conditions would have been fine, especially as two police constables sat in with him, one next to him, one opposite. The driver of the van slammed the cage door, which spring-locked automatically with a bar. Neither constable took much notice of the identity of the van driver – the rain was still hammering down, he had his cap peak pulled over his eyes and they had been given instructions to keep their eyes on the prisoner.

The driver hopped in behind the wheel and set off from the awning outside the hospital.

Behind, the two armed officers jumped into their Ford Galaxy, and behind them was Jack Hoyle in the Vauxhall.

The little convoy set off fairly sedately, out of the hospital grounds and towards the town.

In Flynn's cubicle, the doctor said, 'I saw your name on the computer, thought I'd say hello.'

'Very nice to see you. How are you doing?' Flynn quickly noticed the absence of a wedding ring, though he assumed that was because wearing jewellery in her line of work was not always wise.

'I'm good, you?'

'Good, too.'

It was all pretty banal stuff.

'Still happily married?'

'I think so.'

'You *think* so?'

'Yeah, yeah . . . you?'

'Was, not any more, but two little kids in tow.'

'Oh, sorry.'

'No probs.'

She handed him a business card. 'The number's different.' She smiled, then said, 'I have to go . . . left a patient wide open on the operating table . . . just kidding.'

Then she was gone.

In the back of the van, the two constables were morbidly fascinated by Tasker.

'You cut out a man's tongue?' one asked in disbelief.

Tasker was staring at the van floor. His eyes did not rise and he remained silent, though a tremor of a smile played on his lips.

'Fuckin' animal,' the other one sneered – he was the one sitting across from Tasker.

The convoy moved on and reached the traffic lights at the junction of Preston New Road where, when they changed to green, the vehicles would turn right towards Blackpool.

But as they changed the van went left, away from the resort on to the dual carriageway that led to Preston.

It took a few moments for the direction change to register with the two cops in the back.

Behind, the ARV turned to follow, and the driver flashed his headlights at the van, then moved out to overtake.

Jack Hoyle also followed, puzzled, suddenly worried.

Then from a side road on the left a car flashed out and rammed into the side of the ARV. The vehicle was a big Toyota pick-up with bull bars across the radiator. It smashed into the flimsier Ford Galaxy and flipped it over on to its side, then reversed away, slotted in behind the section van with a quick J-turn before slamming on, stopping, then hurtling backwards into the front of Hoyle's car.

Hoyle was already in shock at the speed and surprise of the first impact, though he had gathered his senses enough to begin shouting into his radio for assistance, but the fast-expanding image of the Toyota powering backwards cut off his words as he tried to wrench his steering wheel down to avoid the beast. He knew he was too slow – too many hours awake, too much driving, not enough rest had taken their toll and if he was honest he'd been pretty much daydreaming even though he'd been wondering about the odd change of direction the van had taken. He braced himself for the impact. The huge machine smashed into him and crushed beyond repair the front of the Vauxhall, and the Toyota almost seemed to be climbing over his bonnet.

Hoyle threw himself sideways over the passenger seat.

Had the Toyota actually driven over him like a tank it might have killed him, but the driver had only one mission with two aims, to put the ARV and Hoyle's car out of commission.

No sooner had this been achieved, with the ARV on its side, its wheels still spinning uselessly, and the radiator of Hoyle's car a crumpled, hissing mess, the Toyota disentangled itself with a tearing of metal and sped off behind the police van which was now accelerating away from the scene.

Inside the locked cage, Tasker raised his arms, held out his hands towards the officer opposite.

'Release me. If you make this difficult, you will die.'

Stripped down to his boxers, bound and gagged, the unconscious police constable who was to have driven the section van was discovered, shivering, wet and cold, an hour later. The story was that he had been flagged down by two men in an apparently broken-down Toyota pick-up while en route to the hospital to pick up the prisoner. He'd been bashed on the head, dragged out of his seat . . . and after that he did not recall anything until he regained consciousness under some bushes in the hospital grounds.

The police van was found later, abandoned in an industrial area close to the motorway, and subsequently the Toyota was found in a ditch in a field near Kirkham.

The two cops in the van were unhurt, but they were handcuffed together and minus their radios, torches, batons and personal mobile phones.

And Brian Tasker had managed to escape from custody.

As Flynn drifted off to sleep alongside Santiago, he visualized himself standing in the field looking at the burned-out Toyota. Just a fire-ravaged shell, even the tyres having melted. It had been stolen earlier from the resort.

He was with a dithering Jack Hoyle, uninjured but still in shock from the break-out several hours earlier.

'They were good,' Flynn had said to Hoyle. 'No messing about. No fear. No qualms about impersonating a cop, either . . . this helped, though.' It was still raining hard and Flynn looked up into the sky, held his hands palms up.

Just released from hospital with a handful of painkilling drugs in his system now, he felt his anger rise, and with it a determination, no matter what the cost, to bring Brian Tasker to justice.

TWELVE

H is head pulsing with pain, broken cheekbone throbbing and his eye swollen and pulpy, Steve Flynn stood at the front of one of the conference rooms at headquarters, fighting nausea and exhaustion in equal measures as he surveyed the array of sour-faced individuals at tables arranged in a U shape; Flynn stood alone, feeling vulnerable, at the open end of that letter.

He had just given his version of the events of the last twenty-four hours.

His audience consisted of Lancashire Constabulary's chief constable, the assistant chief constable in charge of operations and the detective chief superintendent in charge of crime for Lancashire, as well as high-ranking representatives from the National Crime Squad, the Metropolitan Police, West Midlands Police and various other dignitaries, most of whom he did not know.

However, they all seemed to have one thing in common: they looked as though they wanted to tear Flynn limb from limb.

'So let me get this straight,' the chief constable said. His name was Robert Fanshaw-Bayley, known as FB to his friends and enemies alike. 'You began a surveillance operation based on the say-so of a known drug user, not knowing who you were following and what the implications of that might be—'

Flynn opened his mouth to respond, but FB held up a finger to stop him.

'Do not interrupt me,' the chief said. Flynn's mouth clamped shut. 'I get it,' he conceded. 'Things, events, run quickly and you have to react . . . I was a detective for many, many years, so fine.

I understand. You run things on a wing and a prayer sometimes. It's not rocket science.'

Flynn swallowed.

'So you find the vehicle you're interested in, in north London, and follow it up the M1, M6?' Flynn was prevented from replying by FB's stubby first finger, still hovering upright. 'Not actually knowing who was in it?'

Flynn nodded. 'Correct.' He swallowed again – drily. Few men could intimidate him, purposely or otherwise, but FB terrified him. He oozed authority and did not suffer a fool gladly.

'They stop for a brew at Corley Services and you and your partner' – here FB flicked a dismissive finger at Hoyle, sitting to one side of Flynn, his head bowed – 'kept eyeball on them and then you and one of the other surveillance cars set off just ahead of the target in order to get into position, leaving the third car on the services to drop in behind said target.' Flynn nodded again. FB went on. 'Unfortunately it looks as though this particular car had been spotted by the target and identified as either a police car or, shall I say, a car that was a threat and the target has somehow sneaked up on the two officers in that car and murdered them in cold blood.'

FB stopped there. His words hung like a noose.

Then he ploughed on. 'You kept following the target but sent your other team member back to check on the whereabouts of the other two officers, after you lost all contact with them. They were found dead.'

'Yes, boss,' Flynn mumbled.

'And then you lost the target vehicle.'

'Yes, boss.'

'Absolutely fucking incredible.' FB's lips pursed tightly.

'The weather was . . . and the motorway was . . .' Weakly, Flynn tried to explain the loss.

FB waved him to shut it. 'So you then revisited your informant and forced more out of her than she had previously divulged – something she should have done, anyway. From this, along with some intel from our database, you found the target vehicle and a further bloodbath.'

'Yes, sir.'

'And Brian Tasker, who had apparently just murdered up to four people and cut the tongue out of one of them. A fight ensued. Tasker fired a gun at you and missed, but you put him down. Unfortunately he ended up in hospital and, with the help of his associates, managed to escape from custody. Incredibly, he did not seriously injure any more officers, though more by luck than judgement.'

'Sir,' Flynn confirmed.

FB sat back, his eyes half-closed, looking down his nose at Flynn and Hoyle.

'Two National Crime Squad officers murdered. Two of our local criminals murdered. An escape from custody. A very dangerous madman on the loose. This is a fucking serious omelette in our face,' FB said. 'But you know what? I don't really care about that. As operational officers you are required to make speedy decisions on the hoof, it's part of what we do. We can't always invoke health and safety regulations and they certainly don't apply to the bad guys. However, I want it on record that the deaths of the two crime squad officers could not reasonably have been foreseen, but the fact remains that a tragedy has occurred, as in the case of the deaths of the two known criminals, Don Braceford and Will Carney.' He paused and his nostrils dilated. 'I myself shall shoulder the public side of this in terms of the press, media and publicity, and also the private issues of dealing with the grieving relatives of the families concerned. Do not misunderstand this.' He looked pointedly at Flynn. 'There have been many mistakes here and they will be thoroughly investigated.' Flynn heeded the warning. 'However, I feel, unless I can be convinced otherwise, that what has happened is one of the risks we run as police officers, and what criminals can expect if things go wrong for them. Any PC could walk out of the police station and meet his or her death.' He paused again. 'What now remains is for us to bring in Brian Tasker and put him away for the remainder of his natural life. We do not know for certain whether he pulled the trigger on those two officers, but he is the prime suspect since he appears to have murdered the other man he was with. So to that end I am now officially forming a squad to hunt down and arrest this man. It will be a multi-force operation and I will remain its nominal head.' FB glanced at a detective superintendent from the NCS. 'Mr Rothwell here will be the operational head and I am going to bring in DI Craig Alford from my Serious and Organized Crime Unit to be the tactical head. I fully expect a hundred per cent commitment from all officers concerned and I will authorize any necessary overtime and resources. The operation will last as long as necessary but I expect a result as soon as possible. All officers must clear their diaries of other commitments until it is over because there will be long days and nights ahead until this man is apprehended. Anyone not wishing to be part of this may step down now. That is all . . . other than to say the operation will be called "Ambush".'

FB scooped up his papers and stood up. As he went to the door of the conference room he passed close to Flynn and Hoyle. To them, he said, 'With me.'

In the corridor FB looked at the weary duo.

'Quick resolution,' he said to them. 'Bring that man in. Do not make a hash of it.' To Flynn he said, 'Your cards are marked.'

Then he was gone.

'Bloody hell,' Flynn said, realizing he had been given a second chance. 'We need to get working fast,' he said to Hoyle. 'Get back down to the Smoke, get into people's ribs, find him and fuck him . . .'

His voice tailed off because of the look on Hoyle's face.

'What is it?'

'No,' Hoyle said.

'No what?'

'Just not for me,' Hoyle said tightly.

'What's not for you?' Flynn demanded, perplexed.

'Going after this guy. This could go on for ever. Weeks, months. I got a home life, y'know?'

'So do I, but sometimes—'

'Sometimes what?' Hoyle interrupted sharply.

'Sometimes things got to be done,' Flynn answered simply. 'Your wife will understand. This guy needs nailing to the wall and we're the ones to do it. He's a bad fucker. We go after bad fuckers.'

'Nah, nah,' Hoyle shook his head. 'He's a London guy and we'll be down there all the time by necessity. We won't be able to go to work every morning and come home for our teas every night.'

'Jack,' Flynn pleaded, 'we don't do that now.'

'Exactly – and you know what? I shat myself when that car

rammed me. I shat myself when we saw Tasker with a tongue in his hand standing over Don Braceford's body. These are dangerous guys, Steve. I mean, really dangerous. They kill cops—'

Flynn opened his mouth to protest, but Hoyle held up a finger to stop him, the second time Flynn had been silenced by a digit in a short space of time. 'Don't tell me that's why they need catching. I know it is . . . I just don't want to do this job this time.'

Flynn could tell from his friend's face his resolve was unshakeable.

'If that's what you want.'

'It is, but don't let me stop you, Steve.'

Flynn backed off, a bit confused. He could see Hoyle's point of view. He had a wife and two kids; Flynn had a wife and young son; neither saw enough of their families as it was. They worked long and hard and with dedication. Spending more weeks away would not be good for either family and although Flynn wasn't happy about the prospect of leaving his home for a long period of time, and especially about not seeing his son, he also thought it might be a good thing for his marriage. Maybe give his wife a bit of a breathing space to cope with the phase she seemed to be going through with him. A period of work-enforced separation might be helpful.

However, there was no guarantee how long it would take to hunt down Tasker.

This time tomorrow he could be in custody. Flynn argued this point with Hoyle.

'And this time next year we might still be chasing him,' Hoyle argued back.

Flynn shrugged, defeated.

Santiago gently rubbed Flynn's belly with her warm bottom. He thought she had fallen asleep while he retold these events, but her movement told him otherwise.

'So that was the start of Operation Ambush.'

'Yeah.'

'And how did it end?'

'Badly.'

*　　*　　*

In essence Flynn spent the next four months in and around London and in Spain, chasing the shadow that was Brian Tasker. He seemed to revel in being a man on the run.

The Ambush team, led by Craig Alford and with the assistance of Jerry Tope (brought in to run the intelligence cell), together with DS Dave Carver and DCs Jimmy Blue and Lincoln Bartlett, all from Lancashire, formed the core of the squad.

Flynn put in time and effort, but Tasker always seemed to be one step ahead and his business was flourishing according to the contacts and sources the police plundered remorselessly for information.

Flynn was patient. He knew one day Tasker would make a mistake and he hoped that he, Flynn, would be there to step in and snatch the bastard.

At the end of a four-day stretch of surveillance and the following of four known associates around London, Flynn returned home on the Friday of the sixteenth week of the manhunt, drained and lacking enthusiasm. At headquarters he checked into the incident room from which Ambush was being coordinated (other satellite offices were in London and Birmingham) before going home for the weekend. It was ten days since he had been in the north.

He was eager to get home and hug his son, maybe take him to Blackpool Zoo over the weekend, and with any luck relations between him and Faye might begin to thaw, although he did not hold out much hope on that score.

The incident room was deserted bar one lone figure. Jerry Tope sat hunched at a computer terminal, head down, concentrating. He did not initially notice Flynn behind him and jumped out of his skin when Flynn cleared his throat.

'Don't do that!' Tope said humourlessly. He looked drawn, tired and at the end of his tether.

Flynn leaned over his shoulder. 'What're you doing?'

Tope blew out his cheeks. 'Following the money, but getting nowhere.'

Flynn knew that Tope had been able to access some bank accounts belonging to Tasker, but they had ceased to have any transactions on them soon after the manhunt began. They had been virtually emptied of all funds and the inference was that Tasker had opened new accounts in false names and/or was using accounts belonging to others, as well as using cash to buy stuff instead of debit or credit cards.

A list of transactions filled the monitor.

Tope pulled a face. 'What are we missing, Steve? Even here, surely, there must be something we can pin him down with.' He wafted his fingers at the screen, infuriated. 'Pissed off, so pissed off.' He slumped back in his chair.

'Yeah.' Flynn looked at the numbers and stood up stretching. 'Keep at it, mate . . . no one else around?'

'All gone . . . and I'm with them now.'

Tope made a point of shutting down his computer with a flourish, collected his briefcase and stood up. He looked at Flynn. 'You still here?'

'Good point.'

Flynn lay in bed alongside his wife. He was tight-lipped and unable to sleep following the stand-up row the couple had had earlier in front of their son, who had watched open-mouthed, then run away screaming.

Flynn had not picked the argument – or at least he didn't think he had – but it had escalated like a rocket launch.

Later in bed (he had climbed in after her to find her asleep or feigning it) he had reached over to her with the idea of reconciliation through lovemaking but she had shrugged him off and failed to respond to his trite, 'Sorry' (although in his mind he added, but did not vocalize, 'for whatever it was I did').

Eventually he slid out, grabbed his dressing gown and, after checking on his son, went downstairs, found whisky and necked a shot of the burning spirit. He decided he would try to woo her back and make firm promises about the future; he'd try to get a transfer to something more local and with better hours. A job on Blackpool CID would be a good move, he thought.

First thing, though, was to melt Faye's heart.

Corny as it sounded – and because he was a simple man – he thought a bouquet of flowers in her favourite colours would perhaps be a good step, followed by lunch out – just the two of them. As his mind drifted around possible venues, he suddenly sat up and swore.

He scrambled for the phone and dialled Jerry Tope's home number.

'Saturday morning, six a.m.,' Tope whined. His hair was in disarray and there was a certain indefinable smell about him. He was unshaven. 'This better be worth it.'

'When I came in yesterday evening you were scanning some of the bank accounts Tasker was using before he went off the grid. Put them on screen again,' Flynn said, businesslike.

The two of them were back in the incident room and Flynn towered over Tope's shoulder. It had taken a lot of persuasion to lure Tope back into the office that morning, especially as Flynn had called him up at two a.m., only four hours previously.

'You can always go back to bed,' he added.

'I will do.'

He switched the computer on and after a couple of minutes' searching found the page he thought was on display when Flynn had been there the previous evening.

Flynn leaned forward eagerly, certain he had seen something of interest which had only registered later while he was sipping whisky and thinking about treating his wife.

It was just a page full of numbers, bank transactions from an account that had belonged to Tasker but which had been emptied of all funds, some £4,000, and not used since.

'Is this the one?' he said into Tope's ear.

'Yep,' Tope answered with weary lack of interest.

'Move.'

Flynn nudged Tope out of the chair, sat down and scrolled through the figures. He wasn't the greatest at numbers; sometimes they became a blur to him and he could easily lose concentration. He had not been great at maths at school.

'I'm sure I saw something . . .' He stopped scrolling and said, 'Yes.'

It was Tope's turn to lean over. 'What?'

'Tasker doesn't have a mother, does he?'

'She died a few years back according to the intel on the Tasker clan. Breast cancer. She was the old matriarch of the family but had disowned cute little Brian when his murderous methods made even the Taskers blanch.'

'OK, when did she die? What month was it?'

Tope thought and gave Flynn the approximate date off the top of his head. Sometime in April, possibly four or five years ago.

'So, even though Tasker was disowned by his family of criminal cretins, he may have felt something for his dear departed mum and maybe on the anniversary of her death he'd buy flowers for the grave . . . maybe?'

'Who knows?'

'Any idea of the month of her birth?'

'Er . . . again, April, I think.'

Flynn tapped the screen. 'This entry refers to the purchase of flowers, online from Interflora, for a cost of fifty pounds.'

'But that entry is from September last year.' Tope frowned.

'Exactly. It doesn't correlate.'

'So?'

'Who were the flowers for? Himself?'

'A girlfriend?'

'Do we know of a girlfriend?' Flynn asked. 'We've tracked down a couple of exes and we've been leaning on them down in London but neither of them have seen or heard from Tasker in a long time.'

'So why would a guy like Tasker buy flowers?' Tope asked, going with the flow.

'That's exactly what I was wondering last night.'

The two men looked at each other. Because Tope was still leaning over Flynn's shoulder their faces were only inches apart, which was just a tad too proximate for them both. They reared away from each other.

'Who would he buy flowers for, the old romantic devil? A girlfriend we don't know about, I'd hazard.'

'Worth following up,' Tope said.

Flynn read the bank statement entry again. 'And not only that, this refers to a purchase from an Interflora shop in Blackpool.'

Again their eyes met . . . this time from a suitable, male distance.

'He's got a girlfriend up north,' Flynn declared.

It was Tope's turn to shove Flynn off the seat and retake his rightful position at the desk in front of the computer. He cleared the screen, began tapping away and after a few moments said, 'It's a flower shop in Blackpool North, an independent florist with an

Interflora concession.' He angled the screen so Flynn could see the internet home page of 'Flower Girl', based on Red Bank Road in Bispham. There was an Interflora logo at the top of the screen.

'Well, the big old softie,' Flynn muttered. 'We've been looking in all the wrong places for this bastard. He's right under our noses, I'll bet.'

Tope glanced at Flynn with something approaching veneration. 'What made you think of this?'

Flynn gave him a knowing, smug look. 'Just a great detective's mind,' he said, but then could no longer retain his seriousness. He burst into a lion's roar of laughter.

THIRTEEN

She lived on Shoreside estate. Her name was Ellie Davenport and she was twenty-three years old. She had a council flat and was the mother to a twelve-month-old baby boy called Callum. She lived exclusively on benefits and had never, officially, had a job, although as Flynn found out a little bit more about her he discovered she did a lot of bar work when she had time. A drug user and shoplifter, she was wafer thin and pretty in a wasted sort of way, he thought. Like a very hungry Twiggy.

Flynn discovered all this relatively easily. His search for information began that Saturday morning. Two hours after he and Tope had been at the computer in the incident room he was sitting in his car outside Flower Girl waiting for the shop to open up for business.

In those intervening hours Flynn had been to the police training centre gym and punished himself with half an hour on a rowing machine and twenty minutes on a cross trainer before showering and changing into the fresh jeans and T-shirt he had brought along.

It had taken him twenty minutes to get back across from Preston to Bispham, just north of Blackpool, to be outside the florist at about ten minutes to eight.

He saw a figure behind the shop door opening up for business, a young woman, early twenties, frizzy hair and a round, pretty face with wide eyes and no make-up. She was dressed in a blouse and jeans.

Flynn gave her time to set up the display outside the shop – bouquets in buckets and other floral displays – before climbing out of the car and following her inside, where it was very chilly and smelled of water and fresh flowers.

She turned at the counter and watched him walk in, appraising and coming to a pleasant conclusion.

'Can I help?'

Flynn liked the look of her, too. Fresh and innocent. He knew both characteristics could just be a front for something more sinister, but he doubted it.

He flipped out his warrant card and county badge, although the latter, while looking good, had no legal standing. The warrant card carried the weight. He introduced himself, then said, 'Are you the Flower Girl?'

'Oh, yeah.' Her voice sounded husky and breathless.

'I wonder if you could help me?' His voice, unaccountably, sounded the same.

She proved to be of great assistance and though clearly busy – she had two weddings that day and her assistant was off sick – she took the time to help.

In a couple of minutes she had the Interflora orders that interested Flynn up on her computer screen and, more importantly, the name and address of the recipient of the flowers.

Ellie Davenport, Flat 9, 6 Fairview Road, Shoreside, Blackpool.

Flynn thanked the Flower Girl profusely and ten minutes later he was on Shoreside in his own car, fifty metres along the road from Ellie Davenport's flat.

Sitting there he recontacted Jerry Tope, who had grudgingly decided to remain at work for the duration, and asked him to delve into Davenport's antecedents, if there were any.

There were. The details were not particularly spectacular or interesting, although when Tope told him she did bar work, Flynn asked Tope if he could find out any of the names of the places she'd worked in.

Tope came up with Fat Billy's, a town centre pub in Blackpool – the very one where his informant Janie Miller had overheard the conversation in the men's toilets that had set this whole ball rolling. A name which was cropping up with some regularity.

Flynn asked Tope to call Craig Alford to bring him up to speed with the current situation and let him know Flynn was sitting on an address that could, just might be, that of Tasker's girlfriend; maybe even the man himself was shacked up there. Flynn said he wanted some back-up to keep tabs on anything that might happen and maybe get a search warrant sworn out so they could enter the flat and look for Tasker or anything connected to him.

Flynn realized the Ambush team had the best lead they'd had in weeks and he didn't want to mess things up.

Plus, he knew that he did not have long before his cover was blown on Shoreside. Cops, whether in uniform or plain clothes, were easily identified by the residents. He gave himself an hour, tops, before a crowd gathered and overturned his car with him inside it.

He had heard nothing back from Tope or Alford when a door opened on the landing on which Davenport's flat was situated. From his position he could not be sure if it actually was her flat but when a young woman emerged and came down the steps with a child in a buggy ahead of her, Flynn was reasonably certain it was her. She fitted the description given by the Flower Girl and also the one relayed to him by Tope from the descriptive forms and mug shot.

She was on the move but fortunately walked in the opposite direction to Flynn.

It was only a short walk through Shoreside to cross Clifton Road and enter the huge car park at the front of the Tesco supermarket, then go into the store.

Flynn managed to keep her in sight, happy she had not seen him creeping along behind her like some sort of kerb crawler. He parked up and dived into the store, grabbing a shopping trolley on the way.

It was still quite early and the shop was relatively quiet.

Flynn soon spotted her pushing a large shopping trolley with the youngster sitting in the baby seat, facing her. He assumed she must have stowed the buggy somewhere near the entrance. He passed quite close to her once, got a good look at the child and was astonished to see the unfortunate little mite had Brian Tasker's face on it.

He kept her in view easily, putting a few things in his trolley which he had no intention of buying, pretending to be a customer. As he moved around he called Tope, still waiting to hear back from Alford, who was proving elusive. Flynn seemed to think the DI had the weekend off and was possibly away for a few days.

He hoped he was wrong.

'What's she doing?' Tope asked.

'Shopping.'

'Exciting.'

'Actually it could be,' Flynn said.

The weekly shop looked to be going into the trolley, a shop that included a lot of canned food and soup, packets of pasta and pot noodles; bread, crisps and a lot of booze. All very simple 'heat up and consume' food.

Hoping he wasn't making an assumption, Flynn thought, 'Ideal fodder for a man on the run, holing up somewhere.'

When she joined a queue for the till, Flynn took his trolley to the book and magazine aisle and flicked through a few fishing magazines, keeping an eye on the exit.

Davenport appeared ten minutes later, having made her purchases. Still pushing the trolley, she grabbed the baby buggy from beside the front door, pushed the trolley and dragged the buggy out behind her and went directly to a private taxi parked in the pick-up bay, obviously pre-booked.

The driver knew her. He smiled, patted the baby, heaved her shopping into the car boot and parked the trolley for her. Davenport eased herself and baby Tasker into the back seat of the taxi, which moved away as Flynn, leaving his trolley blocking an aisle, ran low, threading his way between parked cars, and leapt into his. By the time he reached the car park exit, the taxi, with its passengers, was driving east along Clifton Road to the junction with Preston New Road which was controlled by lights currently on red, allowing Flynn to catch up and sit behind with two cars between him and the taxi.

The taxi went right towards Junction 4 of the M55, just a couple of hundred metres away, but then it was driven straight across the traffic island known as Marton Circle on to the A583 towards Preston.

Flynn called Tope, wedging his mobile phone between his left shoulder and cheek.

'She's on the move, Jerry, Preston bound, A583, in a taxi with a lot of shopping, and my phone battery's running low. Have we any news from Craig?'

'Not yet, still trying. Get off the phone and save your power as much as you can.'

The taxi kept going and Flynn stuck with it at a discreet distance.

The area they were travelling through, between Blackpool and Kirkham, the town halfway between the resort and Preston, was wild, flat and open either side of the road, mainly farmland, a few cottages scattered around, a few caravan parks and little else.

If Davenport was on her way to see Tasker and he was hiding out in a property around here, it would be hard to approach without being spotted and it would also be impossible to follow the taxi along any of the country lanes without being blown.

Flynn's face twitched; he was annoyed with himself for being so ill-equipped, even though he could not have foreseen these events – if, in fact, they were 'events'. This could be an innocuous journey and she could simply be taking supplies to her dear old grandma.

Flynn did not believe that for one moment.

She was on her way to see Brian Tasker.

Cop sense, common sense, told him that.

He held back, allowing other cars to overtake on the wide road and slot in to mask him from the taxi. He did wonder if the taxi driver was in on this, watching for a tail. If so, that could be another problem.

A one-car tail was almost impossible to pull off if the target vehicle was being driven by a surveillance conscious crim. It had been bad enough, Flynn thought wryly, following someone with three cars . . . what could have gone wrong with that? he questioned himself bitterly.

Everything, as it happened.

He forced those terrible memories out of his mind and concentrated on the task in hand, sticking behind the taxi and not being made.

They bypassed Kirkham on their left, still on the A583, which widened into a dual carriageway at that point, went past the turn-off for Kirkham Open Prison, still heading towards Preston on quite long, fairly straight stretches of road on which it became more difficult to remain invisible.

Flynn was perhaps 200 metres behind the taxi when it signalled, then turned left off the main road on to a narrow, rural road called Vicarage Lane and, just thirty metres into it, stopped dead. Flynn could just see the roof of the taxi above the hedge line.

An anti-surveillance tactic, simple, but good.

Turn into a side road, stop, see who followed you in. Not hard. Flynn swore.

He knew he had to keep going, which he did, zipping across the junction and resisting the urge to rubberneck, although he did angle his head slightly to look. Out of the corner of his eye he saw Davenport and the taxi driver looking back over their shoulders.

Had he turned in, it would have been game over and the young lady would simply have said, 'Home, James.'

Things would then have got ugly because Flynn would have confronted her.

Fortunately he knew the geography of this area well. Vicarage Lane ran into Church Lane, which ran almost parallel with the A583. It came out at a junction close to the nuclear fuel and uranium manufacturing plant called Springfields. There was the possibility that the taxi might loop back on Vicarage Lane, but Flynn had now committed himself to cutting through the village of Clifton and coming at the nuclear plant at right angles to the route the taxi was taking.

If the taxi had turned, he could have lost it.

He veered left, sped too recklessly through the tightly packed village, then left again towards Springfields and glimpsed the taxi zipping across the junction on to Deepdale Lane, which ran along the edge of the nuclear facility.

Still heading towards open country on quiet roads.

Flynn turned into Deepdale Lane, the taxi some 400 metres ahead now.

He called Tope, updated him quickly.

'I've managed to get hold of Craig and some others are on their way . . . and me, too . . . where should we meet?'

'Tell 'em to make towards the old windmill at Clifton . . . I'm just going to have to see how this goes,' Flynn blabbed. 'It's just a bit fluid.'

'You don't have your PR, do you?'

'No, I don't, and my phone, as I said—'

'Is running low,' Tope finished for him.

Flynn ended the call and lobbed the phone on to the passenger seat.

The road dipped, there was a sharp left and then it all straightened out again with two hump-backed bridges ahead, one after the other, the first over the Preston to Blackpool rail line, the other over the Lancaster Canal. Beyond the second bridge Flynn knew the road carried on for another quarter of a mile to a T junction.

As the taxi went over the first and less steep railway bridge Flynn was well behind, and as it bobbed over the tighter but more 'humpy' canal bridge he lost sight of it for a moment, then saw brake lights come on. The taxi slowed and turned tight left on to a farm track which ran parallel with the canal into an area of flat farmland with many farmhouses dotted across the landscape. Flynn again realized that if he followed, the job would be over.

But he had a shiver of gut-led excitement because he was certain that finding Brian Tasker was now a distinct possibility.

He stopped in the dip between the two bridges, jumped out and ran at a crouch to the canal bridge, hiding behind the roadside wall and attempting to watch the progress of the taxi without revealing his bobbing head.

It moved slowly and the lane angled away from the canal.

Flynn appraised the surrounding landscape through narrowed eyes, seeing farmhouses and several slightly elevated wooded copses.

The taxi went out of sight and Flynn's shoulders dropped in frustration.

He jogged back to his car, gave Tope another update and suggested another location for a rendezvous. He knew these lanes and farm tracks criss-crossed the countryside, but without a map he could not be certain if there was another exit for the taxi and realized he would simply have to wait somewhere inconspicuous until further cops arrived and then all the other exits could be plugged.

As he spoke to Tope he was still parked between the two bridges and his eyes widened in horror when he saw the taxi trundling back down the farm track towards the road.

He hung up without explanation and watched as the car reached the junction.

He expected it to turn back towards him, but it drove away in the opposite direction. Flynn slammed his car into gear, went cautiously over the bridge and accelerated up behind the taxi – which now had no visible passengers on board.

Davenport had been dropped off.

Flynn's adrenalin surge made him gasp.

The road ahead was straight and within seconds Flynn's car was up behind the taxi. He saw the driver's eyes glance in the rear-view mirror, then do a double-take.

'Yeah, right, mate,' Flynn growled. 'I'm right up your chuffer.'

He flashed his headlights and gestured for the driver to pull over.

The man's shoulders seemed to set with determination and he slammed his foot down on the accelerator. The exhaust coughed plumes of purple-grey smoke which enshrouded Flynn's car, and at the same time the taxi accelerated away.

Flynn kept up.

As they reached the T junction, the taxi swerved sharp left, powered down a dip in the road and dinked around a sharp bend, then sped past a pub called the Sitting Goose, which Flynn knew was one of Tope's haunts. The premises flashed by, Flynn making certain his car stuck with the taxi. He steered with one hand and reached across to try and get his fingertips on the mobile phone, which had slithered tantalizingly out of reach on the passenger seat. Then he had to get both hands on the wheel to correct the steering and prevent himself from ploughing into a hedge.

The taxi sped north on Rosemary Lane, shooting over a bridge spanning the M55, then another over the Lancaster Canal, going towards Catforth.

Flynn kept with him. He could see the driver's back; he was only steering with his right hand and was holding his mobile phone clamped to his ear with the other: he was making a call.

Flynn's face set as hard as granite. He accelerated, came up close behind the taxi and touched its rear bumper. This caused the driver to look into his mirror again, set his shoulders – again

– and then try to coax more speed out of the machine. And he was still trying to make a phone call.

As the road went into a sharp right hand bend, Flynn clipped the rear of the taxi again and this time a combination of velocity, the change of direction, uneven weight distribution, the swerve of the car and the fact that the steering wheel whipped out of the driver's hand caused the taxi to spin and suddenly go into a complete 360-degree rotation – and Flynn had a fleeting glimpse of the horrified driver as they came face to face for a fraction of a second before it continued with the circle. Both cars were then as they had been – nose to tail – but the taxi suddenly veered sideways and its nose dropped into the drainage dyke at the side of the road, where it stopped.

Flynn braked hard, but before he could get out, the taxi driver had managed to roll out of his car, scramble up the muddy bank and run at Flynn with a single barrel auto-loading twelve-bore sawn-off shotgun brandished in his hands.

Flynn was half out when he saw the weapon being racked and swinging up into a firing position. The taxi driver's stubby index finger wrapped around the trigger, pulling it back. He stood at the front of Flynn's bonnet and aimed through the windscreen as if he was about to dispatch a rat.

Flynn flung himself across the front seats under the line of the dashboard as with a boom the window disintegrated and a million glass fragments and shotgun pellets sprayed across him like pebble dashing, several stinging as they splattered against his cheek.

But the taxi driver had missed.

Flynn rose, the glass fell off him.

Through the missing window he saw the taxi driver rack the weapon again. The used shell casing spun out as the new cartridge was slammed into place.

Knowing he had missed and swearing, the taxi driver shuffled sideways, intending to blast Flynn through the passenger door window. This time Flynn had no cover, nowhere to hide, and was trapped.

Flynn lurched sideways and tried to time it just right – the opening, fast and hard, of the passenger door. Most car doors do not open quickly, as a house door would. Their weight and the mechanism of the hinges make occupants push the door. The only time Flynn had ever truly experienced a car door opening quickly was once when he had been parked in a police car on a stormy Blackpool sea front and, unthinkingly, had opened the door only to have it ripped from his grasp by the storm wind. Not only had it shot open, the door had almost been torn off its hinges, and it never closed properly again.

That was what Flynn wanted to recreate.

He moved fast, pulled back the handle and forced it open, catching the taxi driver with the edge of the door, banging the gun sideways. The man managed to keep hold of the weapon but staggered back, surprised at Flynn's speed. Almost at once he was recovering and attempting to bring the shotgun round and fire again.

Using the door as a fulcrum, Flynn swung out of the vehicle and grabbed the barrel of the shotgun with his left hand, trying to keep it pointing down and away.

The taxi driver fired the weapon.

Flynn's fingers were wrapped around the barrel and he kept a tight grip of it, aware of the sensation of the cartridge powering down the barrel and the blast as it left the muzzle in a spray of sparks and smoke – but it fired into the grass.

By then Flynn was completely out of his car. The man tried to tear the gun out of Flynn's grip, but to no avail. The driver looked a moderately fit person with his tight T-shirt and bulging biceps and six pack, but Flynn was bigger, fitter and, once riled, more dangerous to know.

There was a short push-me, pull-you contest, but Flynn wrestled the gun from him and tossed it down into the dyke, where it landed in a slurp of muddy water.

The man backed off, but he was dancing on his toes with hatred and determination in his eyes, confirmed when his right hand came from behind him with a short-bladed knife in it.

He did not hesitate. No words were spoken.

He came at Flynn, the blade glinting in the rain as it slashed up towards his belly.

Flynn reared backwards. The knife slashed fresh air – but only just – and Flynn eyed the sharp point as it zipped up past his face.

The man backed off again and hunched low, preparing for another assault.

Flynn responded by revealing his own secret weapon from his back pocket. His police warrant card.

'I'm a cop. Put that down.' He held out the card between his finger and thumb.

'Fuck you.'

Two words that meant Flynn was not going to get a deep meaningful conversation from this man just yet.

'You'd better be very good with that, then,' Flynn advised him, 'because you were shit with a shotgun.' He slid the warrant card away.

He'd hardly said the words when the taxi driver lunged for him again.

The knife slashed up through the air but Flynn was already out-thinking and out-manoeuvring him.

It was an unsubtle, telegraphed and remarkably slow thrust – to Flynn's eyes.

He sidestepped, deflected the arm with the open palm of his right hand, twisted on his heel and, again with his right hand, grabbed the man's wrist, stepped in close, hip to hip, turned and slammed the point of his left elbow into the man's right eye socket while yanking him off balance at the same time.

Flynn pivoted away, still yanking the man forward and down on to his knees, although by that point the taxi driver did not know whether he was picking up a fare or pissed out of his mind; the impact of Flynn's elbow was the equivalent of the man's face hitting the rim of a steering wheel in a head-on collision. A stunning shockwave bounced through his head and his vision tripled.

Flynn eased him to the ground carefully.

He left him there and went to retrieve his own mobile phone and made a call.

After that Flynn spoke to the taxi driver, who was just about regaining some clarity in his brain.

Initially he was reluctant to chat.

He changed his mind after Flynn persuaded him.

Flynn picked a sliver of broken windscreen glass casually out of his face and flicked it away. It was the third he had found embedded in his flesh but, checking his appearance in a wing mirror, he guessed there would be no lasting defacement to his handsome features.

'He says you forced him off the road and then you assaulted him.'

Flynn looked blandly at DI Craig Alford. 'I say he blasted me with a shotgun, then tried to stab me.'

They were standing by the side of the road next to the ditched taxi. The driver was sitting cuffed in the back of a nearby police van, holding a thick wad of paper towel to his face, refusing to speak any more. A traffic car was at the scene with another section patrol. Jerry Tope had also arrived, together with DS Dave Carver, and DCs Jimmy Blue and Lincoln Bartlett.

'He was trying to make a call on this.' Flynn held up the taxi driver's mobile phone. 'That's the problem driving and using a mobile phone. Dangerous. You end up in ditches.' Flynn waggled the phone. 'I don't think he got through, which hopefully gives us a bit of time to get our shit together.'

'He told you Tasker was holed up in a farmhouse?'

'Yep,' Flynn said. 'Then he stopped being chatty.'

Sleepily, Santiago said, 'What happened next?'

Flynn's hands were clasped behind his head.

'Then it all went tits-up, as they say.'

FOURTEEN

F lynn had once spent two weeks living in the back garden of a house belonging to an active member of the IRA in a village on the coast of County Antrim, Northern Ireland. This had been during his time as a member of the Special Boat Service way back in the volatile 1980s in a joint operation run by the SBS, the SAS, the Royal Ulster Constabulary and the security services. He had been dinghied ashore from a submarine, sneaked up the beach and into the long, overgrown garden that backed on to the shoreline. He had hidden himself in a thick hedge of bramble and settled in to watch the activity in the house.

That had been one of the easy jobs which concluded when,

from his intelligence report, the house was raided and two fairly low grade IRA members were arrested five minutes before they were due to set off and plant a bomb in a shopping centre.

There had been many jobs much more hazardous than hiding out in a garden, but that was the one that came to mind as he put on his grey-green combat jacket from his car boot, pulled on a pair of similar-coloured cord pants and then leapt into a field, keeping low, using all the cover he had available – bushes, hedges, the contours of the land, even a cow – to make his way over to a copse called Many Pits Wood. Beyond that he crept across to another clump of woodland, Cookson's Plantation, on the far side of which was the dilapidated but habitable farmhouse Brian Tasker had chosen to hide out in. It was called Old Strike Farm.

He arrived five minutes later, crawled through the thorny undergrowth and, keeping three metres back from the treeline, could see the front elevation of the farmhouse.

All appeared to be peaceful.

There was an old Ford Fiesta parked in the yard. The buggy in which Ellie Davenport had pushed the baby with Brian Tasker's mug was also parked there, just to the right of the old front door.

Flynn settled in and watched patiently.

For five minutes there was no sign of life or movement, bar wisps of smoke rising from the chimney.

Then he saw someone move across one of the ground floor windows. Just a dark shadow, unidentifiable but definitely male.

According to the taxi driver there were three men in total, plus Ellie and the kid. One of the men was Brian Tasker, the other two his bodyguards.

A flicker of a grin crossed Flynn's face at the memory of the short but effective follow-up conversation he'd had with the taxi guy in the back of the section van.

It had been completely illegal but completely necessary.

Craig Alford had cringed when Flynn had said, 'I need to encourage him to be more open.'

'No,' Alford had insisted. He sounded firm (or firm-ish), but the determined look in Flynn's eyes made him waver.

'Tasker might be there but we need to know who else is and whether or not they're armed. He can tell us.' He pointed to the van.

Alford's face suddenly developed numerous nervous tics, but he relented. 'I do not know anything about this,' he said, and turned away with a look Pontius Pilate would have been proud of.

Flynn went to the back of the van where the driver, a PC, stood.

'Chat time,' he said, and gestured with his thumb. 'Move.'

The constable's eyes dropped and he sidled away from the van doors. Flynn wrenched them open, unlatched the inner cage, bent low and climbed in.

The taxi driver's face rose from behind the paper towel he was holding to stem the blood already flowing from his face.

Flynn grinned at him. 'Chat time,' he said again. 'Quick chat time.'

'I demand a solicitor.'

'We're in the middle of nowhere, taxi guy, and like a tree that falls in the middle of a forest, no one can hear it, or you when you scream.'

On the edge of Cookson's Plantation, Flynn smiled proudly at his deeply philosophical pronouncement, wondering where he had dug that up from. Normally his approach was less subtle, his philosophy being more bull in a china shop, but somehow the forest analogy seemed to be the right approach with the taxi driver, especially when Flynn added, 'It's just you and me and I'll be accompanying you to hospital with three broken fingers and a dislodged knee cap.'

More movement caught his eye at the farmhouse. An upstairs room, a bedroom, he had to assume as Ellie Davenport appeared naked at a low window, peering out into the day time and stretching languidly as a pair of hands slid around her, one cupping a breast, the other sliding down to her sex. Brian Tasker began to chew at her neck.

'Confirm Tasker is here. Davenport here and one other male for definite,' Flynn whispered into the radio that had been provided for him. 'Tasker is busy with his girlfriend, first floor bedroom. Where are we up to now?'

'Ready to roll on your say-so,' Alford said. 'Half a support unit serial, one dogman, two ARVs and a few section officers for back-up – and us, of course.'

Flynn totted up the numbers. Maybe seven SU, one dogman, four firearms officers (two double-crewed ARVs) and, say, four from section, so possibly sixteen uniforms (four armed) and the Ambush team who had turned out. Alford had done well to muster them all at such short notice.

'What do we need to know?' Alford asked.

'That you'll be in view all the way up the lane,' Flynn told him, 'so you need to move as fast as possible, split two ways, front and back, one ARV each way. Keep in cover, though. We know from the taxi man they have at least two handguns, so best to be safe. Surround the place, then start to negotiate and coax them out on their hands and knees.'

'Roger that,' Alford said.

'I'll stay where I am for the time being.'

'Roger that, too.'

'ETA?'

'Give us ten minutes.'

Flynn sat on his haunches, began the wait. Ten minutes was a long time, but he was accustomed to it, a skill he had acquired well.

He saw more movement through a downstairs window.

Upstairs, Tasker and the girl had moved away from the bedroom window, presumably back to the bed. Then Flynn's brow furrowed. Something instinctive told him things were not all OK, mainly because he had seen the shadow of only one other person, not two, through the downstairs window.

So where was the other one the bloodied taxi driver had blabbed about?

He could easily be there; maybe hadn't moved since Flynn arrived, possibly sitting watching TV, although there was no sign of an external aerial.

So far he had seen one man, plus Tasker, plus the girl.

He wished he'd seen them all, accounted for them all.

Part of himself said not to worry, this wasn't an exact science; but it was always better if as many items as possible could be ticked off the list.

He tensed.

Perhaps the guy was just having a shit? Shave? Shower?

Flynn glanced down the lane towards the main road, the road he'd seen the taxi turn off not long before, then return after having deposited the woman and child.

He could hear a car approaching.

Then he saw one, an old VW Passat estate, dark red.

He edged forward for a better view: three persons on board.

Always possible it could be someone going to one of the farms further along the track.

To be on the safe side, he radioed Alford.

'Vehicle approaching the farmhouse, Craig, three on board.' He paused. 'Now stopping outside the farm, three males getting out. Stretching their legs. Gone to the back of the car – it's an estate – opening the door. Shit – Craig?' Flynn waited for an acknowledgement. 'Craig, you receiving?'

'Yes – turning into farm track now,' Alford responded excitedly.

'Shit!' Flynn grunted as he watched one of the men reach into the back of the VW and pass a machine pistol out to one of the others, then another to the third guy. 'These guys are armed,' he said, looking down the lane and now able to see the police convoy racing up. The two ARVs were the lead vehicles, followed by the support unit personnel carrier, then the dog van, a couple of liveried Astra patrol cars, then the plain cars driven by the detectives. 'And they've seen you,' Flynn added bleakly.

The men had spun around and they panicked when they saw who was approaching.

One shouted something, a warning lost in the wind and rain, but Flynn got the gist: *Run.*

They split three ways, like a formation flying team, but all of them headed towards the trees where Flynn was concealed by foliage.

Two went either side of him, crashing into the bushes. One came directly at him, charging like a wild animal.

Flynn rose to meet him at the very last moment and the expression of shock horror on the man's face was a brief moment of delight.

He was going full pelt, tried to dink around Flynn and bring the gun up at the same time to spray him with a hail of bullets.

Flynn swivelled at the hips and brought the chopping edge of his right hand into the man's throat, stopping him instantly. The gun dropped and the man clutched his windpipe, his eyes bulging like fat red marbles. He dropped to his knees.

Flynn did not waver. He drove his fist into the man's temple, knowing he had to be put down, out of action. The punch was one he had learned many years before and he hoped he got it right – just powerful enough to pole-axe the man and put him out of business for a couple of minutes without actually causing brain damage or death, just to give him a very sore head.

The man toppled over as his brain went into neutral.

Flynn ripped the gun from him and hurled it aside in two directions – the gun one way, the magazine the other – then hastily rearranged the unconscious man into a recovery position so his airway would always be open.

He glanced up.

The cops had almost reached the farmhouse.

Twenty metres to his right there was the crashing of one of the other men who'd done a runner, as he fought his way through the undergrowth.

Flynn went in that direction. He had half-considered not going for the other two but he thought it could be dangerous not knowing what they were up to. There was a glimpse of the man and his face as it twisted towards Flynn – and another delightful reaction of shock. The man tried to run faster, but his feet were in the dead leaves and branches carpeting the woodland floor.

This was not going to be a stalking job. It was going to be a run down and ram, and Flynn knew he had the speed, strength and stamina to bring this second guy down.

The man ran, but Flynn came up on his flank and was glad to see this one had already discarded the machine pistol he'd run off with.

Flynn was about three metres to one side of him when the man looked at him again but in so doing ran straight into a branch at head height, which was about as effective as being hit across the head by a baseball bat, saving Flynn a job.

His head stayed where it was, but his legs ran on and then he fell flat on his back.

Flynn moved in quickly. He was reluctant to give this man a similar punch to the one he had just landed on his accomplice, so he dragged him, moaning, over to a slim but strong tree, made him hug it and then cuffed his wrists. Flynn patted his head, then turned to find the third escapee. He had lost sight of him, but as he looked around he saw the guy had made it all the way through the copse and was sprinting away across the fields. Flynn let him go.

'See you soon,' Flynn said to the man who was attached to the tree; his head was lolling loosely.

Flynn then heard the unmistakable sound of gunfire from the direction of the farmhouse.

Hunkered down behind a tree that had fallen diagonally against another, he peered through the leaves at the farmhouse.

Two armed officers crouched down behind their vehicle. The other vehicles in the police convoy had rapidly reversed back down the track and were still in a line about 200 metres from the gable end of the house. Flynn had no idea what was happening on the opposite side of the building. From what he could deduce it seemed that the first ARV had drawn up outside; the officers had presumably alighted and immediately been fired on from one of the windows. They had dived for cover behind their car – which, as they would be only too acutely aware, was no guarantee of safety. Bullets easily travel through cars.

Neither appeared injured, though.

Flynn saw a shape at a ground floor window, the glint of a gun barrel, then 'crack-ack' as two rounds were fired at the ARV and the instant clunk as at least one of them ripped into the bodywork and another ricocheted off the ground, sending up a mini-eruption of grit.

The officers crouched and so did Flynn. He was in the firing line if any misaimed shots came his way. He kept very low.

The two officers had drawn their Glocks and were babbling urgently down their radios, words Flynn could not hear because his radio was tuned into a different channel. This was undoubtedly the first time they had ever been under real fire and it was suddenly a very scary world.

Another shot.

Flynn ducked, the armed officers cowered, but this time the shot had been fired not from a window at the front of the house, but from the gable end that faced down the track. Someone inside the farmhouse was firing at the remainder of the convoy, who had retreated to what they had thought was a safe distance.

Flynn guessed the make and model of the weapon being fired. Experience of having been pinned down a few times by enemy fire had made him fairly expert in being able to recognize the type of gun being used to blow your brains out. It was a useful bit of knowledge in a battle, knowing exactly what you were going to be facing.

This time Flynn recognized the gun being fired at the convoy as a Czech Škorpion machine pistol set on single shot. Though not massively accurate at 200 metres, if it hit you it killed or seriously wounded you.

The officers milling about down the lane all hurled themselves down or behind their vehicles as the shooter from the house loosed off more rounds at them.

Cops held down at the front, cops pinned down at the side and, Flynn assumed, cops held down at the back of the house where the second ARV had gone.

He was sure things should have been the other way around. It was the villains who should have been on the back foot.

The people inside the farmhouse had responded very quickly to the situation and it was clear this was all going to end up very messy. In that moment, as Flynn crouched in the bushes, he could not have guessed just how messy.

He saw flickering flames and plumes of smoke at the bedroom window at that moment. The whole bedroom was suddenly engulfed by fire, something whooshed inside like a bomb and the whole window frame was blown out of its casing and came hurtling through the air in front of the explosion. It spun like a huge death star and embedded itself in the side of the armed response vehicle with a crash.

Flynn ducked but the force of the blast still rocked him, hot air shrouding his face as well as bits of grit.

He rolled to one side as a shard of glass shaped like an axe head struck the tree trunk in front of him. A foot to the left and it would have cleaved through his skull and split his brain into two perfect halves, left side, right side.

He looked up through the stems of grass, saw the front door of the farmhouse open and two armed men burst out side by side, firing into the ARV. The two cops dropped to the ground behind it, terrified.

The men were well armed: both had machine pistols with

magazines taped back to back so that when the first one clanked empty it was simply a case of reversing them and slotting the fully loaded one in place.

They were on single shot now, but firing rapidly.

Flynn raised his head. Neither of the two was Brian Tasker, which meant he was still inside the farmhouse, as were Davenport and the baby boy.

The first floor fire seemed to be taking hold and raging. Flames spewed out of the bedroom window, reaching up to the wooden eaves above, which also caught fire quickly.

The two armed cops were still crouching low, their guns drawn, having a heated discussion over the radio and with each other.

'Shoot back,' Flynn thought.

Then movement caught his eye on the gable end of the farmhouse – the opposite end from where someone had been shooting down the farm track. A ground floor window opened, then a leg appeared. A man scrambled out, dropped low and paused dramatically, almost like a pantomime villain.

It was Tasker, and he was armed with a handgun. Flynn expected him to turn and assist the girl and baby through the window but he did not, something which gave Flynn a bad feeling.

Instead, Tasker sprinted away across what had once been a farmyard, vaulted a low fence and dropped into a field.

At the front door, the two gunmen continued to pour rounds into the Ford Galaxy, which was now mortally wounded.

Upstairs, flames whooshed out of the space where there once had been a bedroom window.

Flynn started to run after Tasker, keeping his head down as he crashed through the undergrowth, transmitting to Craig Alford down his radio, 'Tasker's on the move, done a runner from the ground floor window out of your line of sight, and he's armed.' He included Tasker's direction of travel. 'I'm after him.'

Alford acknowledged him. 'Be careful, Steve.'

Tasker ran, still at a crouch, heading north across the fields, then across a narrow track that dissected Cookson's Plantation before turning right in a north-easterly direction and into the next field, heading towards Many Pits Wood. If he got into that it would give him cover.

He had not spotted Flynn who, keeping his own cover in Cookson's Plantation, was tracking him like a leopard on a warthog.

He broke cover just behind Tasker in the field.

Tasker was constantly checking his shoulder, but it must have been a bit of a shock to see Flynn suddenly burst out of nowhere and bear down on him.

Tasker spun, fired on the run, a wild shot from a pistol that recoiled crazily in his hand.

Flynn dropped to one knee instantly, even though he realized the bullet was going nowhere near him.

Away in the distance behind them the bang of gunfire could still be heard from the farmhouse.

Tasker fired wildly again, missed and ran on.

Flynn rose up and after him, cutting the distance between them easily but also knowing that by doing this he was increasing the chance of getting shot. He knew, however, that hitting anything while running with a handgun was a hard thing to do unless the shooter was trained and very fit.

He guessed that Tasker was neither, but nevertheless he only had to get in one lucky shot.

Tasker reached the perimeter of Many Pits Wood and dived into the treeline about thirty metres ahead of Flynn. He disappeared instantly into the undergrowth.

Flynn powered on relentlessly and entered at exactly the same point, a tiny piece of woodland much darker and more densely packed than Cookson's Plantation. He was immediately enshrouded.

If he had been Tasker he would have waited for his pursuer to come in behind him, dropped into a kneeling shooting position and taken him out as soon as he entered the woods.

Bearing this in mind, Flynn dived sideways once he entered the woods, just in case that was what Tasker had done. And indeed it was: he had lain in wait.

He had hidden himself and fired twice, but missed as the cop went sideways. This gave Flynn a brief advantage because, although he could not see Tasker, he saw the double muzzle-flash in the half-light which pinpointed Tasker's exact position.

Tasker fired twice more. Flynn scuttled around on all fours, feeling the whap of air above him from the shots just as he dropped full length behind a fallen log.

Flynn counted up. Tasker had fired six shots, which meant that if he had started with a full magazine he could possibly have nine or up to eleven bullets remaining, but he doubted Tasker would get as far as the last bullet.

Flynn bobbed as Tasker double-tapped, revealing his position again but – more importantly – missing Flynn's head.

Then he heard the sound of Tasker running away, crashing through the vegetation. Flynn rolled up on to his feet and, keeping down, weaved behind him, seeing fleeting glimpses through the trees as Tasker ran to the far edge of the copse.

More gunfire from the farmhouse. This time Flynn recognized the sound of Glocks being discharged. The police were shooting back. He gave a silent hooray and dipped under a branch, coming round wide on Tasker in a one-jawed pincer movement.

Tasker burst out through the edge of the woods, scrambled over a low fence and then was in the next field.

Flynn came out twenty metres to his right and both were in the open again.

Tasker ran fast; the man obviously did not wish to be caught but, Flynn decided, he would be.

Flynn powered up, vaulted the fence easily and came diagonally at Tasker just behind his right shoulder, a place he hoped would be similar to a driver's blind spot.

Tasker was noticeably flagging.

Flynn wasn't.

It was only as Flynn came within touching distance that Tasker saw him and turned.

He was too late to bring the gun around.

Flynn was on him, smacking the gun sideways as he smashed into him, a full body charge, grabbing the gun hand at the same time. Tasker pulled the trigger, fired, but Flynn had control of his hand and wrist. As they toppled over, Flynn hit him with an uppercut from his left fist, jarring his jaw.

It wasn't Flynn's best punch but had the desired effect and, in an involuntary spasm caused by a brief explosion of his brain synapses, Tasker dropped the gun.

Flynn saw it, rolled off Tasker and grabbed it. He did another sideways roll, using the impetus to come back up on to his knees with the gun already in his right hand and, supported by his left palm, pointed it steadily at Tasker, who groaned, sat up and grinned lopsidedly at Flynn.

'Let me walk and there's a million in your bank account tomorrow,' he said, panting.

'Wow, let me see,' Flynn said mock-seriously.

'If not, you're a dead man walking and your family is dead, too,' Tasker said, wiping his face with his hands.

'Oh, it's the money, then,' Flynn said. 'Obviously.' He let the gun swing on his finger.

For one moment Tasker actually believed him.

FIFTEEN

'The two guys who came out of the farmhouse all guns blazing just dropped their weapons when they were empty and stuck up their hands in surrender. Even though the cops did return fire – eventually – no one was injured in the shoot-out, which was amazing, but it just goes to show how hard it can be to shoot someone.'

Flynn was talking to Santiago.

It was the morning after and they were having breakfast on the rear deck of Flynn's boat in Santa Eulalia harbour.

She had fallen properly asleep at the point where Flynn had described Tasker's arrest in the middle of a field and the ineffective attempt to bribe him with a million pounds.

Flynn, too, had dropped off then, but had resumed the story over breakfast when Santiago asked what happened next.

He told her some more about the two men with the guns.

'It had been their job to provide cover so Tasker could get away – y'know, give him a few more minutes' grace . . . unfortunately they didn't know I was in the woods – obviously.' Flynn paused. 'So they dropped their guns and were arrested without a fight . . . subsequently it turned out they were the team who'd sprung Tasker from our custody when he was being transferred from the hospital to the police station. The taxi driver was in on that, too.

'What we didn't know until then was just how long Tasker had been in the north west. Long enough to put his business together, get a girlfriend and a baby. He'd set up with Braceford, but they'd had a huge fallout over money and percentages and skimming and Tasker thinking Braceford was a grass – he wasn't. Braceford, our very own nasty, nasty local drug lord didn't realize he'd got into bed with the devil going under the name of Brian Tasker.

'Anyway, they all eventually went to trial and got their just deserts and Tasker's evil was put on display for the world to see. He got . . . I can't remember . . . five, six concurrent life sentences.

'On his way down from court he stopped and pointed at each one of us who were in that photograph Jerry sent me. One of those very deliberate points, y'know? You, you, you, you, you and you – Craig, Jerry, Dave Carver, Jimmy Blue, Lincoln Bartlett and me.'

Flynn chortled at the memory, recalling every word.

'He paused when he got to me. "You're all dead, you know, and I will never, ever forgive you . . . you all made me do it . . . and I will get my revenge, and it will be hot and sweet." Then they dragged him away.'

'Made him do what?' Santiago tore a chunk off her croissant and placed it in her mouth.

The fire service took over two hours to douse the flames in the farmhouse and damp it down enough for anyone to be able to enter the building. They had tried to get in while the fire had been raging but the intense, hell-like heat had beaten them back. It frustrated them because they knew people were trapped inside, but their brave efforts ultimately proved futile.

Flynn watched from a distance, noting the passion with which they attacked the fire that had so quickly engulfed the farmhouse, spreading downstairs from the first floor. They had been brilliant, brave, but ultimately all they could do was extinguish the flames.

All the while Flynn's eyes had flickered to the child's buggy parked by the front door which, as the fire service had tackled the blaze, was thrown aside, almost discarded, so as not to cause an obstruction.

Flynn knew what would be found upstairs.

His heart had been whamming throughout the incident, a cold

rage in him, a numbness, as his eyes constantly looked at the buggy.

A baby. A mother.

Eventually the flames were extinguished and damped down. Several firefighters tramped out of the building removing their breathing apparatus, leaving black outlines around the perimeter of their faces. Their expressions were grim.

There was little use for the two ambulances at the scene.

The firefighters talked in a huddle, then with Craig Alford and the other high-ranking police officers who had materialized on the scene. Flynn was beckoned over by Alford and asked if he wanted to put on a forensic suit and go in with him and a CSI.

Flynn said he did.

He had seen death in many forms, particularly during his years as a Marine and in the SBS. He had seen death on the streets of British cities and African jungles, but he had never become completely immune to the death of a child.

In that farmhouse, the death he saw was as bad and as brutal as any he had witnessed, death caused simply as a diversion to facilitate escape.

Both bodies had been roasted black. Smoke still rose from the corpses.

It transpired that Ellie Davenport had been shot through the head before the bedroom had been doused with petrol and set alight. The baby had simply been left on a blanket on the floor and had died of smoke inhalation before being consumed by fire.

Just so a man could evade justice.

Flynn looked at Santiago, who was mesmerized by his retelling of these awful events. She had stopped eating her breakfast and drinking her coffee.

Her eyes became moist.

'Steve,' she gasped.

He was staring into space, recalling the scene.

'A man with no redeeming features or qualities. I've come across some villains in my time. But Brian Tasker, psychopath . . .' Flynn did not finish. He shook his head at the memory, which until that moment he had never discussed. It was usually locked away and internalized in a cellar room in his mind, a place where nut jobs were kept at bay, and the key was rarely found.

'Steve,' Santiago said, feeling useless.

'Some images are with you for ever,' he said. He sighed and looked at her. 'It's what you sign up for . . . the irony was, he blamed me, us, for forcing him down that path, but I guess that's just the way his perverted mind works. That said, we treated him with professionalism and courtesy. He was questioned by me and others without emotion.'

'So you never . . .?' Santiago asked.

'Never what?'

'You know – kapow!' She punched the air with a few boxer-like digs.

He turned face on to her. 'Of course I fucking did.'

'Thought you might have.' She smiled at him and her voice softened again. 'I can see why it affected you.'

He nodded. 'In more ways than one.'

Santiago narrowed her eyes questioningly.

'I also found out why my so-called mate, Jack Hoyle, was so reluctant to get involved with Ambush . . . because it meant I would be away, and he and my wife,' Flynn said peevishly, 'could continue their illicit affair behind my back and Jack's wife's back . . . but I only found that out quite a bit later when other stuff happened.'

'I'm sorry, Steve.'

He shrugged. 'Such is life.' He did not go on to mention that he did find some solace in the arms of a very pretty lady doctor and an even prettier Flower Girl. As to those two assignations his lips would remain for ever sealed.

There was a nice charter in for the day, two chilled-out, almost horizontal and very wealthy couples who just wanted to swim, sunbathe and eat. Flynn and Santiago took them out around Tagomago, the private island just off Ibiza owned by a zillionaire German industrialist, then dropped anchor at the tiny inlet of Es Pou des Lleó where they swam, ate at a beachside café and swam again in the tepid water.

Flynn was back by five p.m. and, after receiving a very generous tip, he and Santiago cleaned down the boat and prepared it for the next day. Then they strolled out to the Babylon Beach restaurant for an evening meal on the cliffs.

He had immersed himself in work for the day and forgotten about the real world, although there were a few pensive moments at Babylon Beach when he mulled over Brian Tasker and the deaths of Craig Alford, his poor family and Jerry Tope.

Undoubtedly Tasker was more than capable of committing these atrocious crimes. Yet he was in prison, incarcerated for the remainder of his lifetime . . . though Flynn wasn't convinced that Tasker could not have done them. Maybe he had contracted someone to do his dirty work for him and make his death promises come true.

But from a prison cell? Maybe . . .

Looking out across the calm sea to the Illa de Santa Eulalia and the S'Argamassa headland, Flynn made a decision and picked up his mobile phone. Tasker had to be checked out.

It rang before he had the chance to make a call.

'Flynn,' he answered.

'Steve? Rik Dean,' came a flustered voice.

'I was about to call you.'

'Oh, right . . . look . . . some more bad news, I'm afraid . . .'

Flynn glanced at Santiago and mouthed, 'Rik Dean.' He leaned towards her and tilted the phone so she could hear the conversation. 'Go on,' he said.

'Dave Carver.'

'What about Dave Carver?' Flynn's guts tightened ominously.

Dean drew in an unsteady breath. 'He was in a nursing home, suffering from dementia.'

'I know that.'

'He's dead.'

'You may have to expand on that, Rik.'

'Shot in his room in the home.'

'Suicide?'

'No . . . a nurse was killed, too, undoubtedly a witness . . . signs of a struggle . . . looks like Dave put up a fight . . . and the security tapes have been taken too . . . a professional hit . . . he's been murdered.'

'Shit.'

'That's three out of the six guys in that photograph, Steve – Craig, Jerry, now Dave.'

'That is not lost on me . . . look, Rik,' Flynn said earnestly, 'I've been thinking about this. It's got to be Brian Tasker. He's the link and it doesn't take the Brain of Britain to work that one out, even if he's – and I use this word advisedly – "masterminding" it from his cell.'

'I'd go with that one hundred per cent, except for one thing,' Dean said.

'That thing being?'

'Because he'd have to be masterminding it from the grave . . . he'd have to be a ghost.'

'Grave? A ghost? What d'you mean?'

'Brian Tasker died three months ago in a fatal fire in his cell in Lancashire Prison.'

SIXTEEN

Flynn studied the photograph, the six men, the Lancashire contingent on Operation Ambush, the ones who led the hunt for Brian Tasker, self-styled drug cartel leader (UK version), ruthless killer and not one to shoulder blame for anything. Nothing was his fault, everyone else was responsible.

The six men who had been there, literally, at the death.

The cops who were responsible, as he saw it, for making him kill his girlfriend and baby son. And Flynn, the one who had brought him down in a field and, just for an instant, had made him believe he would take a bribe.

Flynn had been a hard-edged cop, often broke rules and heads, but there was only one thing he wanted and that was to see bad men, and occasionally women, face justice.

He was beyond bribes.

No amount of money would ever have made him deviate from his goal and he had been offered money many times because drug squad officers chasing down wealthy villains were open to it.

In fact, the more money on offer, the more pleasure he took in saying no and then slotting a reference to the attempted bribe into his witness statements, just to make the defendant cringe in court.

He had loved seeing Brian Tasker marched away down the Crown Court steps never to see real light of day again, and Tasker's death threat had made it even sweeter.

Flynn had laughed in his face, which had had the desired effect of riling him into a rage.

Flynn rubbed his face, thought it through.

Three – Craig, Jerry and Dave – murdered in quick succession. Lincoln Bartlett was already dead through natural causes, thereby leaving Jimmy Blue and himself still breathing and possibly the next two targets.

It was always possible Jimmy had already been murdered and the news had not yet surfaced. According to Rik Dean, Jimmy's whereabouts were currently unknown, but he was making enquiries with the pension and HR departments, who should know.

Flynn glanced at Santiago.

They were back at the Mirage, mid-morning, the day after the phone call from Rik Dean. Both were at a loose end after a charter party cancellation, although Santiago was on the phone to her boss in Gran Canaria, who wanted to know when she was coming back to work. Something was bubbling that he needed her for.

Flynn sighed. Although the facts as outlined by Rik Dean stated otherwise, one thing he did not believe was that Brian Tasker was ashes.

Santiago ended her phone call, but almost immediately her mobile rang again. She rolled her eyes and took it, but Flynn didn't listen in. It was in Spanish anyway and his grasp of the language, even after all the years he'd lived in Spain, was pretty tenuous, although Santiago was giving him some personalized tuition and he was becoming quite good at it in some situations, such as ordering food and drink and asking for sex.

She ended the call. 'That was the detective in charge of investigating the armed robbery we interrupted. Would you believe it . . .?'

From the look on her face, Flynn did. 'They got bail?' he guessed.

She nodded. 'The police found their apartment, they'd been renting it for a couple of months, so the magistrate was happy enough there was a permanent residence.'

Flynn wasn't surprised. Even though they had terrorized two shop assistants and been happy to use firearms, the courts were probably more concerned about their human rights. He said, 'So they're as stupid here as they are in the UK.'

'So it would seem.'

Flynn watched the boats in the marina. A big motor cruiser owned by an American billionaire had just berthed and disgorged various occupants, mainly middle-aged ladies shrouded in gold and diamonds and wafting kaftans, stepping into stretch limos on the quayside. Flynn assumed they were being whisked away somewhere glamorous to have their toenails done or bikini waxes updated.

'Do you think you're next on the list, if there is a list?' Santiago asked. 'And if so, what are you going to do about it?'

'Er . . . at the moment I'm not too concerned. No one really knows I'm here for the summer, but once I get back to Gran Canaria people will know, and that includes quite a few crims. I try to keep a low profile, as you know' – here he exchanged a knowing grin with her – 'but somehow my head keeps popping up over the parapet.'

'What about your family?' Santiago almost choked as she said the next two words. 'Your ex?' Then she cleared her throat and said, 'And your son?'

'Faye is away with her latest boyfriend, somewhere in Phuket, I believe, appropriately enough.' Santiago chuckled meanly. 'My lad is trekking somewhere in the Himalayas with his uni mates, so I think both are safe enough for the time being. I didn't know you were bothered about my ex,' he said cheekily.

'Old Frosty, you mean?' She had nicknamed her that after Flynn had once told Santiago about her. She had taken an instant dislike.

He laughed and touched Santiago's hand tenderly. 'Me and you, babe,' he assured her. Santiago's face softened. Then he went on, 'I think it would be wise to make the assumption that Jimmy Blue and I could be the next targets, and what I don't want to do is sit back and let some arsehole sneak up behind me.' He paused, a pained look on his face. 'I need to make the running, somehow, and I kinda think the only way to do that might be to head to the UK and do some digging, make sure Jimmy's OK, and see what worms I can dig up. Rik Dean might be grateful for any help I can offer, though I won't hold my breath on that. I've offered help before and been cold-shouldered by the cops because of my history.'

'I think you need to rephrase part of that,' Santiago told him.

'Which part?'

'The "I need to make the running" part. It should be "we need to make the running".'

'I was hoping you'd say that.'

'But I'm a woman,' she protested. 'Why aren't you saying this is no sort of a job for a girlie like me?'

'Because I'm a modern man,' he boasted. 'I see women for what they are and what they can contribute and not just as sex objects and housewives, and because you're my special girlie – my hot bitch, remember?'

She punched him quite forcefully on the arm.

Rubbing his bicep, he said, 'I'm going to contact Rik Dean and see what he thinks about me going over, but there is one thing we need to do first.'

'And that is?'

'Pay someone a visit.'

Flynn had not been to Ibiza many times before and usually the visits had been fairly fleeting. The last time had been several years before to buy a sportfishing boat to replace one destroyed in a fire set by two enforcers who thought he owed money to a drug dealer. Their belief was wrong but it hadn't prevented the boat being sunk in a terrible explosion. That had been his first boat as a skipper and he still missed her to this day.

He had only ever been to San Antonio once before, the night-club capital of the island. He had been surprised at how pretty the town was but how that all changed once night descended and it became a heaving, sweaty mass of young humanity coupled with pounding disco music of all genres. Not that Flynn would have been able to differentiate any of the genres even if they had been piped directly into his eardrums. He was pretty much an Eighties child as regards music, but even a lot of that passed him by.

The taxi dropped him and Santiago off on the sea front of the town and they took a short stroll to get a feel for the place, knowing that if they were successful in what they had to do it would not take long, and also that they had a little time to kill because their flight did not leave until after midnight.

After the walk and a lingering cup of coffee they strolled up to the old town, into the maze of tight streets set back from the bay, until Santiago led him to the address he was seeking, an apartment above a shop selling lace and trinkets. The entrance was a door to the left of the shop and the buzzer panel showed eight apartments up there, but there were no names in any of the card slots.

Flynn pressed all the buttons several times. Eventually an occupant spoke. Flynn grunted something about a lost key and the entrance door clicked open.

Apart from being tiled throughout, it was much like stepping into any one of the less salubrious apartment buildings Flynn had frequented as a cop. The smell was the same urine/vomit/sweat/food/weed reek, the sounds too – muffled music, someone shouting, someone having sex, possibly with someone else – and underfoot was the same, the crunch that says you've just stepped on a used needle.

'Nice,' Santiago commented.

'Love it.'

Flynn went up the narrow staircase on to the second floor via a couple of tight dog-leg landings until they reached number eight.

He tried the door handle: locked. He knocked politely.

No response.

He arched his eyebrows at Santiago. She shrugged.

'Definitely number eight?'

She nodded.

Flynn stepped back, his body almost touching the opposite wall, raised his right foot, took aim for what he thought was the weakest point on the door just by the Yale type lock and flat-footed it.

It rattled loosely and on the second blow crumpled open as though he had kicked it in the solar plexus.

He gave it a third one to send it clattering all the way open on just one hinge, then stepped inside the studio apartment.

It was empty, but a mess. One unmade single bed and one camp bed, both looking as though they had been slept in for months without a change of covers. Unwashed dishes were strewn in and around the sink, many with black-green mould growing unhealthily in them.

The room reeked of sweat and cannabis.

Flynn flicked through the bedding, looked through drawers and in the minute bathroom and came to a conclusion.

'Done a runner.'

Since Rik Dean had been amenable to Flynn coming back to the UK so he could share his knowledge of Tasker with him – something Flynn found a bit of a surprise – he had booked a flight from Ibiza to Manchester at 00:30 hours. Flynn and Santiago caught a taxi from San Antonio after their breaking and entering episode, arriving at the airport with just hand luggage. They passed quickly through check-in and immigration, then found a pleasant spot in one of the bars in the departure lounge. Flynn drank tea and Santiago decided on a glass of red wine. He didn't travel well on alcohol.

They boarded and took off on time and settled – too snugly for Flynn's wide frame and long length – into a pair of seats on which he felt as if his knees were up to his chin. This confirmed him in his view that one day, when he was a successful international businessman, he would always travel first class and never on a budget airline – unless he owned it.

Santiago, smaller, slimmer, prettier, had plenty of space.

The flight was an uneventful two and a half hours, during which Flynn visited the cramped toilet once.

When he returned to his seat he gently woke the snoozing Santiago and whispered in her ear.

When the plane touched down he and Santiago were first through the door, hurrying from the arrival gate through the quick formality of customs and passport check before entering the arrivals hall, where a weary Rik Dean had agreed to meet them.

Flynn did not have time to explain but quickly asked one of the waiting taxi drivers, who was holding up a clipboard with the surname of a passenger written on it, if he had a spare piece of paper and pen.

Flynn then positioned himself directly opposite the arrivals door he had just come through and held up the piece of paper with the name he'd written on it.

Rik Dean, not having had anything explained to him, looked on bemused.

Flynn and Santiago had been well ahead of the other passengers, who now began to filter lethargically out in dribs and drabs and included a certain Dwayne Assheton, the young man Flynn had chased from the scene of an attempted robbery, now on bail.

As Flynn had earlier stumbled through the plane to reach the toilet and empty his tea-filled bladder, having to keep his head low, he had tripped on someone's outstretched foot and caught himself from falling by grabbing a head rest on the back of a seat. Pulling himself upright in the gloom – the cabin lights having been doused to allow passengers to doze – Flynn caught sight of the sleeping young man in seat 26A, next to a window.

'What the hell are you doing?' Dean hissed in Flynn's ear.

'Meet 'n' greet,' Flynn said.

At these words, Dwayne Assheton came out through the one-way doors and sauntered cockily towards the barrier where Flynn stood in a line of taxi drivers.

Assheton had his hood over his head. At first he didn't see Flynn even though he was standing directly in front of the doors. Then his eyes picked out his name on the A4 sheet of paper, plastered in thick black felt tip pen.

Rising another few degrees, his eyes stopped at Flynn's gurning face.

Recognition took a moment – then the young man's facial expression screamed, *Shit!*

'Taxi for Assheton.' Flynn beamed brightly.

The lad sprinted, and for the second time in a matter of days he found he was being pursued by a man who rarely gave up. He zipped sideways, elbowing between a couple ahead of him.

Flynn dropped his piece of paper and went with him, closely followed by Santiago and Dean, who was just tagging along for the hell of it.

For a few metres Flynn and Assheton were side by side, divided by a steel barrier, but then Assheton upped his pace. Flynn vaulted the barrier but could not quite reach his prey with his fingertips as Assheton veered around a taxi driver bearing a name plate, knocking it out of his hands.

Flynn dodged the man, who spun in amazement and gawped as the two men ran either side of him, followed by another man and a woman.

Assheton was undecided. He moved quickly, agile and lithe, but Flynn was more of a bulldozer, and the young lad's indecision was his undoing. His hesitation gave Flynn an extra metre and he caught him exactly underneath the 'Meeting Point' sign and flattened him.

Assheton struggled but Flynn overpowered him easily and dragged him to his tiptoes by his hood, at which point screams of warning permeated Flynn's skull.

'Stop – armed police!'

Flynn froze but kept his grip on the dangling man, who writhed and wriggled like a fish, but Flynn had caught bigger and heavier ones than him. Flynn slowly raised his left arm in a gesture of surrender to the two armed airport cops who stood, their weapons – which they were clearly willing to use – drawn and pointed.

'Fuck you, fuck you all!'

Dwayne Assheton slouched challengingly in the plastic chair, scowling at Rik Dean and, behind him, Flynn and Santiago.

The appearance of Rik Dean's warrant card and rank had appeased the armed officers, plus the hurried explanation that Assheton had broken his bail conditions set by a court in Ibiza and illegally skipped the country. The police were happy enough with that and happy to haul him away to the detention centre at the airport and book him into custody.

Unfortunately no details of his bail conditions were available on any computer system as yet and it would be later in the morning before it could be confirmed whether or not he was on the run, but Dean and Santiago were convincing enough for the custody officer to keep him.

The police were also more than happy when it transpired he was travelling on a false passport under the name of Harold Bruce.

So for the time being he was going nowhere and when he was hustled into an interview room to face Dean and the other two, he was defiant and obnoxious.

'You can't fuckin' interrogate me without my brief,' he snarled.

'We don't interrogate people,' Dean corrected him, 'we interview them. And this is not a formal interview, anyway. The purpose of this chat is to gather intelligence and information from a willing witness – you. We are not investigating an offence.'

'Not talking.' He folded his arms.

'And anyway, you have spoken to a solicitor on the phone, who saw no reason to get out of his warm bed until the police have confirmed your status as a fugitive travelling with a false passport.'

'Fugitive – very dramatic.'

'Well, that's what you are, Dwayne, a fugitive.'

Assheton continued to scowl, but also squirmed uncomfortably.

'But that's not why we want to chat to you.'

'So what is this about? I know my rights. I should be allowed to have some sleep. I've been locked up often enough to know that.'

'You can have a sleep soon enough,' Dean said.

'And what's he doing here?' Assheton's eyes flickered to Flynn, standing tall and erect.

Dean glanced sideways at him.

Flynn said, 'Something I didn't get the chance to ask you after I'd chased after you and caught you, even though you fired a gun at me.'

'I missed, din I? Anyway, ask me what?'

'Why you had a photograph of me in your apartment.'

'I don't know, do I?'

'You don't know why you had a photograph of me?'

'Nope.'

'It was in the back pocket of a pair of your jeans,' Santiago said.

Assheton pulled his face at her. 'And?'

'Tell us,' Dean encouraged him, but all he did was shrug and avoid further eye contact.

Flynn tapped Dean on the shoulder and jerked his head at the detective. Dean rose and followed him to the corner of the room where they appeared to have a hushed confab with their eyes constantly looking over at Assheton, who continued to shift uneasily.

Nodding in apparent agreement, Dean split away from Flynn and resumed his seat.

'What?' Assheton demanded.

'We've just had a little chit-chat and we're in agreement.'

'About what?'

'Well, to be fair, breaking bail conditions in Ibiza isn't all that interesting to us. Nor, to be honest, is the passport thing, really.'

'What d'you mean?' Assheton was rightly suspicious.

'What I mean is that we're thinking of wiping the slate clean and letting you go. I'm sure I can convince the good people here to let this happen.'

'Why would you d-do that?'

Dean's eyes were only inches away from the prisoner's as he leaned towards him keeping eye contact, then flicking his pupils sideways with just the faintest twitch of his head.

Assheton frowned.

Rik Dean did it again, then whispered, 'The big guy wants to see you in private to discuss things. He seems to think he has unfinished business with you after that fracas in Ibiza.'

Assheton's couldn't-give-a-shit demeanour faded in an instant and he became horror-struck. His lips, previously zipped tight, plopped open with a tiny, bubble-bursting noise. 'You wouldn't,' he almost choked.

'You have his photo and he wants to know why, so yeah, I would.'

Assheton's eyes tore away from Dean and looked into the smirking face of Steve Flynn. 'We have a lot to discuss in private, possibly in the dark corner of a car park with no CCTV cameras,' Flynn explained.

Assheton looked back at Dean. His Adam's apple rose and fell with an audible 'dunk'. 'Bastards.'

'Just tell us why you had his photo, that's all. Simple equation. Tell us now, open up, spill the beans, sing like a canary,' Dean said, enjoying himself, 'and your life will be much less . . . painful, shall we say.'

Assheton rocked back, jerking nervously. He started to gasp, on the verge of hyperventilation. 'Look, I'm just a fuckin' nobody, y'know? I'm just the shit on your shoes. I'm a chancer, a fuckin' scavenger. I deal drugs, I steal to buy 'em too. I use drugs. I rob people. I'm your friendly neighbourhood scumbag, so I don't know nowt, OK?'

'Your release from custody is imminent,' Dean said.

Greater panic consumed Assheton. 'This is all being recorded, right?' he asked hopefully.

'What do you think? I told you, this is information gathering.'

'We were just asked to look out for him.' Assheton gestured loosely at Flynn. 'Given a picture and a phone number, that was it.'

'Who's we?' Flynn asked.

'Dunno. People like me.'

'Where, when, who?'

'Coupla weeks ago, just before I went to Ibiza. A picture and a number to call if you were spotted, like a wanted poster.'

'Where?' Flynn demanded.

'Pub in Blackpool.'

'Name it!'

'I can't fuckin' remember, OK?'

'Name it!' Flynn insisted.

'Fat Billy's, I think . . . they were just like circulating.'

'You mean people were giving out my photograph and telling you to phone a number if I was ever seen?'

'Yeah, wanker! Do you not get it?'

'Who?'

'No friggin' idea . . . five hundred squiddly-doos for it,' Assheton said. 'Do you still not get it?'

Flynn blinked, getting it.

'There's a fucking contract out on you.'

SEVENTEEN

'Five hundred pounds! Five hundred measly quid?' Flynn was affronted almost to the point of apoplexy that such a paltry sum could have been put on his life.

'Darling,' Santiago cooed, 'that was only the price for information leading to your whereabouts.' She was trying to comfort and reassure him but despite the seriousness of the situation she could not keep a grin from her face.

'Yeah,' Rik Dean said, 'I'm sure whoever takes you out is bound to get ten times that.'

Flynn was unimpressed. 'Whatever,' he said tiredly.

The three of them were sitting in Dean's car in the car park outside the Ibis Hotel at Broughton, north of Preston, close to the M55/M6 motorway link. Flynn had booked a room for four nights. It had taken just over an hour to get there from Manchester airport where they had left Dwayne Assheton in custody.

In spite of repeated questioning Assheton maintained that he had neither phoned the number associated with Flynn's 'wanted' poster nor would in the future. Just to make sure of this Flynn had taken Assheton's mobile phone and deleted every number in his contacts list as well as the made and received numbers in case he was lying, so he could not make the call now even if he wanted to. He had also snapped the SIM card in half.

The journey from the airport had been relatively silent. Flynn and Santiago had taken up residence in the back seat of Dean's car and Santiago had curled up, rested her head on his shoulder and slept. He had stared through the windows as the motorways zipped by in a blur.

The £500 whinge had been the only thing Flynn had said, but then the reality of being the target for an assassin or assassins hit him quite hard. If the person – man or woman – who had been awarded the contract was the same one who had already killed Craig Alford and his family, Jerry Tope and the already dying Dave Carver, then even Flynn realized he had something substantial to worry about.

His mind was a whirr of tumbling thoughts as he attempted to piece it all together and draw conclusions.

But now he was tired and needed sleep.

Dawn was almost upon them, some weak British sunshine rising slowly and reluctantly.

Before getting out of the car Flynn had said, 'Can I just chew the fat for a minute?'

'Course,' Dean said.

'If we are right in the assumption – or the fact – that the guys in that photograph are being picked off one by one, three down, two to go, one already dead anyway, and I'm the only one to feature in a wanted poster that's doing the rounds of the Blackpool underworld, can we draw a conclusion from that?'

Dean thought it over.

Santiago stretched, coming groggily awake. 'The whereabouts of everyone else but you are known,' she ventured.

'Could be,' Dean conceded.

'In which case, if Jimmy Blue's whereabouts are known, he could be next on the list and somehow we, you, need to contact him and warn him. I half-remember he always fancied being a farmer, but I would have thought that the pension or HR people should know where he is.'

'It's not an infallible system. Once you retire or leave the job, the pension payments just go to your bank account. They should have an address, but that's dependent on the individual concerned notifying them of any changes. Sometimes they don't, but that doesn't stop the pension being paid.'

Flynn accepted that and moved on, 'But that still leaves the question as to why people are being murdered. Answer that and you could be on a roll.' He sighed. 'Mind's a mush. It's all over the place, need sleep. Look,' he said to Dean, 'I have a rental car being delivered here later this morning. When I get that, the first thing I want to do is visit Marina, Jerry's wife . . . widow. I know you've spoken to her but I think I need to see her and offer my, our, condolences.' He glanced at Santiago. 'Maybe she might have thought of something more.'

'You'll have to show some sort of ID,' Dean told him. 'We have her under guard for the time being – at home, obviously – in view of what happened to Craig's family.'

Flynn nodded and reached for the door handle. 'I know it's a bit obvious, but killing a whole family is extreme, isn't it? It's not really something any of our home-grown organized gangs would usually stoop to, but it is something Mexican and Colombian drug cartels are more than happy to do.' His eyes narrowed. 'And Brian Tasker had ideas about running his businesses along cartel lines, murdering innocent people. That's partly why his own family disowned him – he likes killing too much.' He let go of the handle, sat back. 'And he's not averse to setting fire to people so he can escape from custody. He killed his girlfriend and kid. He has no conscience, no feelings.'

'You talk like he's still alive, Steve,' Dean said.

'Are we really sure he's dead?'

Flynn left the question hanging in the air as he and Santiago climbed out. He thanked Dean and went to the reception desk, then to bed.

'I am so sorry,' Flynn said to Jerry Tope's widow Marina, a slightly rotund woman with the hint of a moustache.

He was perched on the edge of the settee in Tope's living room, leaning across and holding Marina's chubby fingers between the palms of his hands. She seemed numb, almost catatonic in her grief.

'I can't believe he's gone,' she whispered. 'If only I hadn't been away.'

Flynn glanced over to Santiago on the armchair opposite. She smiled sadly.

'He was a good friend,' Flynn said.

'Who would want to do that?' Marina demanded as if she hadn't heard him. 'All he did was sit and mess with computers all day. He wasn't even a real detective.'

'Yes he was,' Flynn said softly. 'He just had a different skill set. He was as much a detective as any of the others, and better than most.'

'Yes, yes, I suppose you're right,' she conceded with a sigh. 'You were a good friend to him.'

'Really?' he said, surprised.

'Covering for him all those years ago, saying *you* were the one who had a one-night stand with a slapper.'

Flynn was shocked. 'I don't know what you—'

'I've known all along,' she said. 'I'm a woman. We know things.' She exchanged a glance with Santiago.

'How?'

'Someone told me the truth, one of the other guys you were out with that night.'

Grab-a-Granny night, Flynn thought. Preston town centre, as it was in the 1980s, before city status. A night out on a detectives' course. Tuesday, known unkindly as Grab-a-Granny night, the night on which tradition had it that the 'older' end of the female spectrum hit town and eventually tumbled down the steps into Squires nightclub to become willing prey for hunting detectives and other cops on courses at Hutton Hall; and the night when Jerry Tope, normally so risk averse, got himself stupidly pissed and into the panties of a lady almost twice his age.

Then the cover-up – and Marina, Tope's young bride, had known all along.

'It made him a wonderful husband,' Marina said. 'In my mind I forgave him as soon as I knew. It was just a stupid night. Didn't make it right, but it was a mistake, and now it's killing me I never forgave him to his face and he will never know.' A tear teetered on the lower rim of her right eyelid, shimmered, then lost its balance and tumbled down her cheek.

She rubbed it away crossly. 'Shit. I already miss him messing about with gadgets, here and in his car, and stuff. Who's going to drink all that home-brewed beer and wine? It's horrible stuff, but he loved it.' She laughed. 'Now he'll never have a microbrewery and a tiny pub . . . never. And what about these bloody cops outside?' She made a wild gesture.

A double-crewed ARV was parked on the avenue outside the house.

'Who would want to kill *me*? I don't know anything.'

'That's not the point, I don't think. It's about keeping you safe,' Flynn said.

'I know, I know.' Her head dropped into her hands. 'Oh, fuck.'

Flynn and Santiago stood outside Tope's house. Tope's car had been returned home from where it had been found, close to the place he had died, and parked on the driveway. Flynn leaned against it and tried to make a contact call with Rik Dean, but got no joy. He thrust his phone back into his pocket and stared glumly at Santiago.

'All those years I blagged him for information by threatening to reveal his dirty little secret to Marina, and she knew all along. And now I feel such a bastard, too. He'd been mentally paying for that one night of idiocy for all these years. It must've been hell for him. Funnily enough I really liked doing it, loved making him squirm . . . what an utter – bah! – I am.'

Santiago touched his arm. 'Don't beat yourself up about it. What's done is done. You two ended up in a good place with each other, so that's what matters.'

'Suppose so.' He turned away, slightly tearful, not wishing to blub in front of her. He placed his hands on the edge of the car roof and leaned against it like a prisoner about to be searched, with his head drooping between his shoulders. Then, raising it slightly, he stared blankly into the car.

The imprint of a ring on the dashboard caught his eye – as if a wet cup had been balanced on the black plastic.

Flynn wondered what it could have been. Possibly a satnav, the type of gadget Tope would have liked; but peering into the car he saw there was a factory-fitted satnav in the dashboard itself.

'What?' Santiago said, noticing his change of posture.

'One second.' Flynn pushed himself off the car and went back to the front door of the house, tapped on it. Marina appeared a few moments later.

Flynn apologized for the inconvenience and asked, 'Did Jerry have a satnav for the car?'

'Er, no.' She scratched her head. 'I mean, yes – it's in the dashboard, came fitted.'

'In that case, what was stuck on the dashboard that would leave a round mark like a cup or a sucker?'

'The mini-cam, one of those things that records journeys, what's happening in front of the car. He had one in the back window, too. He was terrified of those false accident claims, y'know? People claiming you've bumped into them or knocked them over when you haven't, and then going to your insurance company. He said it was rife in this area – and he always took the cameras out when he got home because he said they were a thieving bunch around here.'

'He was a cautious man,' Santiago said.

'Not cautious enough,' Marina said bleakly.

'What are you thinking?' Santiago asked Flynn.

'It's probably nothing,' he said, and turned back to Marina. 'Did he record every journey?'

'Think so.'

'So why are the cameras not in the car now, if you don't mind me asking?'

'I don't know.' She leaned to one side to look past him at the car.

'Are they in the house?'

'Again, I don't know. If they are, they'll be up in his study.'

'What are you getting at?' Santiago asked again.

He gave a helpless shrug. 'I don't know. Do you remember what time Rik Dean said Jerry finished work on the day he was murdered?'

It was Santiago's turn to shrug. Then she said, 'Didn't he finish work about the same time as Craig Alford, but then he got called back later to go to the scene of Alford's death? Then he finished work after that, if you see what I mean?'

'Yeah . . . what if he recorded something of interest during any of those journeys, either on the way home initially or going to or coming away from Craig's house. Wouldn't hurt to have a look, would it, even if there was nothing.'

'If the cameras are here,' Santiago said.

'Mm. Maybe they aren't, and if they aren't that throws up a whole new ball game – such as where are they and who has them?'

'They're here.'

Flynn and Santiago turned, not having realized that while they were talking Marina had gone back into the house, gone upstairs, found the two cameras and returned with one in each hand. She held them out, like a dead bird in each palm. 'Have them.'

Flynn and Santiago had not slept well, just a few hours of tossing and turning until eventually, though wiped out, they'd got up, made coffee in the room and waited for the arrival of the hire car, a Fiat Punto. It was after that they'd gone to see Marina, offered their sympathy and acquired the dash-cams.

From Tope's house Flynn had driven down to Preston Docks, where they ate breakfast in the café at Morrisons supermarket. They then walked across to the edge of the dock.

'If I'm right, from what Rik told me, Jerry was shot along here.' He and Santiago walked in an easterly direction behind the Halfords car spares building, next to which was a customer car park. 'This is about the spot.'

Flynn leaned on the rails and looked at the discoloured water in the dock, imagining the scene. Tope leaning on the top rail, the killer sneaking up behind him, the blinding flash of light and terrible pain, then blackness. Tope would probably not even have known he went into the cold, diseased water; he would have been dead before hitting it. Flynn felt queasy.

'When are we going to have a look at the stuff on the cameras?' Santiago asked.

Flynn fished out his mobile and called Rik Dean.

This time he connected and after the greetings and wellness

checks Flynn put the question to him. 'Have you got a timeline for Craig and Jerry's murders?'

'Yeah, course, why?'

'What time did Craig leave work that night?'

Dean knew the answer instantly. 'He went out through the main gate at headquarters at eight fifteen p.m.'

Flynn sensed the 'why?' question hovering, so he jumped in quickly to the next point. 'He and Jerry were both working on the same drug-bust operation, both in the control room at the same time, is that right?' Dean said yes. 'What time did Jerry leave work?'

'He went out of HQ a minute or so after Craig.'

'Any idea what route they both took home?'

'As far as I know, the usual. They both – usually – went up the bypass, under the bridge and back down the Fifty-nine again. I know for sure that Jerry went that way, just assume Craig did too. Up to reaching the Penwortham flyover, they both probably followed the same route. We've only just sourced some CCTV on those roads, so we'll soon know for sure, probably tomorrow. Why?'

'Bear with me,' Flynn said. 'Is there any suggestion or suspicion that either of them was followed?'

'Not that we know of, but who's to say? Look, what is this, Steve?'

'Jerry had dash-cams in his car, front and rear. We just thought there might be something on them . . . worth looking at, is all.'

'There weren't any when the forensic team did his car,' Dean said.

'We think he took them out when he went home and didn't put them back in when he went out again . . . you said you spoke to him when he was at the Sitting Goose.'

'Yeah, that's right. He'd nipped out for a pint. Anyway, you're right, they must be worth a look, can't do any harm. Where are they?'

'We've got them. Marina gave them to us.'

'Right . . . any chance of you . . .?'

'We'll bring them over and maybe we can watch them.'

'OK.'

'Another thing,' Flynn said. 'Just off the top of my head: even if they weren't followed, do you think there could have been a spotter alerting the killer that Craig was on his way home?'

'Could be worth checking. I'll speak to the telephone unit.'

Twenty minutes later Flynn and Santiago were at headquarters sitting in a room in the FMIT building, sipping more coffee.

A detective constable was setting up a feed from the dash-cams into a laptop computer which was in turn linked up to a ceiling-mounted data projector, and the image from the screen was on the whiteboard at the front of the room.

Rik Dean entered, sat alongside Flynn and nodded at the DC, who pressed a button. The screen changed to a coloured but grainy image of the exit barrier at the front of headquarters, with the corner of the security kiosk just visible at one edge. There was a running time and date stamp in the bottom right hand corner of the screen.

A moment later a black Jaguar drove up to the barrier with headlights on. The barrier rose, the car drove out, one person on board, not clearly defined.

'Craig leaving,' Dean said.

Flynn's mouth dried with fearful anticipation. He took a sip of his coffee and Santiago laid a hand on his arm, picking up on his emotion, knowing what was coming next. He was about to see what had been almost the last journey Jerry Tope had undertaken. It would be hard to watch.

The barrier came down and Alford's car disappeared.

Flynn held his breath.

'Jerry leaving,' Dean said unnecessarily as Tope's car approached the barrier.

Flynn squeezed Santiago's fingers, then pulled himself together.

'This is the dash-cam footage coming up,' the DC said, and began to run the images taken from the front and rear of Tope's car on a split screen which came to life the moment Tope started the engine and reversed out of his parking spot at HQ. They were good, sharp images of the view from the car, Tope driving slowly around the HQ building, then towards the exit barrier. At no time was Alford's Jaguar visible in front of him.

The barrier rose and Tope passed under it, across the junction, then left up the A59 where he turned off left again and under the bridge as expected.

Tope passed a single car parked in the layby a couple of hundred metres up the road from the HQ junction. Just as Tope drove past the driver's door on this car was opening and there was the transient image of a man's face at the crack, checking over his shoulder before getting out.

The rear-view camera caught the same man getting out, closing his door and walking around the rear of his car towards the hedge by the field.

By this time, only a matter of seconds, Tope had reached the turn-off and only moments after that he was under the bridge, then coming back down the road in the opposite direction. There was only a glimpse of the car across the carriageway with the driver still by the hedge, looking downwards.

'Looks like he's urinating,' Dean said.

The remainder of the journey was uneventful, all the way up to the point where Tope drew up on his drive and the screens went dead. At no stage was there any sight of Alford's car.

'Not much to see,' Dean commented. 'Good thought, though.'

'No,' Flynn agreed. 'Can we just spin back to the car on the layby, if you don't mind?' he asked the DC, who said, 'No probs.'

Rik Dean's phone rang so he excused himself and left the room.

Flynn looked at Santiago. 'It's like watching ghosts.'

She nodded. There were tears in her eyes. She had only known Tope briefly and had almost been murdered alongside him in the car bomb in Puerto Rico, so she felt a strong connection and was feeling these re-runs as much as Flynn.

'Here we go.' The DC pressed 'play'.

Tope reversed out of his parking spot and the journey started.

'I know it's a pain,' Flynn said, 'but when the layby comes into view, can we do it frame by frame, as it were?' Flynn knew it was a digital image and frames did not exist any more, but the DC knew what he meant. Slow motion.

Tope went under the barrier, drove out on to the A59.

Then the DC slowed the image right down, forwarded it the equivalent of one frame at a time as Tope's car approached and passed the car in the layby. The make and model were clear but the number plate was just a tad hazy and indistinguishable.

'Any chance of enhancing the reg number?' Flynn asked.

'Sure.'

The next complete pause was on the face of the man peering backwards through the crack in the door, which was quite clear but only showed a vertical strip a couple of inches wide down the middle of the man's face.

Then Tope had gone past and Flynn concentrated on the rear-facing camera showing the man getting out. It also captured the front of the car and the registration plate, which was still hard to make out.

But the man was quite distinguishable, even from a distance and in the fading light of the evening.

He was a middle-aged white man, maybe six feet tall, heavy build or simply overweight.

The DC paused the image and zoomed in, something that could never have been achieved as easily with videotape or old-fashioned film.

An icon resembling a Sherlock Holmes type magnifying glass appeared and suddenly the whole screen was the man's face.

'I think I know him,' Flynn said.

The DC then dragged the icon around and zoomed in on the car's number plate, which was then easy to read; then he went back to the man and positioned the icon on his hand, in which he was holding something that was probably a mobile phone.

'Who is he?' Santiago asked.

'Name escapes,' Flynn said distractedly. 'But whatever, this could be nothing. A bloke in a car in a layby. So what? Having a brew, having a wank . . . these things happen.' He looked at the DC. 'Can you print off a couple of pictures of the man's face and one of the registration number?'

Rik Dean burst back into the room, blowing out his cheeks.

'Two things,' he said hurriedly. 'First, how do you feel about coming to Lancashire Prison today to look at some CCTV footage?' He glanced at the image on the whiteboard as he talked, screwed up his face and went on, 'It was taken on the day of the fire when Brian Tasker died.'

'Supposedly died,' Flynn corrected him.

Dean shrugged a 'whatever'.

'And, yes, we'd like that very much . . . second thing?'

'The telephone unit called me while I was out there . . . they've been in touch with several mobile phone service providers, who are good at supplying us with information without frickin' warrants all the time if we give them specific dates and times to look at.'

Flynn waited.

'After you suggested it earlier, I asked them to look between eight ten p.m. and eight twenty p.m. on the night that Craig and Jerry were murdered, at any calls that were made or texts sent from the area just outside HQ on the Fifty-nine. Incredibly only two calls were made and one text message sent from that location. Craig made two calls, one to his wife's mobile number and one to his home landline.' He paused dramatically.

'And the third, the text?' Santiago asked impatiently.

Dean held up a sheet of paper on which he had scribbled two numbers. 'It was sent from the top number to the second number. You might be interested in the bottom number, Steve, very interested.'

He and Santiago looked. She made a hissing noise. Flynn just shook his head. He did not recognize it.

'It's the hotline number on the Steve Flynn wanted poster,' Santiago said.

Flynn's mouth dropped open.

'The telephone unit tell me it's a pay-as-you-go number, but now out of service,' Dean said. 'Unfortunately it's impossible to read the content of the text.'

'And the other number – the top one?' Santiago said.

Dean turned the sheet back towards himself, then looked at the image on the whiteboard, the face of the man from the car in the layby. 'Don't know who it belongs to – yet – but I'll bet a pound to a pinch of shit it's from him.' He looked at Flynn. 'You know who that sleaze ball is, don't you?'

EIGHTEEN

Lancashire Prison was situated a few miles south-west of the town of Leyland, close to the other prisons in that area, Wymott and Garth, and was fairly modern, built on similar lines to the other two. Flynn had been there in the 1980s, when all three prisons kicked off with major riots and many buildings were overrun by inmates who kidnapped and assaulted the staff and set fire to the places. It had been a time of great unrest in British prisons and Flynn knew it still bubbled to this day, almost thirty years later.

Prisons were never going to be happy places.

Flynn, Santiago, Rik Dean and a DS called Bromilow had been allowed into the prison, but not into the inner sanctum. They were sitting in a training room in which a laptop and projector screen had been set up. A senior prison officer, Milne, had linked the laptop via Wi-Fi to the prison's internal security camera network. He was explaining things.

'It was the night of the twentieth . . . all inmates had been returned to their cells, a rollcall was done and lockdown had just been completed. Just a normal night by all accounts.'

'Were you on duty?' Flynn asked.

'No, I came in the morning after,' Milne said, and went on, 'A fire was noticed in one of the cells at about three a.m. on the morning of the twenty-first, but we're not certain exactly how long it might have been blazing – possibly for some time.'

'Why do you think that?' Dean asked.

Milne winced. 'Part of the alarm system was disabled on the landing of that wing . . . it's called Martin Mere Landing, after the nearby bird sanctuary.'

'How was it disabled?' Dean probed.

Milne shrugged. 'I say "disabled"; it just didn't work like it should have done. It was checked after the fire and was working OK.'

'But it didn't pick up the smoke or the heat?'

'No . . . and it's one of those that can respond to heat and/or smoke, but it didn't go off for some reason. They can be temperamental, but they are checked monthly. This one had been checked on the first of the month.'

Dean was eager to ask more questions but decided they could wait. He and the others were impatient to see the CCTV footage. 'OK, can we see?'

Milne touched a button and the screen showed an image split into two camera angles on Martin Mere Landing, Block C, Wing B. These showed views from each end of the landing, the cameras basically facing each other, with ten cell doors on the left of one screen and the same ten on the right looking the other way.

Nothing was happening. The landing was empty.

Then a wisp of smoke came from underneath one of the cell doors, like a spirit coming through the gap.

The time stamp on the screen was '03:01'.

Smoke seeped out, slowly building until it began to fog the landing. Flynn thought he saw a lick of flame from under the door.

The situation seemed to go on for a while, the time passing with excruciating slowness. It took for ever before '03:04' appeared on the screen.

'I'm assuming that is Tasker's cell?' Flynn asked.

'Yes. He was in there alone.'

'Alone,' Flynn said flatly.

'Yeah, guy like him—' Milne said.

'Gets what he wants?' Flynn eyed Milne cynically.

'Up to a point. Occasionally he had to share,' Milne said. 'And, by the way, he had been a model prisoner for all his time in custody.'

'Sociopath,' Santiago said. 'Playing the long game.'

Almost five minutes after the first wisp of smoke the first prison officers were pounding down the landing, weaving their way through the smoke-saturated air to the door from which the flames were now definitely licking. They fumbled the keys and it was evident, even on this silent video, that they were shouting desperately to each other, until one managed to shove the key into the lock.

Once the door was unlocked they did the sensible thing and ducked behind it as it opened outwards, to protect themselves from severe injury or death. A searing fireball came from within the cell as the rush of fresh oxygen produced an explosion of incredible force, heat and ferocity, as though a bomb had gone off, but missed them crouching behind the steel door.

Dean, Flynn, Santiago and Bromilow stared, transfixed, in awe. Flynn gave a quiet whistle.

'He had an armchair in his cell as a perk,' Milne said, glancing quickly at Flynn for a comment which did not come, 'but it was stuffed with old style foam and it looks like he fell asleep on his bed after dropping a lighted cigarette down the back of the cushion. The smoke killed him and he was engulfed by fire after the explosion when the door opened.

'Fire service took twenty minutes to arrive, during which time the fire raged and we were ineffective in fighting it with our inadequate extinguishers. He had no chance and neither did we.'

'Very convenient,' Flynn said sourly.

The officer pushed a brown envelope across to Dean, who shook out several graphic photographs of the scene after the fire had been put out. They were horrific and the body on the lower bunk bed was barely distinguishable as such. The inside of the cell was a black-charred mess.

'We carried out an investigation,' Milne went on, 'together with the police and fire service, and as far as the coroner was concerned it was death by accident.'

'It was a DI from Leyland, I believe, who dealt with the police side of it?' Dean said.

'Correct.'

'And a post-mortem was carried out?'

'For what it was worth,' Milne said.

'So the death of Brian Tasker has now been done and dusted,' Flynn said. 'How sure are we it really was Brian Tasker in that cell?'

'As sure as we can be. He was locked in at lights out, ticked off on rollcall and checked by an officer on his rounds at eleven thirty p.m. and midnight, when he was seen to be asleep. Why? Do you think it wasn't him?'

Dean answered, 'Not sure yet . . . I don't wish anyone dead, but I hope to hell it was Tasker or heads might be rolling.'

'Hear, hear,' Flynn said.

'Can we go back to earlier in the evening?' Dean asked Milne.

'Sure.'

Milne pressed a few buttons and the image changed from a fiery inferno to a more sedate split-screen view of the prison landing. A couple of inmates leaned on the railings overlooking a quadrangle below; another pair walked along, chatting amiably. Tasker's cell door was open wide and then, suddenly, there he was in the picture, walking along with another prisoner. Tasker paused at the cell door in conversation with the man. They chatted for a good minute, then Tasker casually turned face on to one camera, then to the other one at the opposite end of the landing. After this he went into the cell alone and the other man walked away.

'So, you see, he went into his cell at eight thirty p.m.'

'"Look at me, look at me,"' Flynn said cynically. '"I'm going into my cell."' He remained unimpressed.

'He did not come out again,' Milne said with certainty. 'We've been over these tapes quite a few times and he definitely did not re-emerge that night, except in a zip-up body bag.'

Flynn's mouth twisted. He shook his head at Santiago, then folded his arms grumpily.

Milne ran through the footage until the point where three other men entered the cell a while later, all managing – casually, it seemed – to keep their faces away from the camera lens. One was wearing a cowboy hat.

'This is the pontoon crew,' Milne said.

'The pontoon crew?' Dean asked.

'Yes, you know, Twenty-one, the card game? They were regular players and met up in Tasker's cell to play for matchsticks. They never caused a problem. Just like Tasker himself, in fact, despite his reputation.'

'My arse,' Flynn grumbled, not taking any of this well.

Milne continued, 'They were seen on several occasions by prison officers, one of whom stepped into the cell for a chat on a couple of occasions, as he reported on his log.'

'Who were the men?'

'Tasker you know. The others were Felix Loveday, double murderer; Sam Rawtenstall, in for sexual assault; and Ben Dudley, a serial . . .' Milne caught his words.

'Serial what?' Flynn said. 'Killer?'

'In a way, yes . . . he was responsible for killing three students at their digs in Preston.'

'So, yeah, serial killer.'

'No,' Rik Dean interrupted. 'I know him . . . Henry Christie dealt with him a while back.' Dean looked at Flynn, who fidgeted at the name Christie. 'He was a firestarter, a serial arsonist, from when he was a kid. Used to set fire to rubbish skips, then animals . . . only a matter of time before he killed people; then he did. He was suspected of killing more than three students.'

'So he knows how to start fires?' Santiago said.

'Oh yeah . . . an expert. The other guy,' – Dean looked at Milne – 'Sam Rawtenstall, his name rings a bell, too . . . can't quite . . .' He shot a glance at DS Bromilow. 'Find out who he is, will you?'

'Will do, boss.' Bromilow rose and left the room, his phone to his ear.

'You on my line of thought here?' Dean said to Flynn and Santiago.

They nodded. Santiago said, 'Individuals who could be useful to him.'

'You're making things fit how you want them to fit,' Milne said.

'Maybe, maybe,' Dean admitted. 'Tell us about the other guy.'

'Felix Loveday, a gay man, convicted of double murder when he was a teenager thirty years ago . . . he's the one who went in with the cowboy hat on.' Once more Milne's voice faltered. 'He was released on licence the day after the fire . . . well, the same morning as the fire.'

Flynn, Santiago and Dean rubbed their foreheads.

'Let's see the footage,' Dean said.

Milne skipped through the remainder of the evening in the prison. It was uneventful until, at 22:45 hours, a prison officer was seen standing at Tasker's cell door. Then he stepped into the cell out of camera shot, closing the door behind him. He reappeared a few moments later, closely followed by the three men who had entered Tasker's cell earlier for a night of cards. They were dressed in exactly the same clothes as when they had gone in and fell casually into single file as they came out.

Milne paused the video and pointed at the screen. 'The one in front is Rawtenstall, the one in the middle is Loveday and the one at the back is Dudley.' He started the action again. The men walked along the landing, and the men at the front and rear both appeared happy to have their features recorded by the CCTV; the one in the middle, however, kept the brim of the cowboy hat down over his face, obscuring it, and stayed quite close to the man in front, Rawtenstall, so that his physical features could not be made out.

Flynn rolled his eyes. 'That ain't Felix Loveday,' he said. 'If it is, I'll show my arse in Burton's window.'

A minute later the same prison officer returned to Tasker's cell. He did not enter but stood on the threshold, as though he was conversing with the inmate. He even gave a good night wave before closing and locking the cell door. He walked away.

Milne insisted, 'His report clearly stated that he spoke to Tasker before lockdown.'

The door opened and Bromilow stepped back inside. 'Doctor Sam Rawtenstall, life for serious sexual assaults on four female patients and twelve others lying on file. He drugged them and raped them. He was a GP, now struck off the register for life . . . obviously.'

'Fuck,' Flynn said with exasperation. 'So Tasker goes to bed, sets fire to himself and dies? I don't think so.'

All eyes turned to Milne.

'Prisoners being discharged? I'm assuming that process is videotaped?' Dean asked him.

He nodded. 'I'll have to get the disks for that . . . different system.' He left the room.

'Thanks, mate,' Dean said to Bromilow, who sat down and asked, 'What have I missed?'

'A sleight of hand,' Flynn said.

'Or a sleight of identity,' Santiago said.

'And with the collusion of staff and other inmates,' Dean said.

'Bets, anyone?' Flynn said. 'Because I'll lay odds on three things: one, that Brian Tasker walked out of this prison as Felix Loveday; two, that the prison officer we've just been watching is the one who signed him out when the prison was in chaos the morning after because of the fire; and three, that Mr Loveday, much against his wishes, is now nothing more than ashes.'

'You're faced with this: to all intents and purposes, Brian Tasker was locked up alone in a cell which then caught fire,' Flynn said. 'So it was Tasker who died. Everything points to that. No need to question it. All the evidence appears to be there . . . or not.'

'Confirmation bias, kind of,' Santiago said.

They all looked at her.

'What you see supports what you think happened – to put it in very simple terms.'

'Ahh,' they said wisely.

Tight-lipped, Milne slid a disk into the laptop.

This time the view that came up was from behind the desk at which prisoners to be released were processed. Except that on the day of Felix Loveday's release the camera had somehow been knocked slightly askew and all that could be seen were the feet of the staff behind the counter. According to the duty roster that Milne brought back with him the staff included the officer who was on duty the previous evening and who had visited Tasker's cell on a number of occasions and then locked him up for the night.

Flynn, Santiago, Dean and Bromilow were mute.

'The facts are the facts as they are seen and presented,' Dean said eventually, 'and I can't really jump down anyone's throat for accepting them as such. A body burned beyond recognition, a trustworthy prison officer, CCTV footage that supports everything on the face of it – what could go wrong?' He rubbed his face and looked very pale. 'That said, the DI who dealt with this will be on my carpet first thing tomorrow.'

'What about DNA?' Santiago asked. 'Presumably a sample was taken from the body and tested?'

'I don't know,' Dean admitted. He took a breath. 'Anyway,' he said, looking at Milne, 'I want some things to happen without any fuss. Sam Rawtenstall and Ben Dudley . . . I want them brought here separately. I will then arrest them on suspicion of murder and I want them conveyed – still apart and each unaware that the other has been arrested – to Preston nick and booked in.' He looked at Bromilow. 'Fix that, will you?' Bromilow nodded. 'Then I want the same to happen to that prison officer who, you say, is on duty as we speak. And I want those CCTV images. I'm not completely convinced that your hypothesis is correct yet,' he said to Flynn, 'so let's check it out by speaking to these individuals, and if I have to' – and at that point his eyes flickered to Milne – 'I'm going to break some heads.'

Milne nodded numbly.

'My boss, again,' Santiago said to Flynn, waggling her phone at him.

He responded sadly. 'I know.'

Detective Santiago, now very much a legend in the Canary Island police service despite the short time she had been stationed there, had received further texts urging – almost begging – her to return. As a result she had booked a late night flight back.

'Apparently crime is rife in Las Palmas and he thinks a serial killer is on the loose. He wants me to head the team.'

'Wow!' Flynn said admiringly. 'You should get back for that. Could be a career maker.'

'Except I don't want to go back.' She pouted and batted her eyelashes. 'I want to be with you . . . I've had a brilliant time, just don't want to go . . .'

He embraced her and she moulded herself against him. 'I don't want you to go, either, but I'll be back soon and maybe we can, y'know, see how we can change things. I mean . . . and I'm just spit-balling here, as they say . . . if I could get this Ibiza contract every year from May to September, perhaps you could, uh . . .' Flynn was having problems putting the words together.

'Be with you full time?' she ventured.

'Yeah, something like that. There'd be enough money from that to make sure I could fish from October to April in Gran Canaria, enough for both of us . . . but you'd have to work your ass off, y'know?' He gave said ass a playful pat. 'I'm a hard task master.'

'I'm liking that scenario.'

They were in their hotel room at the Ibis at Broughton. It was early evening and they had just showered after their long day. Both were groggy with tiredness but knew they only had a short time remaining before Flynn had to drive her to the airport to board the flight she had so unwillingly booked.

Each had a bath sheet wrapped around them.

'What are you going to do?' she asked, snuffling her nose into his neck and then biting gently.

'I need to get back to Ibiza. There's a charter in the day after tomorrow and I don't want to let Barney down. What's happening here is for the cops to sort now and I know Rik will do a great job. He's a good man hunter and once he confirms Tasker is alive and well, the game will change.'

'But you'll still be in danger.'

'I'll keep my head down and watch my back,' he promised. 'And we need to warn Jimmy Blue, too . . . once that's done, I'll jump on any flight I can get back to Ibiza.'

'Separate ways,' she said wistfully.

'Another month in Ibiza, then I'll be back to Puerto Rico and we'll be together.'

Flynn looked down into her eyes, just a little overwhelmed by his feelings for her, trying to fight them, if he was honest. The two of them had gone through serious hell to get to this point and maybe the future would be fantastic with her. He knew, as he stood there with just towelling separating them, that he was willing to give this a go and make all the effort needed.

'You really do need to watch yourself, though,' she warned him. 'Tasker moves quickly.'

'I'm good at running away,' Flynn said.

'You never run from anyone or anything.'

'Whatever . . . but he has to find me first, so that's a plus. And I don't think he's the one who's actually killed Craig, Jerry and Dave. That's the work of a hired hand. A good one, mind, but not Tasker himself. I think he's holed up somewhere, directing operations. He won't get me, honest.'

Santiago held him tightly.

'Under the circumstances, and as time is of the essence,' Flynn said, feeling a surge of blood and shortness of breath, 'we should mark our parting in the traditional manner, don't you think?'

He stepped slightly away from her.

Apart from snagging on his erect penis on the way to the floor his bath sheet slid off fairly effortlessly, and Santiago's followed suit. A moment later there was no gap between them.

Flynn watched her walk straight through to the international departure lounge, where she turned at the very last moment and, with her eyes still shining from sex, blew him a sultry kiss, which he found himself catching and planting on his lips while trying to ignore the sniggers of two half-drunk youths who witnessed the moment.

'I,' he said to himself, 'have truly morphed into a soft-arse.'

Then she was gone and he was alone.

He bought a coffee from a kiosk and took it out across to the multi-storey, which had been so packed with cars he'd had to leave his on the third level. He waited patiently for the lift to disgorge a family of four plus luggage, then stepped in and pressed button three.

As the doors hissed shut a man stepped in and stood across from Flynn.

He was youngish with tightly cropped blond hair and a gaunt face, slim built but tough-looking. He had an ex-military air about him. Flynn gave him a nod which was not returned. They both then stood, three feet apart, facing the lift doors.

Flynn sipped his coffee, feeling slightly vulnerable.

This man looked fit, healthy and maybe dangerous. He wore

slim jeans, trainers and a black zip-up jacket . . . did he have an unnatural bulge underneath the left armpit?

Flynn's insides tensed, but he tried to fight his paranoia.

Could this man be an assassin? Come to kill Flynn?

Flynn eyed him surreptitiously and removed the lid from his steaming hot coffee, the first thing that would go into the man's face, followed by a devastating series of punches, if there was even the slightest indication something was amiss.

The man's right hand casually pulled down his jacket zip. His hand went slowly inside.

Flynn visualized the next move, saw the coffee in the face, the pivot of his hips, the blows.

The hand came gradually out of the jacket.

Flynn readied himself, knowing that how quickly he reacted in the next two seconds might mean the difference between survival and death.

The hand emerged with nothing in it.

Flynn relaxed slightly.

The hand dropped to the man's side.

The lift stopped on three, the doors opened.

Flynn made a polite gesture, allowing the man to step out ahead. He turned right. Flynn gave him a couple of seconds, then stepped out to see the man walking along a row of cars.

He exhaled shakily, eased the lid back on to his coffee and went to find his car, muttering, 'You've become a soft-arse in more ways than one, matey.'

NINETEEN

Flynn knew that resorting to violence or threats of violence wasn't always a successful way in which to obtain a confession from a suspect, but sometimes needs must. And because he was no longer constrained by the Police and Criminal Evidence Act, or by any rules whatsoever, he didn't even have to think of a way round it.

He knew he needed a result and needed it fast and sometimes

the only way to get it was to go straight for the jugular – although, to be honest, he didn't actually intend to kill anyone that night.

He left the airport unmolested and gunned his little hire car back down the motorway and eventually towards Preston.

On the way he scolded himself for letting his imagination run riot in the lift, telling himself that not every salty dude he encountered was a killer out to get him – although he imagined quite a few were, not all of them connected to Brian Tasker; and then he recalled the last time he had bundled someone into the boot of a car in order to extract the truth from them.

The villain in that case so long ago was someone suspected of knifing and almost killing a sixteen-year-old lad on a council estate in Blackpool – and there was a suitable, sweet irony to the story as he remembered it while he sped along virtually deserted motorway lanes.

Following a mini-riot on the Shoreside council estate Flynn, then a uniformed constable just out of his probation period and already angling to become a detective, had gone to great lengths to investigate the offence and arrest the youth responsible for initiating the disturbance by sticking a blade into the son of an Asian shopkeeper on the estate.

Once the public order side had quietened down – basically an Asian gang retaliating against the white 'rulers' of the estate – Flynn had homed in on the knife wielder, a young buck called Brent Costain, a member of the notorious Costain clan based on Shoreside. They were an extended family into drugs, theft and intimidation in a big way. Brent was only a peripheral cousin, not really one of the core family members, but was trying to up his street cred by using the knife.

All it did was bring unwanted police attention upon the family.

Flynn 'lifted' Brent as he walked through the maze of streets in South Shore. Costain had spotted him and done a runner but had been brought down by the super-fit Flynn, who in those days ran five miles a day, went to the gym twice a week and played squash and men's hockey.

Flynn had speed, strength and stamina and ran Brent down like a hunting dog, enjoying every moment as the unhealthy youth sagged to his knees, his young body already undermined by drugs, alcohol and cigarettes.

In the police station Brent remained silent and defiant, sitting with his arms folded, staring disrespectfully at Flynn, who, to be honest, was a little naive in those days and did not have a great deal of actual evidence against the lad. Flynn knew for certain that Brent had done the stabbing, but fearful witnesses were not keen on putting pen to paper. Much relied on Brent's confession, which was not forthcoming.

During the course of Brent's time in custody, Flynn was assisted by the CID in the shape of Terry Mulligan, a spiv-like detective constable with the pencil moustache and slicked-back hair of a con man, a super-smooth operator who, Flynn had already heard, was more style than substance.

Mulligan was on the verge of losing his temper throughout the interviews and only the hawk-like presence of Brent's solicitor kept him in check.

Brent admitted nothing and was released on police bail pending further enquiries.

During the release process, as Brent signed to receive his property from the custody sergeant, Mulligan took Flynn aside and hurriedly whispered in his ear at the same time as fumbling a set of car keys into the palm of his hand.

'CID car, the old Montego, get in it, reverse to the back door, quick.'

Flynn frowned, puzzled.

'Don't you want to get this little fuck-faced cunt to cough?'

'Yuh, course.'

'Then do what I say . . . stand by it, have the boot open and follow my lead. We'll take this little shit for the ride of his life.'

Flynn scuttled out and found the Montego, which had seen much better days. It was on the ground floor covered yard of the police station, a dark concrete place with many shadows in which he imagined people might hide. He reversed it back to the door leading to the custody suite, climbed out and opened the boot – which, as he recalled, was quite spacious.

DC Mulligan and Brent Costain appeared from the custody corridor, apparently quite chatty, as though neither had a care in the world.

'Yeah,' Flynn remembered Mulligan saying, 'just one of those things.'

'Well, you'll never find anyone to go up as a witness against me,' Costain boasted.

'Maybe not, maybe not.'

They walked towards Flynn.

Mulligan glanced around. The car park was devoid of other people, so no spectators.

As they drew level with the Montego, Mulligan had a hand resting on Brent's back between his shoulder blades. A non-threatening, friendly gesture.

Until Mulligan's eyes caught Flynn's and he gave him the nod.

Flynn frowned again, unsure about what was about to happen or what was expected of him, though he did have an inkling.

Mulligan took control. With one powerful thrust he propelled Brent towards the open mouth of the boot, then, in a well-practised movement while Brent, taken by surprise, was off balance, he grabbed him by the shoulder, tripped him and shoved him into the boot.

He held Brent face down on the grubby, oily carpet, pulled his hands behind him and cuffed him expertly, then forced an oily rag into his mouth.

Though he struggled and kicked out ferociously, Mulligan easily slammed the boot lid down and said to Flynn, 'Let's go for a country ride.'

He jumped in behind the wheel while the bemused and wary Flynn got into the passenger seat.

'Sometimes,' Mulligan said with an evil smile, 'needs must.'

The bouncy ride through the countryside, the hinterland behind Blackpool, was worthwhile.

A dazed and battered Brent Costain eventually decided that his best course of action would be to admit the offence. Although he threatened to expose the two officers, Mulligan claimed that no one would ever believe him. Kidnapped? Tortured? Interrogated under duress? In the boot of a car? The end result was a pathetic police caution for Costain, but it was a result of sorts.

Mulligan spent the next few weeks leaning on Flynn so he wouldn't crack and admit to anyone what had happened.

'No one,' he said, 'will keep the secret, except us two.'

Flynn had no intention of saying anything but he did learn a valuable lesson at Mulligan's hands – never involve anyone else

in iffy schemes; always carry them out alone, because you are the
only person you can trust.

It was a good lesson for Flynn as he matured as a cop and
became more confident at leaning on crims to scare them.

A few years later Mulligan went too far and a very scared young
cop who had become entangled with him – something involving
a drunken man in a pub, an assault, a theft . . . a very murky
scenario, Flynn seemed to recall – could not live with what had
happened and made a furtive call to the 'rubber heel' squad, the
Discipline and Complaints Department as they were then called,
the cops who police the police.

Mulligan went soon after that, career and life wrecked.

Flynn pulled off the M6 on to the M55 at Broughton, where he
returned to his room at the Ibis. He took another shower and ten
minutes later drew up in a cul-de-sac on a council estate in Preston,
switched off the engine and sat in the shadow between the arc of
street lights, watching a particular block of flats.

He deliberated on whether there was enough room in the boot
of his hire car in which to compress a fully grown man.

Folded carefully, he thought there would be, as he visualized
it. If a dead spy could be stuffed into a holdall he was fairly certain
he could get a live man into a hatchback.

It was now time to experience the sweet irony of the Brent
Costain boot ride.

He got out, walked along the pavement to the front of the flats
and easily entered the foyer, which should have been secure but
was not. He took the stairs up to level two, flat one, the address
that Rik Dean had 'accidentally' allowed him to see.

He paused, listened. Just the normal noises again. Voices. TVs.
Music. Shagging.

The door to the flat was locked and daubed with crude
graffiti.

Flynn knocked, just a tap.

Then harder, louder.

The person inside shouted an obscenity.

He was home.

Flynn knocked again, only to be met by more slurred obscenities,
which suited Flynn. A bit of alcohol down a man could make a chat

go much more easily, exactly why interviews with drunks were strictly controlled under PACE.

He knocked once more, received more abuse, then stood back, braced himself and flat-footed the door just by the lock. It shattered instantly and clattered open. Flynn still got a great deal of pleasure from kicking doors down.

He stepped directly into the living area of the minuscule flat and found the occupant slouched on a tatty two-seater settee dressed in only a stained vest, boxer shorts and ankle socks, with a half-bottle of nameless cheap whisky balanced on his pot belly.

'What, what the shittin' . . .?' the man said, trying to heave himself into a sitting position to challenge the intruder. Beyond him was a large screen TV showing some free late night soft porn, a naked girl on a phone encouraging people to call in while she wobbled her boobs at the camera. The rest of the room was untidy, unpleasant.

In essence, the man had not really changed since Flynn had last seen him. He did have the pot belly now but his legs and arms were spider thin and his torso reminded Flynn of a dung beetle. His face, though aged, was just the same, with the same pencil moustache, his little trademark.

'Fuck outta here,' he shouted at Flynn.

'Terry Mulligan, get your pants on, you're coming with me,' Flynn said.

The former detective jerked a middle finger up. 'Who the fuck you think you are?' he demanded.

The reek of alcohol, sweat and bodily emissions made Flynn's nose twitch. He stepped forward. 'Remember me, Terry?'

His bloodshot eyes showed no sign of recognition. 'Should I?'

'Maybe not. Doesn't matter – now get dressed or don't get dressed, I don't care. You're coming with me because you've been a very naughty man.'

'You can fuck off out of here.' Mulligan stood up and staggered towards Flynn, who hit him once. He sank to his knees.

Five minutes later Flynn had folded him neatly behind the back seats of the Punto with the parcel shelf closed over his head. Not very secure, Flynn realized, but it would have to do for the time being.

Time for a ride in the country.

*   *   *

Flynn chose the scenic route. On to the A6 – driving past Craig Alford's house – then left on to Station Lane and the narrow, bumpy, winding, bucolic roads of that area, not so far away from the farmhouse where Brian Tasker had holed up with such fatal and far-reaching consequences all those years before.

First there was a bridge over the main western rail line between London and Glasgow. Then a narrow but very pronounced hump-back bridge over the canal, where the Punto took off and landed like a stock car, throwing the body in the boot around with a thud, a cry and then another thud.

Flynn slammed on to make a point, and felt and heard Mulligan smack into the back seats.

He set off just as suddenly, throwing Mulligan back with another thud, groan and curse.

Flynn drove the little car hard, braked hard, cornered tight until he drew up after a few kangaroo jumps on a deserted car park in front of a country store. He ran around to open the hatchback and hoisted Mulligan out. The guy staggered and went down on to all fours, vomiting and making very miserable mewing sounds. Flynn towered over him, careful not to put his shoes into the sea of sick. But for good measure he kicked Mulligan hard in the ribs, flipping him over on to his back; he rolled over into a foetal position crying, 'What have I done, what—?'

Flynn balanced on his haunches, grabbed Mulligan's hair into the ball of his fist and wrenched his head around.

'You know exactly what you've done,' he growled. 'Now then, you talk right now or you go back in the car and we go round and round Beacon Fell until you beg to talk.'

'You can't do this, you can't fucking do this. I have fucking rights, human rights, what about PACE?' Mulligan protested. 'You've assaulted me.'

'Yep.'

'I'll fuckin' complain . . . I recognize you now, you're a cop. This isn't legal, not allowed.' He spat out phlegm and some porridge-like lumps of spew.

'What makes you think I'm a cop?'

'I recognize you. I can't remember your name, but I bleeding recognize you.'

'And I'm just taking a leaf out of your interview technique book, Terry . . . remember?'

'Oh, God, I remember it all . . . and you're not a cop any more, are you?'

'Which is why I don't have rules.'

'Shit.'

Mulligan sat on the edge of the open hatchback, breathing heavily.

'I don't know, I don't know, OK? It was just a job, nowt else, a bloke on a phone.'

Flynn stood in front of him. Inside he could feel his heart trembling as he fought to control his utter loathing for this man and the desire to mash him to a pulp.

'I'm a private investigator, a snoop, you know?'

'Sleaze ball, you mean?'

Mulligan's eyes rose maliciously. 'I lost my job. Since then I've done every dirty job that comes along. I'm broke. I won't draw any pension for years and when I do it'll be pitiful; so when some guy rings up and says he's got a simple job for me at a ton a shot, I take it, OK?'

Flynn swallowed drily, his adrenalin overdosing into his system. 'Who was he?'

'I . . . don't . . . know . . . name didn't matter, money did.'

'What did he ask you to do?'

'J-just watch Craig Alford go to and leave work each day for a few days and send a text when he drove past, that's all. Use a different phone and SIM each time.'

'So you're not averse to spying on former colleagues?'

'Former colleagues got me fired, so no.'

'You're a scumbag, Mulligan . . . do you know what you did, sending those messages?'

Mulligan's head drooped.

'Essentially notified a killer his victim was on the way . . . nice one . . . where are the phones you used?'

'In a drain. Like I said, I was told to get a burner for each one out of what I got paid.'

'A drain as in next to where you sat in the layby?'

His head shot up. 'How did you know I was in a layby?'

'Lucky guess.' Flynn was struggling to keep the hatred off his face. 'Anything else to tell me?'

Mulligan blinked, but even in the darkness Flynn could see something shifty in the expression.

'What else?' Flynn said.

'Look – whoever it was – and I don't know who it was – asked me if I could get some details and pass 'em on.'

'What details?'

'Some, uh, contact numbers and addresses for retired cops.'

'And could you?'

'I, er, still have a contact in HR, a woman I've known for a long time . . . was shagging her way back.'

'Whose names did you get?'

'He asked me for four names and addresses . . .'

'Whose?'

'Dave Carver, Jimmy Blue, Lincoln Bartlett and . . . shit, now I know your name . . . it's Steve Flynn. Fuck, now I really do remember you.' He held his head in his hands.

'What did you do with the names?'

'Passed them on . . . but . . .'

'But what?'

'Lincoln Bartlett was dead, Dave Carver was in a nursing home and for some reason there were no addresses for you or Jimmy Blue . . . except . . .'

'I need you to finish your sentences, or I'm really going to get cross,' Flynn warned him.

'I managed to find out where Jimmy Blue lives. I passed it on . . . but I couldn't find your address. Got your photo, though.'

'How did you pass the information?' Flynn asked.

'Like old-fashioned spying . . . a dead letter drop. I never saw who picked it up.'

'Anything else?'

Mulligan's eyes closed. 'I got addresses for two serving officers, too.'

'Who?'

'Craig Alford and DC Jerry Tope, I think it was. I'm really, really sorry.'

'How much did you get paid for that information?'

'Two-fifty per address.'

'What's the name of your bent contact in HR?'

'Lizzie Dawn . . . look, keep her out of this, she just did a favour for an old mate.'

'Fuck that,' Flynn said. 'As far as I'm concerned you set up Craig Alford and his family, Jerry Tope, Dave Carver and a nurse who was caring for him . . . and they're still coming after Jimmy Blue and me. Get back in the boot.'

Twenty minutes later Flynn drew up on the car park outside the new police station in Preston. Not exactly purpose built – it was formerly a water board depot – it had been refurbished and modernized. A cell complex had been added, and because it was just on the periphery of the city centre there was more space to operate and more room for staff to park than at the old station.

Flynn knew that Rik Dean was still on duty and dealing with the two inmates and prison officer from Lancashire Prison who were now detained at the nick.

Flynn called him on his mobile. 'I'm outside, any chance of a catch-up?'

'Give me ten.'

Flynn ended the call and tried to phone Santiago who, if her flight was on time and his calculations were correct, should just have landed in Las Palmas, Gran Canaria.

She picked up instantly. 'Steve . . . I'm just walking towards passport control.'

'Good, you landed safely. How was the flight?'

'OK, but I wish you could have been with me.'

'We'll be together sooner rather than later,' he promised her.

'You know I've fallen in love with you, don't you, Steve Flynn?'

He swallowed and, though fighting it, became misty-eyed. 'You could have told me earlier.'

'Why?'

'Because I might've told you the same,' he stuttered. Suddenly his palms were very damp.

'You can tell me now.'

There was a tapping on the driver's door window. Flynn jumped and looked to see Rik Dean with his face up to the glass.

'Rik's here . . . look, let's speak soon.'

She laughed, that light tinkling sound he had grown to love. 'OK, Steve, not a problem.'

He hung up, knowing it was a problem, knowing that time was running out for him and he had to grab this opportunity with both hands and go for it. In that instant he made plans: get all this Brian Tasker crap out of the way, finish the season in Ibiza, chug back to Gran Canaria, then get down on one knee and do the decent thing for himself and her.

Good plan . . . yet somehow there was a cloud of premonition at the back of his mind.

He shook it off, got out of the car to speak to Dean.

From the side door of the police station two uniformed cops hurtled out, dragging on their jackets and fitting their appointments into the requisite holes before scrambling into a liveried patrol car, reversing out of the parking slot and accelerating towards the gates, blue-lighting as they went.

Rik Dean waved them down.

The car lurched on its front suspension. The policewoman in the passenger seat lowered her window.

'What's the rush?' Dean asked.

'Apparently there's a drunken guy in the middle of the road junction at Broughton just in his underpants, trying to stop traffic.'

Dean waved them away and turned to Flynn. 'I kinda miss jobs like that.'

'Me, too,' Flynn said, all innocent.

TWENTY

The car had been stolen by two teenagers who lived on a council estate in Ribbleton, Preston. They had been on the prowl for some high-octane adventure and had known they were unlikely to find anything of interest on their estate. They'd been on speed all evening and wanted something external to match their inner surge of energy.

They found the big BMW on a good class estate in Fulwood and were soon into it. It wasn't a new car, not protected by modern technology, and both of the lads were adept at getting into such cars and being on the road within a minute.

They worked in silence to steal the beast and resisted the temptation to rev the engine as it rolled off the drive. That pleasure was kept on hold until they were out of the cul-de-sac.

Then they floored the accelerator.

'Can't wait to see this one,' Joanne Farmer said. She was the female officer in the police patrol dispatched from the station to investigate the drunk in the road at Broughton. 'Always love a piss-head in skivvies.'

This made the PC at the wheel chortle.

He drove out of the police station yard up to the junction with the main road, the A6, which at that point was called North Road. He stopped and began to pull out, but slammed on as a speeding BMW shot past, just missing the nose of their car, heading north like a mini-rocket.

It was late, it was dark, but Joanne Farmer recognized the scowling face pressed tight against the front passenger door window and also the profile of the girl in the corresponding seat behind him.

The face of the young man was etched in her mind because Farmer had come on duty four hours before her night shift to deal with this lad, who had reported to the station on police bail to face an allegation of taking a motor vehicle without consent. A BMW.

Although she did not quite see the driver of the speeding BMW, she could guess that it was the lad's best mate, who had also reported for bail earlier.

So, three hours before, the lad in the passenger seat, Wayne Dixon, and his friend, Billy Collins, charged with car theft offences, had been given bail to appear at Magistrates' Court in two weeks' time and a release. Then they had simply gone out and repeated the crime within hours, stealing yet another BMW and giving their girlfriends the ride of their lives.

'Wayne Dixon, you little shit,' Joanne Farmer said as the car flew past. The circle of life, she thought.

The PC at the wheel went after the car. It was going in their direction anyway.

Farmer was on the radio, at the same time clinging to her seat belt.

'Suspected stolen vehicle, a BMW, heading north on the A6, North Road towards Garstang Road, just approaching the lights at Moor Lane. Four on board including Wayne Dixon, probably Billy Collins at the wheel and two females in the back seat. Excessive speeds.'

By the time the police car had turned on to the A6 proper, the BMW had shot through the red lights at Moor Lane, then Aqueduct Street, and was on the straight stretch that was Garstang Road.

The driver of the police car proceeded with more caution, even though the blue lights and, now, the two-tone horns were respectively on and blaring.

The lights at Watling Street Road were dealt with in a similar fashion by the BMW, which swerved to miss another car legitimately crossing the junction in front of it.

'Speeds excess of eighty mph,' WPC Farmer said into her PR.

Ahead she saw the flash of a speed camera on the next stretch of road, which was still in a thirty miles per hour zone.

Moments later the police car made the camera flash too and both cops cheered at that moment of sheer pleasure – legitimately breaking the speed limit.

The BMW did not slow for the next major junction with Sharoe Green Lane, though the police car did.

Less than a mile ahead was the motorway roundabout at Broughton, and thinking of this gave Farmer a sudden concern.

On her radio she interrupted the chatter of other patrols shouting up and making their way, and asked, 'Has anyone managed to get to the guy at Broughton lights yet? Because if this BMW goes straight up, he could be in real danger if he's still in the middle of the road.'

'Negative,' the comms operator responded, also seeing the danger. 'No one there yet.'

As the police car sped through the next set of lights at Lightfoot Lane there was just a glimpse of the BMW, now with all lights out, screeching around the motorway roundabout and staying on the A6 northbound, less than half a mile to the next lights in Broughton.

'Hope the idiot's gone,' Farmer said bleakly, 'or this little bastard might wipe him off the face of the earth.'

But Terry Mulligan had not gone. He was still about two hundred metres from where Steve Flynn had pulled into a layby just north of Broughton, hauled him out of the back of the Punto and told him to walk home.

Mulligan had cried pitifully as Flynn drove away abandoning him in just his vest, underpants and socks.

He had tried to get a lift back towards Preston, waving down the next southbound vehicle. The driver had skilfully avoided him.

Distraught, Mulligan saw the traffic lights in the distance and thought that standing in the middle of the junction would give him more chance of bumming a lift.

He was wrong.

Eventually he was right in the middle of the junction, desperately windmilling his arms at any car, travelling in any direction (and they were few and far between at that time of night), crying, 'Please give me a lift, please . . .'

No one did. A man in his vest and underpants was not an appealing sight or prospect.

Mulligan heard the scream of the engine coming from the direction of Preston. He turned to squint towards it.

Even in his half-inebriated state – he had sobered up somewhat after the journey in the back of the Punto – he could tell the car approaching was travelling fast but he saw the lights were on red, so surely it would stop. And when it did he would get into it, no matter where it was going. All he wanted to do was get warm and drunk again.

He began to spiral his arms once more.

The BMW hit him at eighty-two miles per hour.

Santiago slumped into the back of the taxi at the head of the rank in front of the terminal building at Las Palmas airport.

Despite all that was going on she had a grin of pleasure on her face, so pleased she had worked up courage to tell Flynn how she was feeling about him. They had been through so much in such a short space of time, some of it intense and shocking, but Flynn had been there for her and eased her through the pain and now it was time for her to be there for him – and she would be.

She could almost visualize the shock on his face when she'd said she loved him.

Total shock, in fact.

But it did make her wish she'd told him when they were face to face.

Her grin turned into one of lopsided pleasure and she settled in to the journey in the comfortable back seat of the Mercedes taxi as the car left the airport and headed south along the GC1, Gran Canaria's motorway, towards Puerto Rico, where she and Flynn now shared a small apartment at the back of the resort. Before meeting him she had lived in Las Palmas but moving to Puerto Rico had been a natural progression for them both. Flynn had limited means of transport since his car had come to a sticky end a few months before and she was mobile with her work as a detective and did not mind driving to Las Palmas each morning, because she loved the journey back and the laid-back evenings in Puerto Rico with Flynn.

'Come on, pass, you idiot,' the taxi driver muttered in Spanish.

Santiago raised herself and glanced over the back seat. A car, headlights on full beam, was close up, tailgating.

'Any closer and we'll be lovers,' the taxi driver said.

Amazingly the taxi driver had actually slowed down to let him pass but the car seemed intent on clinging to the bumper.

'Don't worry about him,' she said to the taxi driver, 'he'll go when he's ready.'

He lifted both hands off the steering wheel in a gesture of extreme frustration.

Santiago smiled, settled back down again.

They had reached a section of road parallel to the Punta del Corral outcrop of coast when the car moved out from behind and drew level.

Santiago had her eyes closed, beginning to dream.

She heard the metallic crash and scrape of a collision, felt the impact and lurch at the same time, opened her eyes instantly as the taxi veered out of control. The overtaking car, it seemed, had deliberately rammed the taxi. The driver fought hard to keep the Mercedes on the road, but the car connected again, smashing the taxi sideways.

The section of road had been well chosen.

There were no safety barriers, and this time as the taxi left the road it plunged into a steep, volcanic gully. Santiago grabbed her seat belt, but she was still thrown around inside the vehicle and then, as it rolled sideways on to its roof, she was somehow flung by the weird physics of centrifugal force out of the back window, which had exploded out of its seal in one piece.

She crashed bodily against a rocky outcrop, smashing the back of her head. She blacked out, regained consciousness, blinked, feeling the intense, furnace-like heat of agonizing pain searing through her skull. Her whole body felt out of line, something possibly fractured around the hip or femur, and pain radiated from the organs beneath her rib cage.

Her mind cleared.

She shouted for help.

Then she heard footsteps, someone making their way down the slope towards her, then the black shape of a man – her rescuer – standing over her. Laughing.

TWENTY-ONE

'A very nice little team,' Rik Dean said.

He and Flynn were in the CID office at Preston police station. Flynn wore a visitor's badge, the first time he had worn any formal ID in almost ten years. He glanced around. A CID office was no different from any other office the world over. Desks piled high with paperwork and junk; waste bins full to overflowing; empty mugs, personal photographs, football team names, calendars. What, of course, made a CID office unique was the content of the files and the material on the walls – people and crime: wanted posters, intelligence bulletins, stolen property lists, and so on. Everything impacted on someone's life.

Flynn felt a passing pang, but no more. Time had moved on for him and being a cop was now a different country for him. The organization had not wanted him, he had left under a cloud of suspicion, subtly hounded out by a detective called Henry Christie who would not let go, but who had later learned the truth: Flynn was completely innocent. A million pounds' worth of drug dealers' money had not gone into his back pocket as alleged.

By then it was too little and too late. The split was permanent with no chance of reconciliation.

Flynn's face twitched, then he spotted a coffee filter machine gurgling away on top of a cupboard.

Now that was what he needed.

Dean noticed the look. 'It's for us,' he said of the coffee.

'Good . . . what do you mean, team?'

'I'll come to that in a second, but I'll just bring you up to date with one or two things. My DS has been working the phones and found out a couple of things of interest.'

Flynn waited, but what he really wanted was coffee.

'First off, Felix Loveday, supposedly released on licence because all convicted murderers are subject to this for all their lives, should immediately have reported to a probation officer. Didn't show.'

'Ahh,' Flynn said.

'Second, he was allocated a room at a bail hostel in Inskip. Guess what?'

'Never checked in?'

'Correct. And, as far as we can see, no one who should have been in contact with him has been. It's all been reported.' Dean winced. 'He should have been circulated as wanted but . . . cock-up somewhere along the line between us and the probation and prison service . . . not done.'

Flynn laughed cynically and tried not to roll his eyes. 'Not that it would have made much difference,' he conceded, 'because without everything else that's going on, he'd just stay missing and no one would be any the wiser.'

'Correct.'

The filter machine gurgled its last hiss of steam: the coffee was ready.

'And a DNA sample was taken from the burned body, but it came back inconclusive . . . coffee?'

The two men walked over to the machine and found a couple of relatively clean, mould-free mugs on the way. As Dean poured the steaming brew he said, 'So it's looking more and more likely that Tasker staged his own death, as you thought.'

'I'm blushing,' Flynn said. 'So what about this "team" business?' He sipped the coffee, which tasted wonderful.

'A bent prison officer and two convicts with special areas of expertise, one a doctor, one with a passion for fire.'

'The arsonist?'

Dean nodded.

'What have they said so far?'

Dean smiled a detective's smile. 'They've pretty much crumbled, but two are still being interviewed as we speak. I've just been talking to the prison officer and I'm going back after this break. He didn't have a leg to stand on and became particularly perturbed when I mentioned bank accounts to him. Then he just hung his head and said, "Twenty grand." I said, "What?" and he said, "If you check my current account you'll see twenty grand deposited three days after Brian Tasker supposedly died."'

'So he definitely isn't dead?'

'Seems not . . . looks like Loveday is the victim, drugged up by the struck-off doctor and toasted by the arsonist, who made it look like an accident . . . cigarette burning, accelerant . . . in fact, I'm going to have a very long chat with him, because I know of several mysterious fires in which people have died that have never been properly explained. He could easily have committed more murders.'

'I assume the prison officer facilitated it all in exchange for the said twenty Gs?'

'He did, and this included getting Loveday to pre-sign all his release forms the evening before, "just to speed up the process", he was told, and the tame PO then opened the front door for Tasker to walk out – after knocking the CCTV camera so it didn't actually record who was leaving. They spent a few weeks setting it all up and then it happened. And the doctor and the arsonist happily gave false witness statements about the night, which were presented to the coroner. There was an inquest of sorts and the coroner ruled death by accident . . . a lazy investigation made lazier by just accepting what appeared to be the facts and not following the first rule of an unexpected death.'

'Treat it as murder, then work back,' Flynn said.

'Exactly,' Dean sighed.

'Hey!' Flynn said mock-brightly. 'If a health authority can get away with not investigating twelve hundred unexplained deaths and the prison service can release over five hundred murderers by mistake, anyone can get away with anything if they're clever enough. It's only just begun to unravel and Tasker's had three months' start on us.' He sipped his coffee ruminatively. 'Trouble with prison is that it gives bad men too much time to mull things over.' Then he thought fleetingly about Santiago, assumed she would now be tucked up in bed.

'How did you get on with Mulligan?' Dean said. 'Let me rephrase that. When I say "How did you get on with Mulligan?", I don't actually know anything about it, if you get my drift?'

'Yeah – I didn't accidentally see his address on a piece of paper you accidentally let me see.'

'And?'

Flynn's face tightened. 'Some unknown person contacted him and asked him to report on Craig's comings and goings, to and from work. He didn't know what it was about but guessed after hearing about Craig's murder. Mulligan also has a friend in HR who gave him contact details for retired officers which he passed on to this unknown person. He was paid cash and the exchange was by a dead letter drop. Apparently my contact details aren't on the HR system – which I need to check, of course. I'd hate to miss out on my pension when it's due.'

'You got the name of the HR person?'

'Lizzie Dawn . . . she must have access to historical personnel records. She looks like being the source of my ugly mug on the wanted posters, too.'

'I know her,' Dean said. 'She's based at headquarters.' He sighed sadly again. 'I hate corruption, especially in public office.'

'Me too.'

They sipped their coffee in philosophical contemplation.

'So, where are we up to?' Flynn said at length.

Dean's head rocked from side to side – more contemplation. 'I need to ensure these three are dealt with and get statements, admissions, off them, pin 'em down.'

'Have you asked if they know where Tasker is?'

'I have; they don't – and I believe them. So, to answer your other question, there's a few things running. I need to continue to investigate the murders of Craig and his family, Jerry Tope and Dave Carver, none of which, I believe, were actually committed by Tasker himself. I think, as you do, it's a hired killer or killers and they are still out there, after you and Jimmy Blue, so I need to provide adequate protection for you and him . . . but what about your family, Steve?'

'They'll be OK. My ex is out of the country and my lad's somewhere up a mountain in Asia. They'll be all right for a while.'

'Then we need to make sure Jimmy Blue's OK and then start a manhunt for Tasker.'

Despite his reservations and commitments, Flynn found himself saying, 'Can I tag along, somehow? In a non-involved, consultancy capacity . . . I'm very cheap.'

'You can't be hands on,' Dean said, reluctantly and after consideration.

'I get that, but I spent a long time chasing Tasker. I know a lot about him and I could be valuable, could possibly pick up on something you might miss.'

'You can't be in on any interviews but I'll keep you up to date on everything we do, how's that? You've already done enough, Steve, and it is appreciated. I can't even begin to see why Henry Christie hated you.'

They both laughed sheepishly.

'Tasker has killed people I cared for . . . I just want to be around, but not under your feet.' Flynn knew he had to get back to Ibiza, but didn't need to get a flight until next evening – which he still needed to book – so he would be at a loose end all day, which did not appeal to him. It would kill some time.

'Fine.'

'And if he comes for me with you around, I can use you as a human shield.'

'Thanks for that.'

'Where do we go from here, then?'

Dean checked his watch. 'I'm going to go back and interview the prison officer . . . there's an A/V link just off the custody unit. You can watch and listen if you like.'

Flynn said that would be very nice.

The new police station at Preston had been bought from United Utilities and refurbished long after Flynn had resigned from the cops, so he had never been in the custody suite.

The custody sergeants' desk reminded Flynn of Captain Kirk's bridge on the Starship *Enterprise*. It was a curved desk on a raised platform from which the sergeants could look down on the prisoners and their arresting officers and was a fairly effective barrier preventing the said sergeants from being easily assaulted.

Flynn had done a very short spell as a custody officer, a requirement imposed by the organization at the time he had been newly promoted to sergeant. The thinking was that six months behind the desk would be beneficial for any sergeant, especially those with aspirations to be detectives. It showed them the pressures of the position, the stresses that custody sergeants had to endure, and would make the wannabe jacks a little more empathetic in future.

Flynn hated every single minute of it, having to deal with drunks and violence and everything that went with the detention of offenders. The position put the sergeants between the devil and a hard place: protecting the rights of the individual (although clearly, Flynn learned, many did not deserve rights) while trying to ensure that the investigating officers could do their jobs effectively.

He knew some sergeants relished the role, and could appreciate that. Once a sergeant got the hang of it, the process was much like shelling peas.

But it took a person of a particular character to do it and enjoy it.

Flynn was not that person, but he did enjoy the physical side of it because not a week went by without a prisoner having some sort of dig at him and a legitimate, reasonable response was always in order.

Having to avoid shit being hurled at him, though, never went down well with him and twice he had been subjected to prisoners throwing their faeces at him.

He had been relieved to get the stint over with, never to return except with his own prisoners in tow, and he would find he had completely forgotten just how hard a job it was when he himself tried to bypass rules and regulations to get a result.

As Rik Dean led him into the custody office the back door opened and two young men were dragged in under arrest, kicking and fighting and spitting (Flynn had been spat on almost daily when a custody officer), even though they were handcuffed.

One was pitched into the holding cage and the other bundled up to the custody desk, where he continued to struggle and try to head-butt the arresting officer. Flynn recognized her as the police-woman who had earlier turned out in response to the report of a man in his underpants flagging down traffic.

Flynn's natural reaction was to wade in and help. He didn't. He left it to Rik Dean to step forward and give a hand.

The struggling youth did not spend much time in front of the custody sergeant, who took one look at the situation and announced, 'Cell.' A gaoler, another PC, the arresting PC and Rik Dean carried him between them into the cell corridor and deposited him in a cell, where he was pinned down and searched. His shoes and belt were removed and his handcuffs taken off; then he was left in the cell. He began to pound on the door, screaming obscenities.

The WPC came back into the custody office, breathing heavily after the exertion, followed by Dean and the others.

The custody sergeant, who hadn't moved, smiled benignly at her and asked, 'Circumstances of arrest?'

She caught her breath. 'We turned out to the report of a man in the middle of the road at Broughton lights and just as we got up to North Road a BMW shot past with matey at the wheel' – she gestured with her thumb at the prisoner in the cells – 'and the other one' – she indicated the holding cage – 'in the passenger seat. Two females were in the back seats. I recognized the lads, Wayne Dixon and Billy Collins, and suspected the car might be stolen. It sped away, refused to stop and went through several sets of red lights on the A6 northbound at excessive speed. Went down across the motorway roundabout at Broughton and unfortunately ploughed into the guy who'd been in the road. He's dead. The BMW veered off the road and embedded itself in the corner of the pub on the crossroads. Somehow none of the occupants were hurt. We arrested all four for vehicle theft and causing death by reckless driving. The two girls are in the back of the other section van. And I'm pretty sure the driver is over the limit, but he wasn't amenable to a breathalyser. Traffic are still at the scene, plus ambulance, plus supervision.' She shook her head. 'The poor guy was, like, cut in half. Not identified yet.'

Flynn listened. His teeth grated. *Shit*, he said to himself, but try as he might he could not start to feel guilt or sympathy for the dead man – who he was certain would be Mulligan – because of what he had done to others.

He decided the best course of action was to say nothing to Rik Dean, believing that ignorance might be bliss in this case.

Maybe later.

But only if he felt he had to.

The custody sergeant tapped details into the computer, then glanced up at Rik Dean and said, 'Boss?'

'Interview with the prison officer, Birtwell, please.'

There was a large whiteboard on the wall behind the custody desk with cell numbers and their occupants written on it in black felt tip ten. Birtwell's name was on the board with the names of the other two detainees from the prison. Other names were there, including a couple of prisoners with the word 'Aquarius' written in above them. Flynn jolted slightly, realizing these were two of the people arrested following the raids put together by Craig Alford and Jerry Tope, the big drugs bust orchestrated by Alford, the results of which he would never see.

The custody sergeant asked one of the gaolers to bring Birtwell from his cell and put him into an interview room.

Dean sidled over to Flynn and said, 'That sounds a bad one,' referring to the death at Broughton. 'I'll tell the night duty jack to get himself involved in it.'

'Good idea,' Flynn said with an inner cringe.

Dean had seen Flynn looking at the whiteboard. 'I still need to oversee the operation Craig was running. There are a couple of bods still in custody here. There's so much to think about,' he moaned.

Tell me about it, Flynn thought.

Listening to the interview did not really help Flynn. It actually made him feel inconsequential as regards the whole investigation; because of that and the unfortunate fate of Mulligan (again, although he tried he could not dredge up much guilt) he decided that, even though he had thought he would perhaps delay Ibiza, he now wanted to get back as soon as possible, finish the contract, then get home to Maria Santiago, truly – and cornily – the love of his life.

Realistically, he had probably contributed all he could, sent the investigation off on to the right track, and there was nothing more he could do; he was now a spare part. He could not go out knocking on doors, knocking heads together, asking questions. He had to let the real cops do it now, and as he listened to Rik Dean questioning the prison officer, he knew things were in good hands.

Tasker would soon know, if he did not already, that he had been rumbled and his faked death – at the expense of some other poor sucker – had been exposed. He could no longer act under the cover of his demise.

He was alive, the cops knew it, Flynn knew it – and he would be caught.

The interview was concluded and the prison officer was returned to his cell.

He had readily admitted everything and pointed one finger squarely at the ex-doctor, Rawtenstall, for whom he had smuggled in the knock-out drugs required to put Loveday to sleep; his next finger was pointed at the arsonist, Ben Dudley, who knew enough about fire to fix it so that only badly charred remains would be left of the body of Loveday/Tasker.

Rik Dean found Flynn in the A/V room. 'We need to call it a night,' he said. 'I'm bushed and beginning to hallucinate, don't know about you?'

'Yes, need sleep,' Flynn agreed.

'Any observations?' Dean asked him.

'Not really. Just confirms that if you're presented with a fait accompli you generally accept what you see. I wouldn't be too hard on the DI who investigated the fire . . . it was probably just one of those jobs he could have done without, a burden on top of all his other burdens.'

'We'll see,' Dean said, not convinced. Volume of work, in his estimation, should not contribute to a lack of professionalism. 'I'll make him poo his pants at the very least.'

'Your prerogative,' Flynn acceded. Then, wincing, he said, 'Uh, there is one thing . . .'

'Go on?'

'The guy run down by the stolen car?'

'What about him?'

'Could be Mulligan.'

'Eh? On what planet would that be the case?'

'Er, I took him for a drive and a chat.'

'In his underpants?'

'And vest. And socks. His decision not to get dressed.'

'Go on,' Dean said, feeling his lungs contract.

'We had our chat and I dropped him off at Broughton so he could walk home.'

'And again I say, in his shreddies?'

'I guess.'

'You mean you dumped him in the middle of the road?'

'Not exactly. He was annoying me a bit, but I did leave him on the side of the road.'

'And now I regret accidentally showing you his address. If that comes out . . .'

'I won't tell anyone if you won't.'

'Fucking hell, Steve . . . I agreed you could come and offer some assistance and now I suddenly see what Henry Christie saw in you. You're a bloody liability.'

Flynn was back in his hotel room fifteen minutes later, stretched out on the firm but comfortable bed, two miniature whiskies from the mini-bar clutched side by side in the palm of one hand so he could drink both at once.

Although tired he could not sleep. He wondered about booking the return flight to Ibiza and thought about his lovely boat, looking forward to getting back on board, working the few weeks until the end of summer, then returning to the Canaries with a big enough chunk of cash in hand to get the sportfishing business back up and running.

At the back of his mind, though, was a dark feeling that this Tasker stuff would not be going away soon.

His mobile phone woke him at ten a.m. He had been asleep for almost five hours, a black and dreamless sleep, the kind he liked.

Groggily he answered. 'Flynn.'

'Hey, Steve, my boyo,' came the jovial, Scouse-accented voice down the line. He recognized the tones of Jimmy Blue instantly, the last surviving member, besides himself, of the Ambush team photo. He had rubbed along well enough with Jimmy and for a time they had been good drinking buddies, but once the operation ended they had returned to their respective units, Blue to Blackburn

CID and Flynn back into the drug squad. They had rarely seen each other since.

Flynn shot upright.

'Jimmy, my man . . .'

'I'm hearing we're the last men standing,' Blue said buoyantly, not a whiff of fear in his voice. 'Some very tragic news indeed.'

'Yeah, yeah . . . how are you? How have you heard?' Flynn said, his brain still a bit muzzy.

'I'm good, family's all good, local cop came round to tell me to watch my back, but I'm fine, we're all fine. Got a shotgun, ain't nobody going to get near us.'

'That's good to hear, but these are dangerous men, Jim.'

'I got that, mate . . . and on that note, I only got half a story from the local cop . . . any chance you can fill me in on the whole thing? I know it'll be inconvenient, I'm way out in the sticks, but I'd like to know what you know and then I can really protect my brood. I hear you're over here.'

Flynn hesitated; again, his thinking was just a mite muzzy.

'Steve,' Jimmy Blue said, sensing the hesitation, 'this is serious stuff . . . I could do with talking it through with someone who really knows it and I know that's you. We could set up a Snapchat thing on the phones after, maybe, so we keep in touch, or do Facebook or something.'

'I was going to go back to Ibiza today.'

'I'd be really appreciative, and Ruby would love to see you. You can have a look at what sort of set-up I've got here; you could stay over if you wanted. I think we do need to talk, put a strategy together so we can keep in touch. Thing is, I'd come across there, but it's lambing season and I need to be on hand for my ewes – sixty of the buggers all ready to drop.'

'OK, you talked me into it . . . give me the address and a couple of hours.'

Flynn showered, taking a long time over the process, thinking about Jimmy Blue, the man who had always wanted to be a farmer. Which was a shame, because Jim was one of the best thief takers Flynn had ever known – but he had a dream to chase. He had finished in the job around the same time as Flynn, but whereas Flynn had left with his tail between his legs, Blue had gone out head held high with six chief constable's commendations and a long service and good conduct medal behind him.

When dried and shaved Flynn sat on the edge of the bed and made a call to Santiago, which went straight to voicemail. Checking the time, he assumed she would be back in work chasing a serial killer.

He dressed in the same jeans and T-shirt he'd been wearing for far too long, packed his hand luggage and checked out. He had no intention of returning to the hotel and once he'd finished at Jimmy Blue's (he intended it to be a flying visit) he would head for Manchester airport for the midnight flight to Ibiza. He had just booked this via the hotel, and the ticket had been printed off for him.

In the morning he would step aboard *Maria*, the second love of his life.

TWENTY-TWO

F lynn tried to enjoy the drive east across Lancashire towards the Rossendale Valley where Jimmy Blue had bought a run-down farm in the steep, harsh hills above the town of Bacup, midway between Burnley and Rochdale.

As a cop Flynn was never stationed in the valley, but because he had done a lot of roving on drugs branch he'd spent quite a lot of time there – a small valley with big secrets, he often quipped. So he knew how to get there and, more or less, get himself in the vicinity of Blue's farm.

He tried to enjoy the drive, but couldn't quite do so.

For one thing he just did not want to be bothered, but knew that Jimmy Blue should be told first-hand what was going on with Tasker. Flynn could not begrudge him that, even if it was an inconvenience, and he was probably the best person to do it. He would rather have mooched about today, got to the airport early enough for a leisurely meal and a drink and a bit of cut-price shopping for some of that Chanel perfume Santiago loved so much.

Also, something in his brain was chipping away like a

woodpecker, trying to tell him something, but he could not work out what.

Not having heard from Santiago was troubling him but only because he wanted to hear her voice, not because she hadn't even replied to the cheeky/rude text he'd sent her.

Even if she was interviewing a serial killer she had no right not to respond to him, he thought – and chuckled. He guessed her boss was on her case, big style.

His route took him from Preston on to the M6, bearing left on to the M61 and then on to the M65, arcing across the county from east to west and passing the old mill towns of Blackburn and Accrington, with Darwen somewhere in between.

Once past Accrington (home of the once world famous Nori brickworks) but before reaching Burnley, he hooked right on to the A56, which took him spectacularly across Moleside Moor and dropped him into Rossendale at Rising Bridge. From there he decided to do a little town run, came off the A56 and then drove through Haslingden, then on to the A681 into Rawtenstall itself where, as ever, he saw sheep grazing on the grassy roundabout that was Queen's Square. He went straight on, not even thinking twice about farm animals grazing in a town centre, because it was the kind of thing that went on in this neck of the woods. Nothing unusual.

He blinked.

In his mind, something came and went, was gone.

'Duh!' he said, and clonked his forehead with his knuckles. 'Think, doom-brain.'

The A681 carried on towards Bacup and soon, turning on to the A671, he wasn't too far from Jimmy Blue's farm, which was somewhere on the moors between Bacup and Burnley.

In Bacup town centre, his phone rang.

Rik Dean had had an ugly night, not least because of what Flynn had told him about Mulligan. As much as he tried to convince himself that Flynn was blameless for the unfortunate death – the man had been sliced in half by a car travelling at over eighty miles per hour – Dean was not happy. Nor was he happy he had allowed Flynn to see Mulligan's address and given the nod and wink that it was OK to go and have a quiet word with the corrupt, useless ex-cop. If that chain of events ever surfaced, he would be for a very high jump and a sudden stop.

A lesson learned.

Keep cop things for cops, not renegade individuals who could not be trusted not to compromise you. Flynn, useful at first, had sunk in Rik Dean's estimation and he was very cross with himself.

Fancy taking him for a midnight run in his underpants!

Fuck, what was I thinking? Dean pummelled himself mentally.

Bleak thoughts about Flynn were not the only things keeping him from sleep in those early hours.

The complexity of what had happened over the last few days was almost overwhelming him. From the brutal murder of Craig Alford's lovely family to the point he was at now – discovering the murder in prison which was a cover for the break-out of Brian Tasker – it was blowing his mind.

In some respects he was glad of Flynn's intervention; otherwise a lot of time could have been wasted chasing false leads. They would probably have been working on the assumption that Alford and Tope had been murdered because of their link to Operation Aquarius and wouldn't have made any connection to the death of Dave Carver . . . until, perhaps, a forensic or ballistic link had become evident. That would have wasted even more time. Possibly other people would be dead and he would still think that Brian Tasker was dead.

Over a coffee he tried to focus his mind on the day ahead.

Briefings were at eight a.m. at Preston nick with regards to interviews, and then nine a.m. at headquarters, and he had to be very prepared for them, which was why, only a couple of hours after climbing into bed, he had climbed out again, trying not to disturb his wife and going down to the kitchen.

He had sat with his coffee in the dining room with a pad and pen and tried to get his brain around things.

He had been back in work at seven a.m.

Once the prisoners who had hit Mulligan with the stolen BMW, and their two girlfriends, had calmed down and passed out, the cells at Preston nick, though full, became relatively quiet and no other prisoners were brought in that night. The custody sergeant could get his paperwork in order and the gaolers prowled the cell corridors, eyeballs regularly to peepholes.

Most prisoners were asleep under their rough blankets. Ex-doctor Sam Rawtenstall and arsonist Ben Dudley slept soundly, glad of the change of venue. Also, although they had been rumbled in their association with Brian Tasker and the events of that night (and everything leading up to it), nothing would change for them. They were both lifers and if they ever got out they would be old and haggard. Both were resigned to dying in custody anyway.

In another cell was the prison officer who had been bribed by Tasker to do the dirty work. He had initially tried to deny any wrongdoing, but the weight of evidence was against him, especially when the other two blabbed. And, like them, he was guilty of murder, plus many other things.

He knew he was right royally screwed, so he cried and whimpered pitifully all night and did not sleep.

Another prisoner in another cell not sleeping for a whole different reason was called Lawrence (Loz) Digson.

He was too busy working out percentages and odds, and the dangers and benefits of a decision he had yet to make.

'Steve, Rik Dean.'

'Morning.'

'Just a contact call.'

'Contact made,' Flynn said coolly.

'You finalized your plans?'

'You mean my "fuck off out of town" plans?'

'No . . . yeah . . . sort of.'

'I'm returning to Ibiza tonight . . . I'm just on the way to see Jimmy Blue at his farm in Bacup. He wanted to have a heads together and a chat through things, but he seems OK. Local cops have been to see him, so thanks for that . . . oops.'

Flynn negotiated a tight right hander at Broad Clough on Burnley Road, one controlled by double white lines. As he did this a car coming in the opposite direction inadvertently crossed the lines, causing Flynn to swerve to avoid a collision. In so doing he dropped his phone at his feet when he grabbed the wheel with both hands.

By the time the manoeuvre was over, the sharp swerve had

made the phone slide underneath the seat, out of reach of Flynn's fingers.

'Steve . . . Steve . . . shit . . .' Rik Dean shouted down the phone, and looked accusingly at the device when it showed the call had been disconnected. He redialled, muttering to himself, 'I haven't said anything to the local bobbies yet.'

The line came through as engaged.

Flynn slowed right down and took a left turn on to the very narrow and steep Bacup Old Road. He knew this was a section of the ancient route from Bacup to Burnley, superseded many years ago by the A671 and still only just about wide enough for a horse and cart.

The road climbed steeply and Flynn had to slow down to a crawl to negotiate the bumps caused by old water run-offs that siphoned water off the adjoining fields in diagonal channels across the road. He scraped the sump of the Punto on one, but didn't seem to have done much damage, so he continued without even checking whether he was leaking oil. The road carried on rising until it eventually levelled out at its highest point, where he pulled in and looked across some quite magnificent moorland in all directions, west across Lancashire and east over Yorkshire, and he really could believe that he was in the land of the gods. Hundreds of thousands of acres of land on which about the same number of sheep seemed to be wandering.

'Mm,' he thought, selected first gear and drove on, looking for a farm track which, according to Jimmy Blue, had a hand-painted sign on it pointing to Cunliffe Clough Farm. A couple of hundred metres further, there it was, and he stopped to look at it. 'Cunliffe Clough Farm. James and Ruby Blue and family. Fresh free range eggs. Please drive in.'

Flynn nosed the Punto on to the track and passed two other farms before reaching the farmyard named Cunliffe Clough. He turned in between the huge concrete gateposts and parked in front of the farmhouse, old stone built and very substantial. From the back he guessed there would be great views across the moorland at all times of year.

He got out and stood by the car, looking around the yard and beyond to where a number of sheep were grazing, and a chill wind made him shiver.

Something slotted into place, but before he could make sense of what he was thinking he heard a voice behind him.

'Flynnie! My man!'

He turned and saw Jimmy Blue emerge through a Judas gate in the large barn door across the yard. Jimmy waved and started across to Flynn. He was in a wax jacket and wellingtons, looked the part of a farmer.

Flynn could not help but smile, and he walked to meet him.

Jimmy's face was round and red but healthy-looking and the two men hugged and patted each other's backs. He was as tall as Flynn, but heavier and rounder and less fit.

'Welcome, welcome,' he said effusively to Flynn. 'Thanks for coming, marvellous to see you after all these years. Very grim situation, this.'

'Good to see you, Jim . . . this place looks great.'

'Thanks, it is.'

'And how are you doing, you and the family?'

'Making a real go of it . . . best thing I ever did.'

Flynn watched him carefully because his body language did not seem to fit the verbal language. His face, in particular, did not match the words coming out of his mouth. His eyes were red raw and his expression serious.

'Good,' Flynn said. 'I'm pleased, mate.'

'Hey, come and have a look at the family first . . . we're all in the barn, just doing something. Then we'll go have a brew and you can tell me just what the hell is going on; how does that sound?'

'Yeah, good.'

He beckoned with a jerk of his head, but again his expression, Flynn thought, was odd. It was as if he was trying to convey some sort of message to Flynn, but he was perplexed by it and followed Blue to the door inset in the bigger barn door.

Once there, Flynn paused as Blue opened up and waved a hand for Flynn to step ahead of him. Flynn stepped over the high threshold with his right leg and then stopped and frowned at Blue as that 'something' he had been churning over in his mind suddenly became clear, now that he had driven past the livestock in Rawtenstall town centre and then seen sheep in fields, where they should be.

'Jim, I thought you said your sheep were lambing? I don't see a lamb anywhere.'

Flynn was halfway through the door when he said those words, one foot in the barn, the other still in the yard, so he was slightly off balance as he turned to Blue and posed the question.

'Sorry, Flynn,' Blue said darkly, and as he spoke he pushed Flynn hard through the door into the barn, causing him to trip and stumble to his knees. Blue came in behind him and closed the door.

Flynn was on his hands and knees but was raising his head to complain when another man came on his flank and smashed him hard on the side of his head, stunning him. He rolled sideways, clutching his head, knowing that whatever had hit him had been hard and metallic and had caused a deep cut on his scalp-line.

'Sorry, sorry, mate,' Jimmy Blue said, and knelt down next to Flynn, 'I kinda tried to warn you.'

Even through the haze that was his brain Flynn understood what was being said, and he replied with a moan, 'I'm not a fucking farmer.'

'I know. I'm sorry.'

'What's going on?' Flynn asked. His vision was a little blurry and he moaned again as he moved and took his hands away from his face to see blood in his palms from the wound.

Blue eased Flynn into a sitting position. His head and vision cleared and he looked around the barn. Then everything really did slot into place.

Rik Dean had made his phone call to Flynn after he had conducted two fairly swift briefings and had returned to Preston cells to see how the interviews were progressing with the contingent from Lancashire Prison. One of the items on Dean's to-do list was to put a call through to Jimmy Blue. He had intended to back up the call by getting a local bobby to pop around to check that all was well with Blue, but because of pressure of work he hadn't quite got around to it. He would have made the call after talking to Flynn, even if Flynn hadn't dropped the bombshell that Jimmy Blue had already been visited by the local police.

At first Rik Dean thought that maybe someone else had made the call, and after he could not reconnect with Flynn he'd called the Major Incident Room at headquarters and asked the office manager whether someone had made the call to Blue without telling him. The man assured Dean that no one from the MIR had contacted Jimmy Blue.

Stalking down one of the cell corridors with his mobile phone to his ear, Dean redialled Flynn's number. It rang out but was not answered and then clicked on to voicemail. He left a brief message for Flynn to call back as soon as possible. Next he keyed in Jimmy Blue's home number which had been lifted from his old personnel record. But there was no reply. There was no other contact number listed for Blue.

He strode back down the corridor with a horrible creeping sensation in his guts.

'Boss, boss.' One of the prisoners rapped on his inspection hatch. Dean stopped and looked at the name by the door, but did not drop the hatch. The inmate was called L. Digson. Dean knew he was one of the Aquarius prisoners on remand, one of the big drug dealers caught by Craig Alford's textbook operation. He ignored him and carried on back to the custody office where he scooped up a phone from a desk and dialled an internal number connecting him to the patrol sergeant based at Rossendale police station, now the only cop shop covering the whole of the valley.

'Sorry, Flynnie,' Jimmy Blue said. 'They were going to kill my family if I didn't.'

Flynn said sourly, 'I get it.'

He wiped blood from his eyelids and looked at the hooded man who had smashed him on the head with a heavy calibre pistol. Slim – young, he guessed. Flynn gave the man a venomous look, then tore his eyes away and looked beyond, around the barn, at a situation which reminded him of the photographs he had seen over the years of Nazis and their atrocities.

Three people were on their knees in a line, facing towards Flynn. Their hands were bound behind their backs and duct tape had been wound around their lower faces, over their mouths, over their noses, round and round their heads.

Jimmy Blue's family. Flynn recognized his wife, Ruby, and assumed the other two were his teenage children, a girl and a boy. Flynn could see abject terror in their eyes as well as disbelief.

All that was missing was a grave for them to fall into.

Another man stood behind them, a gun in his hand resting at his side. He was dressed in similar attire to the one who had struck Flynn, dark clothing, zip-up jacket, black jeans, lightweight black boots and a balaclava pulled over his head with eye and mouth slits.

Both guns, Flynn noticed, had some kind of mini telescopic sights affixed along the tops of the barrels, at least that was what Flynn assumed them to be.

'I did what you asked, I got him here,' Jimmy Blue pleaded to the men. 'Now let them go, please, please.'

Each of the three hostages was crying; tears rolled down the outside of the duct tape. Flynn felt outrage course through him because he knew that no one in this barn was going to live. Brian Tasker had achieved his revenge.

'Let them go,' Flynn said. 'They've done nothing.'

The man nearest to him simply shrugged, rotated his head slightly and nodded to the man behind Blue's family.

He moved quickly, without hesitation or warning, and with cold precision.

Three shots, loud and echoing in the confines of the barn, one fired accurately into the back of the head of each kneeling family member. Their bodies pitched forward one after the other, legs twitching in death, and the man then coldly leaned forward with the gun and repeated the move, firing one more shot into their heads; then none of the three moved. He stood back.

Jimmy Blue must have been too shocked to react for a moment, but then he exploded.

'You bastards!' He went for the man closest to him, his arms outstretched, but the man simply raised his gun and fired into Blue's face three times, the bullets entering around the vicinity of his nose and cheekbones and exiting horrifically through the back. Jimmy dropped to his knees and slumped forward and the man put two more into his neck.

Flynn recoiled as Jimmy Blue's blood and brain matter flicked across him, but he made no other move as the man slowly revolved and pointed the gun at his face.

Flynn looked deep into the muzzle. The man leaned towards him and shoved the gun into his forehead, screwing it tightly into Flynn's skin.

'If you're going to pull it, pull it,' Flynn growled.

The man stopped the screwdriver motion, then slowly drew the weapon across Flynn's face, stopping at his mouth. Flynn gritted his teeth as the man, using the muzzle, parted Flynn's lips and tapped the gun against his teeth, sending a reverberation around his skull. Then he continued on the journey down Flynn's chin, and underneath into the soft flesh of his neck where he twisted the gun again before placing the muzzle against his Adam's apple.

Flynn braced himself as he stared into the man's eyes behind the mask.

The other man had joined his colleague and was standing about ten feet away, covering Flynn.

'Shoot me, you fucker,' he said.

He could tell that the man was smiling.

The gun continued to pass downwards across Flynn's body, pausing over the heart, then down across his stomach to his groin, where the man jabbed the muzzle a few times into his cock and balls before moving on and stopping on the hard muscle of Flynn's outer right thigh, where once more the man shoved the muzzle in and then fired the gun.

Flynn screamed and rolled away, clutching his leg as blood pulsed from the wound between his fingers.

The last thing he remembered was the stunning blow to the side of his head and the feel of a hypodermic needle being inserted into his neck just below his left ear, before complete blackness engulfed him but did not take away the pain.

'Six-three-seven receiving?'

'Yep, go ahead,' PC Dale Allen responded to the radio call from his patrol sergeant. Allen's beat that morning, with only one other mobile patrol out and about, was to cover the east side of the Rossendale Valley, the towns of Bacup and Whitworth, with just a smidgen of Waterfoot thrown in for good measure. It had been a steady morning, two break-ins and a minor road accident, giving Allen a bit of spare time to follow up on some other burglaries he had attended the day before and was investigating. He had a pretty good idea who the offender was, but proving it was just a tad difficult.

'Are you free, Dale?' his sergeant asked.

'I'm free.'

'Good . . . got a little job for you . . . just a welfare check, if you don't mind.'

'No probs, fire away.'

They bundled a now loose-limbed but still heavy Flynn into the back of a Renault van. His hands were now bound behind his back with tape, as was the whole of his face, the tape wrapped around from his chin to his forehead with just a gap under his nostrils. An Adidas polyester school pump bag had been forced over his head and the string drawn tightly around his neck. His ankles were also bound together and he was trussed up, his ankles taped to his wrists.

He lay on his side – there was no other way to lie – and the van set off from the farm.

PC Allen took the same route as Flynn up the very narrow Bacup Old Road to Cunliffe Clough Farm and did the same thing with the police Astra as Flynn had done with the Punto, bottoming the sump with a clunk on one of the diagonal water run-offs. The grounding of police cars in Rossendale was a perennial problem, though few police drivers actually admitted it when it happened.

Allen found the turn-off and drove slowly down the even tighter track, arriving at the farm a minute or so later.

He pulled into the farmyard behind a Fiat Punto – Flynn's hire car, although Allen did not know that at the time. There was also a Land Rover parked next to the barn and a small tractor by the farmhouse.

To Allen, it all seemed too quiet.

He got out of the Astra, fitted his flat cap – he was a smart cop – and walked across to the front door of the farmhouse. He knocked on it: a hollow, no one home sound. He tried the door handle and it opened. He did not go too far because the snout of a seemingly friendly sheep dog snuffled in the gap; although he could see the waft of the tail, Allen never trusted dogs.

He called through. No reply. He drew the door shut behind him and looked around the farmyard again. He set off over to the barn.

Rik Dean sat in the inspector's office at the police station with a feeling of dread beginning to enshroud him, hoping that he was completely wrong. That Flynn's phone had just run out of battery life, that Jimmy Blue was not answering his phone because he was in the fields, shearing sheep or something.

The custody sergeant poked his head around the door.

'Mr Dean?'

He nodded.

'That prisoner in number eight wants to speak to you. He says it's urgent.'

'Oh, that Digson guy?'

The sergeant nodded.

'What's it about?'

'Won't say, other than it'll be beneficial for you.'

For a few minutes, Rik Dean had nothing better to do.

'What?' Dean said through the closed hatch in the cell door.

'You the guy in charge?'

'Depends what you mean.'

'In charge of the thing that's going on?'

Irritably, Dean said, 'What thing?'

'The prison thing.'

'Yeah . . . and?'

'Can you drop this hatch?' The man's mouth was at the air vent in the door, a circle of holes drilled into the metal, and Dean could see his lips moving.

'Why? I'm pretty busy.'

'I can help you.'

'How, exactly?'

'Drop the fucking hatch and I'll tell you.'

Dean closed his eyes with frustration, took a breath and lowered the hatch. Digson pushed his face up to it. 'What?'

'C'mere,' Digson whispered.

'What, so you can spit in my face?'

'No . . . c'mere, so only you can hear.'

Dean leaned forward slightly. 'Close enough for me.'

And close enough to hear the words 'I have some good information for you' come from the man's lips.

Dean was about to respond when the custody sergeant appeared at the top of the cell corridor and shouted, 'Boss – urgent.'

TWENTY-THREE

'How many bodies?' Rik Dean asked.

'Four. Two male, two female,' PC Allen replied.

'Are any known to you?'

'The older male, yes . . . he used to be a detective: Jimmy Blue. He owns this farm . . . it's a bit of a brew shop for one or two of the older PCs around here.'

Rik Dean sat back and rubbed his neck. 'The other male?'

'His son, Aaron . . . and the young lass is his daughter, Megan. The older woman is the wife, Ruby. I know who they are, but I don't want to spoil the crime scene by clambering around.'

'Yeah, sure. Anyone else?'

'No, not that I can see, certainly not in the barn.'

'Right, OK.' Dean's mind worked overtime. He was not liking being on the phone to Allen because, although the officer had described the scene well, to be there physically would be better – and he knew he had to get there sooner rather than later. 'Have you had a look around the place?'

'Again, yes, but I don't want to disturb anything, just in case. Can't see anything, though, or any other bodies.'

Dean was back in the inspector's office at Preston, in contact with Allen thirty miles away in Rossendale. Allen was talking over his personal radio which, like all modern PRs, was equipped with the facility to call landline and other mobile numbers directly. The desk phone was on loudspeaker.

'OK. And you say there's a Fiat Punto in the yard?'

'Yes.'

'Have you looked through it?'

'Do you want me to, boss?'

'Just see if you can find anything of interest in it, such as an ID – but before you do that, have you got your own mobile phone with a camera?' Allen said he had. 'Take some shots of the scene and send them to me, will you . . . just to me. Nothing fancy, just so I can get a perspective.' He gave Allen his mobile number.

'Will do, boss . . . but if you don't mind me giving my two penn'orth, it looks like a gangland execution.'

They hung up. Dean rocked back in the chair. He knew local supervision was on the way to the farm as well as two local detectives, but he had also got the ball rolling with other support, such as CSI and support unit . . . and once he heard back from PC Allen, he himself was going to set off across the county.

A couple of minutes later several photographs landed on his phone and he tabbed through them with a feeling of dread.

'Shit,' he breathed.

The desk phone rang again. It was PC Allen.

'Boss . . . I'm with the Punto. There's what looks like airplane hand luggage in the passenger footwell and some folded documents on the seat itself.'

'Be careful, but have a look.'

'I've got my latex gloves on.'

Dean heard some rustling over the line, then Allen came back on. 'Printed flight tickets, Manchester to Ibiza tonight, midnight . . . and a UK passport in the name of Stephen Flynn . . . you think this guy could be involved?'

Dean said, 'Yeah, he's involved all right . . . I'm just surprised you haven't found his body, which may yet turn up. OK, thanks for everything. Protect the scene and I'll be across in about an hour.' Dean hung up just as the custody officer poked his head around the door again.

'Boss, I know you're busy, but Digson is still after talking to you.'

'Tell him to fuck off . . . politely. I'll catch up with him when I can.'

Flynn was awake and had been propped upright in a chair, but was still in complete darkness with the pump bag still tied over his head and tape wrapped around his face. His hands were taped to the chair arm, his ankles to the legs. A nauseating, pulsating pain emanated from the gunshot wound to his thigh, and he had to swallow back so as not to vomit, knowing that if he did there was every chance of choking to death on it because there was no exit via his mouth.

And he was frightened. More terrified than he had ever been in his life. He had always thought himself a brave man – almost to the point of stupidity sometimes – and he would never back down from conflict if he thought that to strike back was the right thing to do.

But his ability to hit out had been taken away from him. He was injured and therefore weakened and his mobility and speed were compromised; he knew he was dealing with people who would put a bullet in his head without even thinking about it. And he had been drugged, making him woozy and slightly out of it.

He whimpered as pain flooded up from his leg and into his lower abdomen. The nauseating sensation returned and he swallowed everything back down, but realized it would not be long before he could not suppress it any longer. Vomit was designed to come out, not go back and forth in the throat.

He heard the scuff of a footstep and someone close by, breathing. He tensed and attempted to regulate his racing heartbeat by breathing slowly through his nose, but that was not great either because his nasal passages were getting blocked now. Soon, he thought, even if I don't choke to death on my spew, I'll suffocate anyway.

There was the scratch of something on the floor, maybe a chair being repositioned.

Something touched his chest. He flinched. Someone laughed.

And said, 'Steve Flynn.'

Rik Dean tore across the county in his Mercedes estate, gripping the steering wheel, making himself concentrate on driving and nothing else. He knew he had to get there safely; to have his mind wandering and trying to work things out could have been hazardous.

He was at the scene in forty-five minutes, having activated a couple of speed cameras en route. Five minutes after that he was in a forensic suit, gloves, mask and elasticated shoes over his own, and talking to PC Allen. Dean always made a habit of chewing the fat with the first officer on the scene of a murder or other major incident and draining them dry of their observations and thoughts. Allen was good, precise and professional, and Dean thought that maybe he would go far in the job.

After this, he and Allen threaded their way through everyone else who had landed, and Allen talked him through his arrival and what he had found.

Inside the barn, Allen had ensured that everyone who had to have access to the crime scene stuck to the same route in and out and around the bodies in order to minimize the possibility of the destruction of evidence by size eleven police boots.

Two CSIs were at work recording still and video footage.

Dean walked around the prescribed route and spent a lot of time looking at each body. It was similar to the Alford family's murder, but the MO was not quite the same. A complete family, the wife and children killed ahead of the father, who was then gunned down once he had witnessed their deaths. It didn't seem as deliberately set up as that murder, though, so he was already thinking that the killer or killers were different people.

Different people, same objective.

His heart rate had subsided slightly, his desire to be sick under control for the moment.

Flynn sat there, listening, trying to work out what was beyond the hood over his head.

It felt quite chilly, but he was sure he was indoors. Maybe a cellar or a warehouse.

He tried to test the strength of his bindings, moving his wrists and ankles. There was little stretch.

Suddenly he was instinctively aware of someone standing next to him, breathing close to his left ear.

Then the whisper again. 'Steve Flynn.'

'I know I'm being a pain, boss.' The custody officer from Preston was on the phone to Rik Dean, who was sitting in his car, parked on Bacup Old Road – the full length of which had been cordoned off to all unauthorized vehicles and people – sipping a milky coffee from the urn he had ordered to be brought up to the scene of the murder. Strangely, it tasted wonderful, even out of a polystyrene cup that he could bite chunks out of and spit away.

'It's not a problem,' Dean said generously, even though it was. 'What is it?'

'That prisoner, Lawrence Digson, the drug dealer guy.'

Dean faintly recalled the man's earlier insistence. 'Oh, yeah . . . what *does* he want?'

'To speak to you – urgently, he says. Well, he would, wouldn't he, because he's been charged with some serious trafficking offences now and he'll be put before a court tomorrow.'

'Is he specific?'

'No.'

'Then, if you don't mind, go and ask him to be, then get back to me.'

'OK, boss.'

Dean got out of his car still sipping the coffee and walked across the farmyard, a hive of activity now even as evening began to approach. Emergency generators had been brought in and set up, flooding the farmyard with bright, unnatural light. He walked over to the Fiat Punto, the hire car Flynn had been using and in which Flynn's mobile phone had been found underneath the driver's seat. The last call recorded on it was from Rik Dean himself.

He closed his eyes and said to no one, 'Where are you, Flynnie? What have they done to you? They've taken you, haven't they?'

Dean's phone rang and he answered.

'Me again, boss . . . custody sergeant. I've spoken to matey in the traps—'

'And?'

'Still not all that specific, but he says I have to say "BT" to you: Bravo Tango.'

'What?' Dean placed his coffee cup on the roof of the Punto and clamped his spare hand over his spare ear.

'He said I have to tell you "BT", and that you'd understand.'

It took a few blinks to register, then Dean was running back to his car.

TWENTY-FOUR

Flynn began to retch. He swallowed, but this time there was no chance of holding it down; it had been there and back too many times. His whole abdomen convulsed and he brought it all into his mouth – from which there was no escape – and through his nostrils. He fought with maniacal strength, bucking against his bindings, gagging and heaving desperately, unable to keep his cool and knowing that he was going to die a horrific death . . . so much for the heart attack he had promised himself at the age of eighty-five, catching a thousand-pound black marlin off the coast of Australia the morning after the night before, when he'd made love to six or more women and got royally drunk.

This was going to be a squalid death, but maybe over soon at any rate.

Suddenly the pump bag was ripped off and someone grabbed his head in a lock to steady it while another person tore off the strip of duct tape over his mouth, leaving him still blind with the tape over his eyes. Like a volcano the sick erupted in a crazy burst from his mouth and nose.

He gagged continually for a further half-minute, spitting out down his chest, clearing his nose by blowing down it, clearing all the passageways. His stomach muscles contracted and screamed in protest. Eventually it all subsided and he could suck in clean air and begin to recover – until the tape was put back in place, the pump bag went back over his head and the drawstring was pulled even more tightly around his neck, like a noose.

And the voice at his ear: 'Steve Flynn.'

Flynn gathered all his strength and attempted to smash his head into the face of whoever it was, but connected with nothing but air.

'Steve Flynn.'

Dean rushed into the custody office to be met by the sergeant he had been in contact with, who led him straight away to Digson's cell.

The sarge opened the door to find Digson stretched out on the bed/bench reading an old paperback book, a Jack Higgins thriller. He glanced sideways at the two men at the door, reminding Dean of the big bad wolf.

'What's so urgent?' Dean demanded.

Digson closed the book and rose slowly into a sitting position, a smile playing on his lips.

'Not here,' he said.

'Don't piss me about, Mr Digson,' Dean warned him. 'I have a short fuse and will not be arsed about with.'

'But I have something you need. I know I have,' he said confidently.

'What is it?'

'Not here . . . interview room with proper coffee and a KFC Boneless Banquet, please . . . then we talk.'

'Up yours.'

Digson tilted his head and shrugged before starting to lie back down and open the book again. 'A coffee and a KFC is not a great price to pay.' He found his page again and said, 'BT.'

The jet of freezing cold water hit Flynn's head, jerking it back. It took him by surprise, although he had been listening intently to some movement in front of him, unable to work out what was going on – until the water struck him.

He tried to avoid it, to duck and shift the chair, but he had already discovered the chair was fastened to the floor and was immovable.

Then it was over and he was drenched and soon began to shiver, while at the same time the wound in his leg burned fiercely and a weakness came to his head.

'Steve Flynn.'

He looked calm, comfortable and smart. Clearly someone had been allowed to bring him a change of clothing. There was a filter coffee in front of him, and the remnants of the Boneless Banquet acquired for him from the KFC on Preston Docks. He wiped his mouth with a dry serviette, and then his hands with the fragranced wet wipe. He sat back and sipped the coffee.

'Maybe you should look into providing all prisoners with KFCs; you'd certainly get more confessions.'

Rik Dean eyed him. 'What do you want?'

'Freedom? Liberty?' Digson chuckled. 'Not much chance of either of those for a while, now.'

'You shouldn't traffic drugs.' Dean raised an eyebrow pointedly.

'I've learned my lesson . . . at least that's what I'll tell the parole board when I reach that point. In reality . . .' He winked.

'I really, really do not need a sideshow, Mr Digson.'

'Trust me, detective superintendent, I am just the sort of sideshow you do need.'

*   *   *

'Steve Flynn.'

The blow knocked Flynn's head sideways. A flat of the hand smack, but delivered with enough ferocity to set his brain on fire and burst his eardrum.

He screamed behind the tape at the new pain lancing through the side of his head, but as he moved he also shifted his wounded leg, which he had made almost comfortable, and fresh pain arced up into his belly again.

Digson leaned forward and put his elbows on the table, steepling his fingers, the gesture of someone who believed they had power.

'Now then, I know how the wheels of justice turn, Mr Dean; wheels within wheels, deals within deals. I want to make a deal.'

'In exchange for what?' Dean sneered cynically, not even remotely warming to this man.

'Information, of course.'

'What sort of deal?'

'A sentencing deal, a prison deal . . . guaranteed. I know it can be done. I live in the real world.'

'You were found in possession of several million pounds' worth of cocaine and several million pounds in cash from the cocaine business. Looking on the bright side, you're looking at, at best, twelve years. That's the real world. For you, anyway.'

'And that is the maximum. I'll be out in six years . . . but I want to be out in three, or less for good behaviour – and I will behave. I want a guarantee of a maximum sentence of six years so I'll be back out in three. I'll plead guilty but I won't drop anyone in it who was arrested along with me. If no deal, then not guilty, and a very long, protracted trial will ensue which will probably end up as a retrial – because, believe me, witnesses and juries will be intimidated – and will all cost more money than I had in drugs.'

'Law is about principles,' Dean said. 'It doesn't matter how much a trial will cost.'

'You know it does, but if you deal, not only will I plead guilty, but so will all the people you arrested with me . . . that's a promise. You can sentence them to whatever the court sees fit, but for me, maximum of six years. Deal?'

'You're doing my head in. You've offered nothing yet except a couple of initials, BT.'

'OK . . . I'll give you Brian Tasker on a plate . . . and I know how much you want him.'

'Welcome, Steve Flynn.'

The pump bag was eased off his head, the duct tape slowly and painfully unwound.

He blinked as he gasped for air and his eyes adjusted themselves to the semi-darkness. He glanced around to see he was in the cellar of a pub, with beer barrels stacked up alongside wine and spirits and boxes containing crisps and confectionery. And, bizarrely, four large screen TVs in a row, all at the same height and facing him. Then his gaze settled on the man sitting on a chair about a metre or so in front of him.

'Welcome to Fat Billy's, the pub I've owned in Blackpool for many years now. Bet you didn't know that, did you?' Brian Tasker said. There was a gun in his hand, one with those attachments Flynn had previously thought were telescopic sights on the barrel. He rested it on his lap, pointed in the general direction of Flynn's body. 'How is the wound? Sore?'

'Just a tad.'

'Well, tell you what, Steve, I'll make that better, for a while anyway.'

Tasker nodded past Flynn's shoulder. A hooded man came into view on the right with a syringe in his hand, which he plunged into Flynn's right thigh, thrusting the plunger down with his thumb, then withdrew the needle.

'Just a gram of the hard stuff, because I'm caring like that and I need you to concentrate for just a little while longer.'

Almost instantly the pain from the gunshot wound started to ebb and Flynn looked down at his leg and was horrified by the sight of his blood-saturated jeans.

'I just wanted to make sure you were fully incapacitated, Steve, because I know you're a real handful if not. Too tough for your own boots.'

Flynn was feeling a warm glow inside now and his shivering ceased. He guessed morphine.

'You've been rumbled,' he managed to say. His voice sounded like stone being grated. 'Faking your death.'

'My little ruse?' He laughed, shrugged and pulled a face.

'To be honest, it only needed to last for as long as I stepped out of prison, then it didn't matter. I'm surprised it's taken so long, actually, but that just shows how incompetent the police are.'

'They'll be here very soon,' Flynn said.

'But they don't know where "here" is, do they, Steve Flynn?'

'It's like all the drugs trade,' Digson said. 'Like all big business – very complicated.' He interlocked his fingers. 'Lots of connections, lots of subsidiaries, lots of people in chains of command, and the thing is this – by arresting me and some others, you lot seem to think that you've got the top of the pile. Nah.' He shook his head dismissively. 'Nowhere near, and not only that, it's not even a dent, *not even a dent*. What's fucking eight million when we're talking billions? Nothing. That said, the big players are abroad and untouchable, so you'd never get to them anyway, even if I told you who they are. Pointless.'

'Maybe you should get to the point,' Rik Dean said, getting restless.

'The point is this: ever since Brian Tasker was sent to prison he has still been operating his business from his cell. This latest bust you've made is just the tip of the iceberg of the hundreds more that you've missed, and I was unfortunate enough to get caught. Happens. Name of the game. Done the crime, do the time . . . or less time than necessary.'

'OK, all very interesting, and I would like to chat about it in detail. Talking about which, you give me the detail of where Tasker is right now and you'll get your deal . . . at the moment, all the rest is marginal.'

'Clearly I know he is out of jail, has been for about three months. He's been pulling various deals together, one of which was the one I was involved in, which also involves a lot of very nasty people from central Europe. But he's the boss man.'

'Where is he?'

'Probably much closer than you think.'

Tasker leaned towards Flynn.

'Do you know something, Steve? People are queuing up to kill you, but I'm right up there at the front.' He showed Flynn the gun with the strange sights affixed to it that had puzzled him. 'What do you think?'

Flynn said nothing.

Tasker raised the weapon and pointed it at Flynn's face. It was then Flynn realized it wasn't a telescopic sight but a digital video recorder shaped rather like a mini Maglite torch. Tasker drew a breath, then exhaled. He stroked the gun. 'You're probably wondering who else could possibly be interested in your death . . . does the family name Bashkim mean anything to you?'

It did – and jolted Flynn. It was the surname of the Albanian family who ran the crime gang he and Santiago had effectively destroyed and who had tried to kill Santiago and Jerry Tope by means of a car bomb – and failed.

'They would love to see you dead, and these guys' – Tasker pointed to the two men standing behind Flynn, the ones who had brought him here after killing Jimmy Blue and his family – 'are both related to Aleksander Bashkim, who is now unfortunately dead, because of you. I am now in business with them. Prison, that wonderful melting pot of culture, criminality and bad men, brought us together. But there is another fucking irony here, Steve . . . the first consignment of drugs we brought in has been seized by the cops in an operation led by – would you believe it? – Craig Alford, RIP.'

Flynn simply stared at him, tensing his wrists and ankles, trying to loosen the tape. 'Good,' he said.

'The other irony,' Tasker said as though he had not heard Flynn, 'is that he was on my kill list anyway, as were you and some others . . . and do you know why you are on my list? *Because you destroyed my family.* Yes, you.'

'I may have said this before . . . you're fucking barmy.'

Tasker crashed the gun against Flynn's head.

The first of the four TV screens flickered to life in front of Flynn. He was back to being woozy again; Tasker had pistol-whipped him mercilessly before recovering his composure.

'You need to watch this, Steve . . . then you can start to think about what it's like to lose a family.'

Flynn could hardly keep his head upright but tried to look at the TV screen through the streams of blood flowing from his scalp.

'I call this the killer-cam,' Tasker said chattily. The screen came properly to life and Flynn now saw the reason for the cameras affixed to the handguns. The image of Craig Alford's terrified face filled the screen as the gun circled around behind him. At the same time Alford's family could be seen lying dead on the floor of the living room beyond. The gun was then at the back of Alford's head. It was fired and recoiled as Alford was shot in the back of the head. His head pitched out of view, but then the gun followed him down and another round was put into it.

'Clearly these are the edited highlights, Steve.'

The same sequence began again on the screen and Flynn realized it must be on a repeating loop.

He kept control of his breathing, working out just how he was going to kill Tasker.

The next TV screen came alive.

'These people are really very good at killing,' Tasker said. 'You know, the Bashkim family, another family you basically destroyed, Steve. You're good at that, aren't you? Still, I'll bet you're wondering why you're still breathing . . . I'll come to that.'

Flynn recognized the location instantly. Preston Docks, close to the Halfords motor spares store. In the distance a figure leaned on the railings, obviously deep in thought. It was Jerry Tope.

Flynn's fists bunched tightly as the camera on the barrel of the gun recorded the silent approach of the killer, like a character in an Xbox video game, until the moment the gun was raised to the back of Tope's head and fired.

The sequence started again so now two TV screens were showing brutal, real life deaths, again and again.

'That's enough,' Flynn said as the third screen came on.

'No it isn't, Steve, not nearly enough. I want to torture you mentally – at least for a while – just like you have tortured me over the years, how you made me kill my own family, my son, my baby, and then afterwards in court, how you humiliated me, laughed at me, not forgetting that you also assaulted me. This is why you are still alive, for the moment.'

The third screen showed Dave Carver's death at the nursing home from the viewpoint of a gun barrel, plus the death of the innocent nurse. Flynn saw the dementia sufferer's moment of sudden clarity and how the former DS had tried so courageously to tackle the shooter. Flynn saw a good man die for no reason at all.

The sequence went on to a loop, started repeating itself. Now three TVs were showing death after death after death.

'I take it these are the brave guys who did all your dirty work?' Flynn asked scornfully, nodding his head at the two men who had killed Jimmy Blue and his family, standing sullenly behind him.

'Yes, aren't they grand? Guess what their surname is? Yes, you got it . . . Bashkim! And they work for me now . . . these two and another one. Very good at killing.' Tasker smiled at Flynn. 'The question is, do we watch the murder of Jimmy Blue, which I have not had any chance to edit yet, or move on to the live feed? As you've already witnessed that, I think we'll go live right now to our correspondent in the Canary Islands, because I'm eager to see this one.'

Tasker pointed a remote control unit at the TV.

Flynn saw the image and recoiled in horror. It showed a close-up of Maria Santiago's face, brutally injured, eyes swollen, blood caked on her cheeks. Then the camera drew slowly back and framed her sitting on a chair in a room Flynn instantly recognized. Her head fell forward.

'Do we know her?' Tasker laughed gleefully. 'Yes, we do . . . it's your lady friend and she's sitting in your apartment in, where is it, Gran Canaria?'

Flynn's breathing became shallow and rage crawled through him like a virus.

Santiago looked badly injured. She was tied to one of the dining chairs, but her right leg jutted out at an unnatural angle. A hooded man came into view and stood behind her, grabbing her hair, holding her head upright.

Suddenly Flynn wanted to vomit again. 'You bastard,' he said.

Tasker leaned in front of him, putting his face just inches in front of Flynn's. 'This is what you made me do,' he said.

'Funny how you seem to be controlled by other people,' Flynn said, 'how they make you do things.'

'Yeah, funny, that.'

'Nothing is ever your fault, is it?'

'No, you're right, it isn't.' Tasker stood upright and said, 'You have made me do this.' He pulled out a mobile phone and typed a text, then held the phone in front of Flynn's eyes so he could see the words. 'DO IT'.

Tasker pressed 'send'.

A few moments later the man holding Santiago's hair let it go. Her head flopped loosely down as the man took out a mobile phone from his pocket and obviously read the text Tasker had just sent. The man nodded and made an OK gesture with his thumbs.

'Now we'll see something, unless he bottles out . . . but he won't, he's a Bashkim . . . he loves his job.'

The man stepped out of shot, then reappeared a moment later. He took hold of Santiago's hair and yanked her head upright, tilting it slightly backwards, exposing her neck. His right hand then came into shot and in it was a huge panga, an African machete. He placed the blade across Santiago's throat.

'Jesus, no,' Flynn said. 'What the fuck do you want, what can I give you?'

'*Want? Give me?*' Tasker sneered. 'Just everything I had that you took away.'

The man drew back the huge knife, angled his torso slightly to the right and the blade sliced through the air into Santiago's exposed throat.

It took four slashing cuts, the last one being the toughest. The man had to work through the gristle and bone of Santiago's spine before her head came free. He lifted it and danced towards the camera with it jiggling in his hand until her face was right up against the lens and out of focus.

Then the screen went blank just as the cellar door burst open and a stream of armed police officers, weapons drawn, crashed through and swarmed down the cellar steps, screaming orders, fanning out in a well-practised manoeuvre.

Tasker and the hooded men instantly dropped the guns they were holding and fell down on to their knees with their hands raised as arrest teams surged through and pinned the three of them to the ground and cuffed them.

All through this Tasker's eyes stayed locked into Flynn's, a grin of triumph on his face, until he was finally pulled to his feet and frogmarched away by two officers.

Steve Flynn started to cry.

*   *   *

'You need to go to hospital,' Rik Dean was telling Flynn, who was sitting in the back of an ambulance, being treated by paramedics.

They were parked outside Fat Billy's pub in Blackpool surrounded by a mass of emergency vehicles from all the services.

'I know,' Flynn said mutedly.

'I'm so sorry,' Dean said.

'Well,' Flynn said, 'problem is, you can't account for madness coupled with intelligence . . . a lethal combination.'

'He'll never see the light of day again.'

'And that makes me feel better?'

'I doubt it.'

'Have they taken him in yet?'

'Not yet, he's still in the back of a van.'

'Let me see him, Rik.'

'No chance . . . you can't be trusted. Let's put him back into the system. That's what he deserves.'

'No he doesn't.' Flynn shook his head vehemently.

'I can't let you see him and that's final, Steve, you know that.'

Tasker was alone in the steel cage in the back of the section van. He was still handcuffed and sat there waiting to be taken into the custody office at Blackpool police station. There was some kind of delay and he'd been told he would have to wait a while longer.

The back door of the van opened and the inner steel cage was unlocked.

'About time,' Tasker said irritably. He started to stand up but a big hand shoved him backwards against the bulkhead, where he slithered down on to his backside.

Steve Flynn clambered into the back of the van and closed both sets of doors behind him.

Flynn was still drenched in his own blood and even though the paramedics had tidied him up a little he made a terrifying sight. He fought through the agony that consumed his body, from his head down to the bullet wound in his leg.

From his sitting position, Tasker sneered at him. 'I knew you'd come, just didn't know when.'

'Better sooner rather than later,' Flynn said. It took all his remaining strength to haul Tasker back on to a bench and then sit alongside him. Tasker did not resist, even when Flynn slid his right arm around his neck and said, 'I want you to know you made me do this.'

Tasker's neck broke with the most satisfying crack Flynn had ever heard in his life.